I
Did Not
Kill My
Husband

I
Did Not
Kill My
Husband

A NOVEL

Liu Zhenyun

Translated by Howard Goldblatt and
Sylvia Li-chun Lin

Arcade Publishing • New York

Arcade Publishing books may be purchased in bulk at special discounts for sales promotion, corporate gifts, fund-raising, or educational purposes. Special editions can also be created to specifications. For details, contact the Special Sales Department, Arcade Publishing, 307 West 36th Street, 11th Floor, New York, NY 10018 or arcade@skyhorsepublishing.com.

Arcade Publishing® is a registered trademark of Skyhorse Publishing, Inc.®, a Delaware corporation.

Visit our website at www.arcadepub.com.

10 9 8 7 6 5 4 3 2 1

Library of Congress Cataloging-in-Publication Data is available on file.

Cover design by Li Xueting

ISBN: 978-1-62872-426-4
Ebook ISBN: 978-1-62872-467-7

Printed in the United States of America

Chapter One

Prologue: Way Back When

1

Li Xuelian first met Wang Gongdao—Justice Wang—when he was only twenty-six, a thin youngster of pale face and body, light-skinned with big eyes. Normally, people with big eyes have bushy brows, but not him. His sparse brows were so thin they nearly ceased to exist. She felt like laughing the moment she laid eyes on him, but you don't laugh at someone you've come to for help. Besides, it hadn't been easy, getting to see him, that is. His neighbor said he was home, but she knocked and knocked until her hand was sore and still nothing stirred inside. She'd come with half a sack of sesame seeds on her back and an old hen in one hand. Now her hand ached and the hen, hurting from being held by the wings, cackled loudly; eventually, it was the hen that got the door opened. Wang answered in his underwear, a judge's rope draped over his shoulders, which gave her a peek at his paleness, along with the newlywed "Double Happiness" paper cutting pasted on the wall. It was past 10:30, and now she knew why it had taken him so long to open the door. But she'd come at night precisely because she'd expected to catch him at home, and because she had no intention of traveling more than thirty li for nothing.

"Who are you looking for?" Wang asked with a yawn.

"Wang Gongdao."

"And who are you?"

"Is Big Face Ma from Ma Family Village your maternal uncle?"

He scratched his head and thought a moment before nodding.

"His wife is from Cui Family Shop, you're aware of that, aren't you?"

He nodded again.

"And Big Face Ma's wife's younger sister is married to someone in Hu Family Bend, you know that, too, don't you?"

He scratched his head again, but shook it this time.

"Well, a cousin of mine, my aunt's daughter, is married to a nephew of one of Big Face Ma's wife's sisters in-laws."

"What do you want anyway?" Wang asked, this time with a frown.

"I want a divorce," Li Xuelian said.

Wang invited her in and had her sit in the living room of the newlyweds' house, partly so she'd put down the sack of sesame seeds, but especially to calm the cackling hen—though, in truth, it was neither for the sake of the sesame seeds nor the hen, but a chance to get rid of her as soon as possible. A woman stuck her head out from the bedroom, and quickly disappeared.

"Why a divorce?" Wang asked. "Trouble with your husband?"

"It's worse than that."

"A third party?"

"Worse than that."

"This isn't about murder, is it?"

"No, but I will go home and kill him if you don't do something."

That got Wang's attention. He got up to pour tea.

"You can't kill him, since you won't be able to get a divorce if he's dead," he said, the teapot suspended in midair. "By the way, what's your name?"

"Li Xuelian."

"And your husband?"

"Qin Yuhe."

"What does he do?"

"He drives a truck for the county fertilizer plant."

"How long have you been married?"

"Eight years."

"Did you bring the marriage certificate?"

"I have the divorce paper," she said, unbuttoning her coat to retrieve it from the pocket of her blouse.

"You're already divorced?" Wang was flabbergasted. "One divorce is all you get."

"This one's a fake."

He took the wrinkled divorce decree from her and examined it, front and back.

"It's not a fake. Your name is on it and so is Qin Yuhe's."

"The paper isn't a fake, but the divorce was."

Flicking his finger against the paper, Wang said:

"That doesn't matter. With this paper, it's considered a legal divorce."

"That's the problem."

Wang scratched his head thoughtfully.

"So what exactly do you want?"

"I want to file a lawsuit to prove that this divorce was a sham, and then I'll marry that son of a bitch, Qin Yuhe, so I can really divorce him."

By now utterly confused, Wang could only continue scratching his head.

"If all you want is a divorce from this Qin fellow, why go to all this trouble? Isn't that pointless?"

"That's what everyone says, but not me."

2

Li Xuelian had not wanted to go through all that trouble, since she was already divorced, and the most she'd get for her trouble would be a second divorce. The original plan had been to make a clean break by killing Qin Yuhe and letting that be the end of it. But he was over six feet tall, with bulging arms and powerful hips, which meant she might well fail in her attempt. She'd actually married him precisely for those bulging arms and powerful hips, in other words, a strong man, but those positive attributes turned negative when it came to murder. To kill him, she'd need help. Her younger brother was the first person who came to mind. Li Yingyong was also over six feet tall, and also had bulging arms and powerful hips. He drove a converted tractor, buying and selling grain and trading cotton and pesticides in the surrounding area. So she made the trip home. They were at lunch when she arrived; he, his wife, and their two-year-old son were sprawled across the dining table, slurping noodles in bean sauce.

"Come outside, Yingyong. I need to talk to you." She was leaning against the doorframe.

He looked up from his bowl.

"Oh, it's you, Sis," he said. "We can talk in here."

"It's for your ears only," Xuelian said with a shake of her head.

With a glance at his wife and son, Yingyong laid down his bowl, got up, and walked with his sister to the hill behind the village. It was mid-spring and the river ice had melted, sending water surging downstream.

"Tell me, Yingyong, what kind of sister have I been?"

"Pretty good," he said, scratching his head. " You lent me twenty thousand yuan to get married."

"I want you to do something for me."

"Sure, Sis."

"Help me kill Qin Yuhe."

Yingyong froze. He'd known about the "divorce" fiasco between his sister and brother-in-law, but how had it come to this? He scratched his head again.

"I'd be glad to help you slaughter a pig, Sis, but I've never killed a man."

"Nobody goes around killing men, not unless the situation requires it."

"The killing's easy, but I'd have to take a bullet for murder," he said.

"You don't have to do the actual killing. Just hold him down for me so I can stab him to death. I'll be the one getting the bullet. You'll be fine."

"If I held him down for you, I'd still have to go to prison."

"Am I your sister or aren't I?" she said, angered by his waffling. "Don't you care that he's tormenting your own sister? If you won't help me, I'll forget about killing him, and go home and hang myself."

"All right, Sis," he blurted out, frightened by what she said. "I'll help you. When do you want to do it?"

"You can't put off something like this. How about tomorrow?"

He nodded. "All right, tomorrow. Since we're going to kill him, the sooner the better."

But when Xuelian returned the next day, Yingyong's wife told her that her accomplice-to-be had left in his tractor the night before, off to Shandong to buy cotton. Hadn't they agreed to kill Qin Yuhe? Then what was he doing, off buying cotton? And hadn't he always bought it locally? Why go all the way to Shandong? Obviously, he was avoiding her. Xuelian sighed. Now she knew that her brother was neither a hero (ying) nor brave (yong). She also realized that the saying "It takes a blood brother to kill a tiger, and you go into battle with your own soldiers" had it all wrong.

Old Hu, the town's butcher, was her next candidate for an accomplice. He lived in a town called Round the Bend. A man with a ruddy face, Hu butchered pigs around three or four in the morning, in order to cart the meat to the marketplace before sunup.

The pork was piled on the counter and hung from hooks; pig heads and guts filled the basket under the counter. She'd bought pork from him in the past. He'd slice off a piece and dump it into her basket, or toss her a handful of guts he'd plucked out of the basket. But the guts hadn't come without strings, for he'd called her "Babe" with a leering glint in his eyes. On occasion he'd even walked out from behind the counter to feel around, but she'd always cursed him into backing off.

"Old Hu," she said as she walked up to his counter. "Let's go someplace quiet. I need to talk to you."

After giving her puzzling invitation some thought, he laid down his cleaver and followed her to an abandoned mill behind the market.

"How would you rate our relationship, Old Hu?"

"Not bad, Babe." His eyes lit up. "I never gave you less meat than you paid for, did I?"

"Then I want you to do something for me," she said.

"What's that?"

Having learned a lesson from her brother, she avoided mention of murder.

"I'm going to bring Qin Yuhe over here so you can hold him down while I slap him around a little."

Hu had heard what was going on between Li Xuelian and Qin Yuhe, and since holding one person down so someone else could slap him around didn't present a problem, he agreed unhesitatingly.

"I've heard what happened. That Qin Yuhe is a bastard." Then he added, "For you I'd do more than hold him down. I'd even beat him up myself. What I need to know is, what's in it for me?"

"You help me out and then you and I can do you-know-what."

Overjoyed, he put his arms around Xuelian and began to paw her.

"If you let me do that, Babe, I'd kill him if I had to."

"No talk of killing." She shoved him away.

"All right, we'll stop at a beating." He sidled up to her again. "Let's take care of our business first, then we'll beat him up."

She shoved him away. "No. We beat him up first." She got up to leave. "Or no deal."

He hurried after her.

"No sweat, Babe. We'll do it your way. First we beat him up, then we do it." He added:

"But no backing out."

"I'm a woman of my word." She stopped.

"So when do we do it?" He thumped his chest happily. "With something like this, the sooner the better."

"How about tomorrow? I'll go over today and bring him out."

So she went into the city that afternoon, planning to lure Qin Yuhe away from the Xiguan Chemical Fertilizer Plant. With a two-month-old baby girl in her arms, she hoped to trick Qin into going with her to the civic affairs office to discuss child support. A dozen or more smokestacks towered over the plant, noisily spewing white smoke into the air. She made the rounds inside, but was told that Qin was delivering a truckload of fertilizer to Heilongjiang and wouldn't be back for at least ten days. He was avoiding her, just like her brother. She'd have to travel through four or five provinces to reach Heilongjiang if she wanted to find him. Besides, he'd be in his truck and on the go the whole time. Obviously, killing someone was easier than finding him. He'd managed to buy himself a couple more weeks of life. Choked with resentment, she left the plant. Her bladder felt like it would burst, and she spotted a pay toilet by the entrance. The middle-aged woman in charge had a hen's-nest of permed hair. Xuelian handed over twenty fen and left her daughter with the attendant as she went in to relieve herself and open up space for the anger surging inside. The baby was bawling when she came out, so she gave the girl a savage slap.

"It's all your fault, you little witch!"

The child was the root of the entanglement. She and Qin Yuhe were parents of a son born in the second year of their marriage; he was now seven. Then, in the spring she'd discovered that she was pregnant again, an obvious miscalculation. She should have made him wear a condom; instead, he'd had all the fun, and she'd wound up pregnant. A second child was against the law. If he'd been a peasant, they could have had the baby after paying a few thousand yuan in fines. But as a fertilizer plant employee, in addition to the fines, he'd lose his job and the pension he'd spent twelve years working toward. So they'd gone to the county hospital. Only in her second month, she hadn't felt a thing yet, but all of a sudden, there was movement in her belly after she took off her pants, climbed onto the operating table, and spread her legs. Abruptly snapping her legs shut, she jumped off the table and put her pants back on. The doctor thought she was going to the bathroom, but she walked straight out of the hospital, trailed by Qin Yuhe.

"Where are you going? They give you a shot. It doesn't hurt a bit."

"Let's go home and talk," she said. "Too many people around here."

They didn't speak while the bus traveled the forty li to reach their village. As soon as they were home she went into the cow pen, where a cow had just calved a few days before. The calf was suckling at the teat of the cow, which mooed hungrily; Xuelian brought out some hay. Yuhe followed her into the pen.

"What in the world were you thinking?"

"The baby was kicking. I have to keep it."

"We can't. I'll be fired if we have another child."

"Let's think of a way to keep the baby *and* your job," she said.

"That way doesn't exist."

"Let's get a divorce." She stood up.

"What's that supposed to mean?" That came as a shock.

"That's what a fellow in town, Zhao Huoche, did. Once we're divorced, we're each on our own. I'll have the baby, and it'll be mine, not yours. You can keep our son. That way we'll each have one child, what the law allows."

Still somewhat confused, Qin scratched his head, but he was beginning to catch on.

"That's not a bad idea, but we can't get a divorce just because you want another child."

"We'll do what Zhao did. Once the baby's entered into the household registry, we'll get remarried. The second child will have been born after the divorce, so we'll each have a child when we marry again. No law says couples with one child each can't marry. We'll just have to make sure not to have another one after that."

Yuhe scratched his head again, but this time to show how impressed he was by the fellow she'd mentioned.

"Zhao Huoche has a twisted mind. How did he come up with that idea? What does he do anyway?"

"He's a veterinarian," Xuelian said.

"He shouldn't be a veterinarian. He should go to Beijing and take charge of national family planning. He'd close all the loopholes."

He stopped and studied her. "You're not only carrying a baby, but a bag of tricks to boot. I've underestimated you."

So they went into town and got divorced, after which they stayed clear of one another to avoid speculation. But months passed, and when she had the baby, Xuelian learned that Qin had married Xiaomi, the owner of a hair salon in town. And Xiaomi was already pregnant. Li Xuelian's sham divorce had turned real. She had followed in Zhao Huoche's footsteps, but bewilderingly reached a different destination. So she went to see Qin Yuhe, arguing that the divorce was a sham; he was adamant that it was real, and showed her the decree to prove his point. By losing the argument, she realized that *she* had underestimated *him*. The divorce was easier to accept than the defeat; worse yet, she had no complaint, since it had been her idea in the first place. Not much you can say when someone deceives you, but she'd dug her own grave this time, and was humiliated. It was so maddening she decided then and there to kill him. But now he was off in Heilongjiang, too far for her to carry out her plan, so she vented her anger on her two-month-old daughter. One slap was all it took to silence the crying baby, but that slap infuriated the toilet attendant.

"What do you think you're doing?" she demanded with a stomp of her foot. "What have I ever done to you?"

"What do you mean?" a baffled Xuelian asked.

"Go somewhere else if you want to punish your child. You could kill a baby that way. If you did, you might get off because you're her mother, but no one would want to use this toilet if they knew someone had died here."

Grasping the woman's logic, Xuelian took the baby and crouched down on the steps in front of the toilet.

"Fuck you, Qin Yuhe. How am I supposed to go on living after what you did?"

The baby caught her breath and began to cry along with her mother. The profane outburst revealed to the toilet attendant that the crying woman was Qin Yuhe's ex-wife. News of their divorce had spread throughout the factory and even reached the public toilet at the entrance.

"Qin Yuhe, you're no damned good," the attendant cursed.

Her sympathetic words endeared her to Xuelian.

"It was a sham divorce. How did it turn real?" Xuelian wondered aloud.

To Xuelian's surprise, the woman replied:

"I wasn't talking about your divorce."

"What were you talking about?" Xuelian was confused.

"Qin Yuhe is a rotten guy. In January he came to use the toilet when he was drunk. It's a pay toilet. I get a percentage of the fee, and my family depends on this toilet. But he refused to pay the measly twenty fen, saying he worked at the plant and didn't have to. When I chased after him, he hit me and chipped one of my front teeth."

She opened her mouth to show Xuelian; sure enough, she had a chipped front tooth. Back when they were first married, Xuelian had thought he was a reasonable man, so it came as a shock that he'd be so different after the divorce. She had misread him.

"I didn't find him today," Xuelian said. "If I had, I'd have murdered him."

That didn't shock the attendant. "Murder's too good for that bastard," she said.

"What do you mean?" a stunned Xuelian asked.

"You murder a man, and he lies dead on the ground. It's over in minutes. If you ask me, what that son-of-a-bitch deserves isn't death, but tormenting. He remarried, so if you want to work out your anger, then torment him. Make it so that death's too easy and living's too hard."

That was an eye opener. So there actually are even better ways to punish someone, Xuelian realized. Murder only complicates matters. Tormenting him till he doesn't know which side is up and his family is splintered could take a matter that had been turned upside down and flip it right side up. Not just in regard to what was turned upside down, but for the fundamental logic in turning matters upside down. Xuelian had taken her child to the fertilizer plant intending to murder Qin Yuhe and left with the intention of legal action. And the woman who'd figured out what to do was a gatekeeper for people wanting to relieve themselves. She'd borne a grudge against Qin Yuhe over a chipped tooth, but without intending to, had saved his life.

3

The second time Li Xuelian met Wang Gongdao was in a courtroom. Wang, who was in his judge's robes, had just adjudicated a complicated property case. The parents of the two brothers of the Chao family on East Street had died when the boys were still young. When they grew up, the brothers invested in a hot-and-spicy soup shop at a busy intersection, opening their door each morning at five o'clock. In time they had a thriving business. But then, the year before, the elder brother had married, introducing a third person into the sibling mix, and trouble followed. A feud culminated in a clamor to divide the family property. Everything but the shop was easy: 50/50. But both brothers wanted to hold on to the shop, and neither was willing to give in. Which brought them to court.

Wang Gongdao greeted the elder Chao brother, who had been a primary school classmate. Then he turned to mediating the dispute. Whoever was willing to pay the other brother a certain sum of money, he suggested, could retain ownership of the shop. Elder Brother agreed, but Younger Brother raised a new issue. For the two years following the marriage, he said, his brother had stopped getting up early, so opening up each day had become his responsibility, and he demanded that the first order of business was for his brother to pay him for his efforts. But what about the eight thousand yuan we spent to repair your stomach ulcer last year? Elder Brother replied. Back and forth it went, until the brothers appeared to be on the verge of fisticuffs right there in the courtroom. Seeing that his mediation had failed, Wang declared the court out of session, withholding final judgment for another day. Younger Brother would have none of that:

"If you hadn't brought up my stomach operation, we could have settled this amicably. But since you did, we can deal with the shop later. Now it's all about my operation, and no one's leaving this courtroom till we get to the bottom of this!"

By this time he was hopping mad. "I got an ulcer in the first place because of the anger they caused."

"Your ulcer operation," Wang Gongdao rushed to make clear, "is outside the bounds of this case."

To everyone's surprise, Younger Brother lost his head, rushed up to Wang, pointed a finger at him, and declared:

"I know you two went to school together, Wang, and if you engage in favoritism, you won't get off easily! He rolled up his sleeves. "Just so you know, I fortified myself with a couple of drinks before I came here today."

"What is that supposed to mean?" Wang asked. "You're not threatening to hit me, are you?"

"It hasn't reached that point," Younger Brother said, his face white with anger. We'll see if it does!"

Wang Gongdao shook with anger. "I am not a part of this dispute," he growled. "I've got no stake in it. I'm trying to help, and you're threatening violence."

He banged his gavel. "Thugs, you're a couple of thugs!"

He ordered his bailiff to throw the two brothers out of his courtroom. Li Xuelian wasted no time in rushing up to the bench.

"Now it's my turn, Cousin."

Still in an ugly mood in the wake of the dispute between the brothers, Wang did not recognize her at first.

"Your turn for what?"

"My divorce," she said. "That matter I spoke to you about at your house. I'm Li Xuelian. You told me to come back in three days. Well, that's today."

Now Wang knew who she was, and his thoughts migrated to her from the Chao brothers. He sat down behind the bench and reflected on what Li had told him. He heaved a sigh.

"What a nuisance."

"Who's a nuisance?"

"Everybody is. I've thought this case of yours over, and there's no easy solution. First you. You're divorced but you want to get divorced again, yet to do so you have to prove that the first divorce was a sham. Then you need to get remarried, so you can get re-divorced. Now wouldn't you call that a nuisance?"

"Nuisances don't bother me," Xuelian said.

"Then there's your former husband. What's his name?"

"Qin Yuhe."

"If he were still single, we might be able to manage. But he's already got a new wife. If we can prove that your divorce was a sham, and you want to marry him again, he'll have to divorce his present wife or be guilty of bigamy. Then you two will get remarried so you can get re-divorced. Wouldn't you call that a nuisance?"

"That's exactly what I want."

"And don't forget the court. This is unprecedented. What looks like a single case in fact involves several legal actions. Passing judgment on each of them, from one divorce to another, would take us right back to the beginning, like walking in circles. Wouldn't you call *that* a nuisance?"

"Dealing with legal nuisances is your job, Cousin."

"But that's not the real issue."

"Then what is?"

"Let's say your divorce from Qin Yuhe last year was a sham. Well, that makes it a major nuisance."

"Why's that?"

"If your divorce was a sham, any sensible person can see that you wanted a divorce so you could have a second child. That would put you under suspicion of making a mockery of family planning. You know what family planning is, don't you?"

"It means you're allowed only so many children."

"It's not that simple," Wang replied. "This is national policy, which makes it quite serious. If it's determined that you two were involved in a sham divorce, they'll look into your and Qin Yuhe's background, which would involve your child. You think you'd be lodging charges against someone else, but you'd really be lodging them against yourself. And in the end what that means is, you'd be lodging charges against your own child."

That stunned Li Xuelian. She thought for a moment.

"Could she receive a death sentence?"

"Nothing like that," Wang said with a chuckle.

"How about me?"

"Not that either. It would be something administrative, like a fine or the termination of public employment. But that would be sort of like 'the egg breaks when the hen flies off,' wouldn't it?"

"But a broken egg is what I want," Xuelian said. "A fine doesn't worry me, nor does losing public employment, since I don't have that. I sell soy sauce in the market, so the worst they can do is tell me to stop. That son-of-a-bitch Qin Yuhe is a public employee, and I want him fired."

Wang Gongdao scratched his head.

"If you won't take no for an answer, my hands are tied. Did you bring your complaint with you?"

Li Xuelian handed it to Wang. It had been prepared by Old Qian's Law Offices on North Avenue, and had cost her three hundred yuan. Three sheets at a hundred yuan per. Xuelian had complained about the cost.

"This is a big case," Old Qian had said with a glare, "a very big case. Your complaint has several components," he added, "but I only charged you for one. So please, no gripes about the cost. Break this down and you'll see I lose money."

Wang Gongdao took the complaint from her.

"Did you bring the filing fee?"

"How much?"

"Two hundred."

"That's less than I gave the lawyer. It's worth two hundred to solve my problem."

With a glance at Li Xuelian, Wang Gongdao headed out of the courtroom. "Pay the fee at the bank and then go home and wait for a letter."

"How long will I have to wait?" she asked his retreating back.

Wang thought for a moment. "Once your complaint is in the system, it'll take at least ten days to get a ruling."

"I'll come see you in ten days, Cousin."

4

Over those ten days, Li Xuelian accomplished seven things.

One: she took a bath. Obsessed with the idea of murdering Qin Yuhe, she'd gone two months without bathing, ever since the birth of their child, and had begun to smell bad, even to herself. Now that her problem was about to be solved, she visited the public bath, where she soaked in hot water for two full hours, working up a sweat and getting puffy before lying down on the wooden platform to be scrubbed. The bath cost five yuan, the scrubbing another five. In the past she'd always scrubbed herself, but this time she happily spent five yuan to have someone else, a squat, overweight woman from Sichuan with strong hands, do it. The moment she started in, the woman gulped in surprise.

"I haven't see this much caked-on grime in years!" she said.

"Scrub me good and clean, Cousin," Xuelian said. "Something big is about to happen in my life."

"Getting married?"

"Yes, I am."

The scrub-lady examined Li Xuelian's belly.

"You look about the age for this to be your second marriage," she said.

"Yes, it is."

Reflecting on her comment, Xuelian was satisfied that she was telling the truth, for the whole purpose in taking Qin Yuhe to court was to marry him again and then re-divorce him. When she walked out of the public bath, she felt pounds lighter, a spring in her step.

Old Hu the butcher spotted her as she walked by. Like a fly smelling blood, he threw down the slab of meat he was cutting and ran after her, in his haste forgetting to leave his cleaver behind.

"Hey, Babe, hold up. I thought you needed help beating up Qin Yuhe. What happened?"

"Take it easy," she said. "He's off in Heilongjiang."

Hu stared at Xuelian, whose face was rosy; her hair, which was piled atop her head, was dripping wet after the bath. Her full post-partum breasts gave off a milky smell that seemed to envelop her entire body.

"What say we carry out the second half of the arrangement now, my dear?" he said as he drew near.

"No, we'll do it the way I said—we get together only after the beating."

Truth is, a beating was no longer necessary. Only days before, murder—and not a beating—had been the plan. Now both had been replaced by the act of tormenting. But Xuelian did not dare reveal that to Hu, not knowing what he might do, since his thoughts were on what followed the promised beating.

"Waiting around to beat the man is getting to me," Hu said. "I really think we should take care of our business, then I'll go to Heilongjiang and kill him for you."

Since now even a beating was no longer necessary, murder was a non-starter. So, with an eye on the cleaver in his hand, Xuelian said, "We'll have no more talk of killing. Do that and you'll get a bullet in the head."

She reached out and rubbed his chest.

"We're in no hurry, Old Hu. Impatient people don't get the hot tofu."

Old Hu, hand pressed against his chest, was hopping up and down.

"That's easy for you to say, but I'll fold up and die if this goes on much longer."

He pointed to his eyes.

"See that? They're bloodshot from a lack of sleep."

He paused.

"We keep delaying, and if I don't murder Qin Yuhe pretty soon, I'll have to murder somebody else."

Li Xuelian patted him on his muscular shoulder.

"We're in no hurry, Old Hu," she said, trying to comfort him. "Revenge will be sought, but the time is not hot. When the time has turned hot, revenge will be sought."

Two: she changed her hairstyle. After seeing Old Hu off, Xuelian went to a beauty shop. It was time to lose her ponytail in favor of short hair. She'd have to face Qin Yuhe if she was going to torment him, and an argument could spiral out of control. It had happened before. Long hair was easy to grab; short hair was not. That would give her the opportunity to spin around and kick him in the balls. She emerged, hardly able to recognize herself with short hair. That was a good thing. It was time for a new Li Xuelian.

Three: After leaving the beauty shop, she went to a clothing store, where she spent ninety-five yuan on a new outfit. Wang Gongdao knew what he was talking about when he said this was no simple case, that it was, in fact, several cases in one. How long such a trial would take was anyone's guess; during the course of the trial, she'd be in the public eye daily, and mustn't look like a slattern. She hated the thought of appearing to be a woman scorned, for that would make it hard to explain away the sham divorce of the previous year.

Four: She spent forty-five yuan on a pair of high-top athletic shoes with sixteen eyelets on each side, hugging her feet closely when she pulled the laces tight. She examined herself and liked what she saw. To torment him she'd also have to torment herself, since what she had in mind would require lots of walking.

Five: She sold off an old sow, along with a pair of piglets. She'd need the money for the trial, and wouldn't have time to tend to the animals. No sense worrying about pigs when human affairs were still up in the air. But she didn't sell them to Hu, the local butcher, afraid that might complicate things. Instead, she took them to a butcher in the next town over, a man by the name of Deng.

Six: She took a bus some fifty li to entrust her two-month-old daughter to a schoolmate, Meng Lanzhi. Originally, she'd planned to leave her daughter with her brother, Yingyong. But not after the way he'd run off to Shandong when she'd sought his help in murdering her husband. He was not dependable. He'd known he could depend on her if he was in need, but when the tables were turned, he'd been a disappointment. There'd be no more brother-sister issues of reliability after this. Xuelian and Meng Lanzhi had not been particularly close in school; in fact, there had been some bad blood. All because they'd had their eyes on the same boy. But he'd gotten chummy with a girl two grades ahead of them, which left them both in the lurch. The ensuing heartbreak turned them into lifelong friends. When Li Xuelian showed up with her daughter, Meng was also nursing a child—that was made to order. No need for Xuelian to go into the details of why she was leaving her daughter with Meng, since her situation was a hot topic throughout the area.

"I won't have to worry about her if she's with you. I'll spend the next two months tormenting him, until either the fish dies or the net breaks. I ask you, would you do what I'm doing?"

Meng shook her head.

"Then do you agree with people who think what I'm doing is wrong?"

Again Meng shook her head.

"Why's that?"

"You and I are different," she said. "I can put up with a lot, you can't."

She rolled up her sleeve. "See here, this is where Old Zang hit me," she said, referring to her husband. "A person can put up with stuff all her life or not. I'm a coward, but I respect people who aren't. You're stronger than me, Xuelian."

Xuelian threw her arms around Lanzhi and wept. "After hearing you say that, I don't care if I die doing this."

Seven: She prayed to the Bodhisattva. That thought had not occurred to her at first, but on the bus ride home after dropping off her daughter, she passed Mount Jietai, where a Buddhist temple housed a statue of the Bodhisattva. She was attracted first by a sutra chanted over a loudspeaker. Then she spotted people, men and women, young and old, climbing the mountain to burn incense at the temple. Xuelian, who believed that her plan was foolproof, suddenly thought of something she'd neglected to consider, and that was the presence of deities in the world. After shouting for the driver to stop, she got off and went straight up the mountain. Visitors swarmed the temple and its grounds, entry to which required a ticket. She bought one for ten yuan and a bundle of incense sticks for five more. Once inside, she lit the incense, raised it over her head with both hands, and got down on her knees in front of the statue amid a crowd of kneeling believers. Everyone else was praying for something good to happen; Xuelian alone prayed for something bad to occur. She closed her eyes and intoned:

"Great and Merciful Bodhisattva, please see that this legal matter ends in the destruction of Qin Yuhe's family."

She paused, then added, "If that's not enough, then let the son of a bitch die a horrible death."

5

Li Xuelian had planned for a two-month trial. Start to finish, it lasted all of twenty minutes. Wang Gongdao was the presiding judge, as the nameplate made clear. A judicial officer sat to his left, a court clerk to his right. A lawyer by the name of Sun represented the defendant, Qin Yuhe, who was not in attendance. Sun's offices were next door to those of the lawyer Qian, who had drawn up Li Xuelian's complaint. After the briefs were disposed of and the documents placed into evidence, each side stated its case and presented its witness list. The documents in evidence were two copies of a divorce decree, which the court determined was genuine. In stating her complaint, Xuelian told the court that the decree was a sham, after which Qin Yuhe's lawyer read a statement prepared by Qin that the divorce approved the year before was legitimate. The first witness was a civil servant named Gu, who had handled the Li/Qin divorce the year before in Round the Bend Township. Gu had stood in the courtroom doorway, leaning against a post and listening attentively to the proceedings. When he was called, he stepped forward and announced that the decree was legitimate. He had enjoyed a perfect record in handling marriage and divorce cases for more than thirty years. An angry Xuelian disputed that:

"Old Gu, how can a man your age not recognize a sham divorce when he sees it?"

Gu, equally angry, replied:

"If that's true, it can only mean that you two conspired to pull a fast one on me." With a clap of his hands, he continued: "And that is nothing compared to pulling a fast one on the government with a

phony divorce. He just read a statement from Qin Yuhe," Gu continued, pointing to lawyer Sun, "who swore that it was legitimate."

"How can you believe anything that bastard Qin Yuhe says?"
Xuelian argued.

"If I can't believe Qin Yuhe," Gu said, "then I'll believe you.
During last year's divorce proceedings, he said nothing. You were the
only one who spoke. When I asked you why you wanted a divorce,
you said the cause was alienation of affection. Are you saying now
that your affections have been de-alienated? Since you haven't seen
each other for a year, how could you have patched things up? Qin
Yuhe didn't even show up in court today, which looks pretty alienated
to me."

Li Xuelian was at a loss for words.

"In all my fifty years and more," Gu sputtered angrily, "I've
never been tricked like this before! How will I be able to hold my
head up in Round the Bend if this divorce is declared a sham?"

To all appearances, Li Xuelian was taking Gu, and not Qin
Yuhe, to court.

Now that the documents had been admitted into evidence
and the witnesses had had their say, the outcome was clear. Wang
Gongdao banged his gavel, and Li Xuelian's charge was dismissed.
She stopped him as he was making his way out the door.

"How could you rule like that, Cousin?"

"That's how the law works," he said.

"It's over, just like that? Even without Qin Yuhe?"

"The law allows for a lawyer to represent him in court."

"I don't understand," Xuelian said, looking stunned, "how
anyone could not see that it was a sham."

Wang handed her the divorce decree.

"In the eyes of the law, this is perfectly legitimate. I told you so,
but you wouldn't listen." He lowered his voice. "I didn't bring up the
matter of the child, for which you can thank me."

"I lost the case, but you helped me out, is that what you're
saying?"

"You got it," a bemused Wang replied.

6

Li Xuelian first met Dong Xianfa—Constitution Dong—in front of the county courthouse.

A standing member of the Judicial Committee, Dong was fifty-two, short and squat, with a pronounced paunch. He had worked in the courthouse for twenty years, following his discharge from the army and his return to the county to find work. At the time, there had been three job openings: one in the Bureau of Animal Husbandry, one in the Public Health Bureau, and one in the courthouse. The chief of the County Committee Organization Department thumbed through Dong Xianfa's dossier.

"There isn't anything in his file that points to a special talent, but his name alone—Constitution Dong—makes Judicial Committee the obvious choice. No livestock or public health for him."

So off to the courthouse he went. In the army he had risen to the level of battalion commander, so he was designated a presiding judge. Ten years later he was elevated to membership on the Judicial Committee. Spoken of as a promotion, the judicial establishment viewed it as a demotion, for it was an administrative position with no real power. His salary and benefits were that of a deputy chief justice, but he was not a deputy chief justice. His authority to hear and decide cases, use government vehicles, and sign his name to be compensated for expenses was inferior to that of a presiding judge. In a word, Dong Xianfa, a one-time presiding judge, had been kicked upstairs. He spent the next ten years on the Judicial Committee, and had nearly reached retirement age. Twenty years earlier, his superiors, both the chief and his deputy, had been older than him.

Those he worked under now were younger. In terms of age, Dong Xianfa was considered a veteran who, in twenty years, had made it only as far as the Judicial Committee, and for that his colleagues held him in low esteem. And no one held him in lower esteem than he himself. His colleagues' lack of respect for him was evident in normal times; his low self-esteem emerged during critical moments. On the several occasions when he ought to have been promoted to deputy chief, he had failed to "strike while the iron was hot." It was common knowledge that a member of the Judicial Committee was closer to deputy chief than was a presiding judge. But other presiding judges had been promoted over him, while he remained stuck where he was. Aren't critical moments more important than normal times? And don't normal times accumulate until a critical moment is reached? Yet nothing was more critical than his colleagues' view that he had failed to be promoted because he was ineffective, while he attributed the cause to his principled nature. He had, he believed, failed because he was not a toady, he did not send gifts to important people, and he was incorruptible. When what was just and proper led to sadness and despair, Dong simply muddled along. Even more to the point was the fact that he disliked legal work. Not because he felt it was unimportant, but because, even as a child, he had preferred bringing things together over moving things apart, and the daily business of law was taking things apart. No one ever came to court when things were going well. Medicine supplies a fine analogy: doctors treat the sick, not the well. Hospitals need patients, courtrooms need disputes. Absent sickness and disputes, hospitals and courtrooms would have to close up shop. Dong Xianfa simply felt that he was in the wrong line of work. In his view, being a livestock broker, bartering over the price of an animal, fit him better than adjudicating cases at law. But a standing member of the Judicial Committee could not simply step down and start selling livestock. That might not have bothered him, but the rest of the world would have gone nuts, certain that he'd lost his mind. So day in and day out he performed his committee work, and was, as a result, miserable. Others attributed his despondence to not having been promoted in twenty years, and when they were out drinking they lamented the injustice he suffered. Dong shared his colleagues' sense of injustice over his lack of advancement, but mainly he wished he could be a broker in the livestock market. Worst of all, he could tell no one why he was miserable, and so, as he muddled along, he developed hostility toward his surroundings and the people who inhabited them. All this wore him down until his favorite activity outside of working hours was boozing.

Back when he'd first been assigned to the Judicial Committee, its members did examine cases, which involved him in the legal process. Plaintiffs and defendants often invited him out for drinks, and as time wore on, people noticed that while he examined and intervened in cases from time to time, he never wielded a gavel. That kept his status below that of an ordinary judge, let alone one who presided, and so no one felt a need to chat him up. When invitations stopped coming from participants in cases, Dong could go drinking with his colleagues, but they knew he was just killing time till he retired, since he obviously wasn't going anywhere. Who wanted to go drinking with someone with no future? Drinking invitations were a daily occurrence, but no one included him in the outings. That was a hard pill to swallow, and eventually he was reduced to hanging around the courthouse to find drinking partners. When plaintiffs and defendants took judges out to drink, they set out directly from the courthouse. If they spotted Dong Xianfa pacing in front of the gate around noontime, they felt obliged to call out:

"Come have lunch with us, Dong."

At first, he'd hesitated.

"I'm busy." But then, before they could respond: "Did I say busy? Hell, it can wait till this afternoon." And, "The ducks can wait till the afternoon to go down to the river."

And off he'd go to lunch with the others.

But after a while, when they spotted him, they anticipated his response:

"We know how busy you are, Dong, so we won't ask you to lunch today."

"I never said I was busy," Dong said unhappily. "What's that all about? You plan to eat by yourselves? Don't underestimate me," he added. "I'm telling you, I've worked in the courthouse for twenty years. I may not be able to help you when you need it, but I can still make things hard for you."

That would embarrass them.

"Look at you," they'd say. "Can't you take a joke?"

Off they'd go together.

Then, in time they began sneaking out the back door, knowing that a fellow by the name of Dong Xianfa was waiting for them out front.

He was pacing in front of the courthouse when Li Xuelian saw him for the first time. She'd never stepped foot in a courthouse before bringing legal action against Qin Yuhe, and so did not know who Dong Xianfa was. But she'd refused to accept the decision handed down by Wang Gongdao, whom she now found untrustworthy, and could not wait to try again. This time, rather than simply sue to have last year's divorce from Qin Yuhe overturned, she'd first sue to overturn Wang's decision. That was the way to start over. Not going to court was one thing; taking a case to court complicated things. The problem was, she didn't know *how* to have Wang's decision overturned; what she did know, however, was that she'd have to find someone who had authority over him. Since Wang was a judge in the county's Number One Civil Court, she went looking for his boss, a man named Jia, who saw at once that this was going to be a tricky issue, brought to court by a hard-to-manage complainant. Worst of all, he could see that the woman had no knowledge of how the law worked, and that trying to explain things to her would be harder than actually sorting out the case. Jia worried that the more he explained things, the more complicated the matter could get, to the point where he himself might be implicated.

Li Xuelin went to see Jia at six in the evening, as he was getting ready to go out to dinner. An inspiration came to him in his eagerness to start the eating and drinking, a way to untangle a thorny problem. He'd shunt the case over to Dong Xianfa of the Judicial Committee. He had no gripe with Dong, but he knew he could not possibly pass this on to another senior official, such as one of the deputy chiefs, and definitely not to the chief justice himself. Besides, he'd always enjoyed his verbal jousts with Dong. When the two men met, the only thing that counted as a greeting was a personal barb. Just the night before, Jia had jousted with Dong over drinks at a banquet, and he was ripe to keep the joust alive.

"This is a thorny case," he said as he sucked air in between his teeth.

"It didn't start out like that," Li Xuelian said. "It got that way because of you people."

"The case has already been decided, it's a court ruling. I'm not high enough to overturn one of those."

"Who is high enough?"

"I'll give you a name," he said after a thoughtful pause, "but you can't tell him where you got it."

"Why the hush-hush?"

"He's had to deal with so many thorny cases I'm afraid one more might send him over the edge."

"Who is it?"

"A standing member of the court's Judicial Committee, Dong Xianfa."

"What does one of those do?"

"In a hospital he'd be a specialist who worked only on rare diseases."

Was Jia correct to say that? Yes, he was. From a theoretical perspective, Dong Xianfa was a judicial expert who, by definition, specialized in thorny cases. In terms of hierarchy, a judicial expert outranked a presiding judge, which made him Jia's superior. But everyone associated with the court knew that the term "expert" was ornamental, and that Dong had less authority than those below him.

On Jia's recommendation, Li Xuelian went to the courthouse, arriving at half past noon the next day, where she encountered Dong Xianfa, who had been pacing in front of the gate for more than an hour. She knew only that Dong was a judicial expert who specialized in important and thorny cases. Dong had no idea who she was. Since they were total strangers, she respectfully refrained from interrupting him as he looked up and down the street, over and over, until it was obvious that he hadn't seen what he was looking for in the half hour she'd watched him.

"Are you judicial expert Dong?" she finally approached and said.

The interruption caught him by surprise. He looked at his wristwatch and saw that it was already one o'clock, which meant he'd have no company for lunch that day. He turned.

"Who are you?" he said.

"My name is Li Xuelian."

That rang no bell. He yawned.

"What do you want?"

"You people misjudged my case."

The fog in Dong Xianfa's brain was too thick for him to recall if he'd intervened in such a case. If he had, he wouldn't have been able to recall anyway.

"The court hears many cases. Which one are you talking about?"

So Li Xuelian told him about her case, starting from the beginning; Dong had heard enough before she was halfway through, especially since all that divorcing and remarrying and re-divorcing, past, present, and future, was so complicated he knew he had never intervened in it, and so complicated he didn't want to hear more. Livestock talk was a lot more interesting than this stuff.

"This case of yours," he cut her off impatiently, "is none of my business."

"None of yours, maybe," Xuelian, "but plenty of Wang Gongdao's."

"Then it's Wang Gongdao you need to talk to, not me."

"You're his superior, and since he misjudged my case, you're who I have to see."

"There are lots of people in court above Wang Gongdao. Why not them?"

"Because they told me you're an expert in difficult cases."

That's when it hit Dong that someone at court was having fun at his expense, dumping someone else's problem on him.

"Which son of a bitch told you than?" he spat out angrily. "Misjudging a case is exactly what you can expect from bad people who don't belong in a court of law. Go talk to whoever sent you to me. And after you do that, I'll look him up."

He turned to storm off, his mind set on a couple of drinks and a bowl of lamb noodles to take care of his hunger, since the others had gone to lunch without him. Li Xuelian reached out and stopped him.

"You can't leave, specialist Dong. You have to settle this for me."

Dong didn't know whether to laugh or to cry. "Why me? The court has plenty of people."

"I did you a favor already."

"What did you do?"

"I took a bundle of cotton and two hens to your house this morning."

Now he really didn't know whether to laugh or to cry.

"Do you honestly expect to gain a hold on me with a bundle of cotton and a couple of chickens? Go get them out of my house."

He pulled his sleeve free and started off again, only to be stopped a second time.

"Your wife promised me you'd look into my case."

"She's good at feeding pigs, and that's about all. She knows nothing about the law."

"According to you, then, I've done all that for nothing."

"Not for nothing," he said, pointing a finger at her. "What you've done is called bribery. Do you know what that means? You're holding me responsible for something I didn't do."

For the third time Li Xuelian delayed his departure, and by now a crowd had formed. Dong Xianfa, who was already stewing in anger, lost his temper at the sight of the crowd.

"You're nothing but a troublemaker. How dare you grab my sleeve in public! Get out of here!"

He shoved her away and walked off.

That night, Dong Xianfa rode his bike back to Dong Family Village, some five li from town. He could smell stewed chicken before he walked in the door. Once inside, he saw that his father-in-law was visiting and that his wife was stewing chickens. He'd put the Li Xuelian affair out of his mind, but it popped right back in as he walked into the kitchen and lifted the lid off the pot in which two stewed chickens, cut into eight pieces, were nearly ready to eat.

"When will you ever learn?" he screamed at his wife. "Do you have any idea what you're doing? You're accepting bribery and breaking the law!"

By the following morning he'd forgotten all about it.

7

Li Xuelian spotted Chief Justice Xun Zhengyi—Impartial Xun—in front of the Pine and Crane Hotel. Justice Xun, who was so drunk he had to be carried downstairs, had held the position for three years, and, at only thirty-eight, was younger than all his peers in neighboring counties. Being young meant he had to think about the future of what was expected to be a long career, which was why he was socially cautious. He seldom drank, having devised five career rules for himself: no drinking alone; no drinking during work hours; no drinking in legal circles; no drinking in the home county; and no drinking Monday through Friday. Overlaps and redundancies were, of course, unavoidable, but they added up to a single phrase: he did not drink without a reason.

On this day he was falling-down drunk. It was a Wednesday, in his home county, and with legal colleagues, all contrary to his career rules. But there was a reason. It was former Chief Judge Cao's birthday. Cao had turned the position of Chief Judge over to Xun, whom he had taken under his wing upon his retirement three years earlier. So Xun put aside his drinking restrictions to celebrate the elder leader's birthday. Cao drank too much, so did Xun. In reality, Cao's cultivation and mentorship had caused Xun considerable anguish. On the eve of Cao's retirement, there had been four deputy chief justices, and Xun Zhengyi had not been Cao's favorite; that honor had fallen to Deputy Chief Ge. Back when Cao had not been adjudicating legal cases, his sole recreational interests had been boozing and playing bridge. Deputy Chief Ge had also been a bridge player. The game of bridge is an ideal test of a man's character. Having gained knowledge of Ge's character via the game, Cao had anointed him as his successor, confident that he would not be disappointed. Which is what made what happened a month before Cao's retirement so shocking. After some heavy drinking during dinner with some classmates, Ge had climbed into his car and sped down a one-way street in the wrong direction, sending oncoming cars swerving frantically out of his way.

"Don't traffic laws apply to you morons," he cursed, "driving the wrong way! It's this flawed legal system of ours. I'll take you all to court tomorrow!"

As he was cursing, up ahead, a fourteen-wheeler with a load of coal was unable to avoid a head-on collision, hurtling Ge's car into the opposite lanes. Ge did not survive the crash. His death opened the door for Xun Zhengyi. The job was his, for which he owed thanks not to Cao but to the driver of the coal truck, or better yet to the quantity of alcohol Ge had consumed and to Ge's classmates. At least that's how Xun looked at it. But not Cao, who considered anyone he handed the position over to be his protégé, which meant that by ascending to the position of chief justice, Xun was in Cao's debt; and since that was how the retiree felt, Xun went along with it. Once he settled into the chief justice's chair, he greeted former Chief Justice Cao by saying, "Lacking virtue and talent, if not for the guidance of the elder statesman, this job would never have been mine."

Finding nothing to fault in that, the former chief justice began to accept Xun Zhengyi as one of his own. Cao knew better than to interfere in courthouse affairs, but he did not hesitate to call upon Xun in regard to personal problems. That clear distinction was all Xun needed to see that Cao was a sensible person, and that he could help his predecessor in his personal life at little cost to himself. For three years, he'd treated Cao with the respect due a former leader. He held a birthday party for him every year, opening the festivities at the dinner table with:

"Kept busy all year long, I have not been a dutiful visitor to our former leader. But on his birthday, I see it as my duty to host a party for him."

One short comment to make up for a year's neglect, but better than nothing, and Cao beamed with delight. The party this year was held on the second floor of the Pine and Crane Hotel, where the birthday celebrant drank a great deal. And since there was a reason to drink, Xun Zhengyi tried to keep up with him. While still sober, he announced, "Our former leader knows that I have five restrictions against drinking. But one day a year I make an exception and join him in drinking to my heart's content."

Cao's happy face glowed. He had been a big drinker all his life, while Xun Zhengyi, who seldom drank, was not. After a lifetime of boozing, Cao had created a unique drinking style, which revolved around cigarettes. "The saying goes," he would say, "that 'smoking and drinking go together.'" For him that did not mean alternating drinks and puffs. No, it was using a pack of cigarettes to determine how much alcohol to pour into a glass. First the pack lies flat, alcohol is poured to that height, and drunk in one gulp. Then the pack lies on its side, alcohol is poured to that height, and it too is finished off in one swallow. Finally, the pack is stood to full height, alcohol fills the glass, and it is drunk down. The height of a flat pack is one ounce, on its side, two ounces, and full height, three ounces. A three-stage pack equals six ounces of alcohol, a so-called "open door red," considered to be the true beginning of a drinking party, launched by finger-guessing games and accrued penalties. By that time it's hard to say how much has been drunk. What Cao did not know was, now that he had retired and Xun Zhengyi was his successor, the people who drank with him—deputy chiefs, heads of the political section and disciplinary group, the office manager, and other leaders—all once his subordinates but now subordinates of Xun Zhengyi—poured mineral water into Xun's glass but real liquor into his. After eight rounds, Cao was drunk and so was Xun. But Cao was blotto, while Xun still had a ways to go. The banquet ended with Cao being carried downstairs from the second floor. His successor too was carried downstairs, where Li Xuelian accosted him.

"Chief Justice Xun, you have to take up my case."

Being stopped on the street by people with complaints was a regular occurrence for a chief justice. But it was nighttime and he was drunk; caught unprepared, he was thrown off balance. He had to act drunker than he really was, since the former chief justice was there beside him, and he did not want his fright to be obvious. But the office manager, who had helped carry him down the stairs, did not try to hide his alarm. He grabbed Li Xuelian's arm.

"Let go!" he demanded. "Can't you see the chief justice is drunk? Anything you have to say can wait till tomorrow."

He shoved Xuelian out of the way and helped Xun Zhengyi over to the car, but was stopped by a shout from former Chief Justice Cao at the hotel entrance:

"What's going on there?"

His speech was slurred, but that did not stop him.

"Does someone need legal action? Come tell me what it is. Things like this are always happening to me."

If he had not been drinking so heavily, Cao would never have stuck his nose into courtroom business. But the alcohol had dulled his recollection of having retired three years before, and he was caught up in the remembered excitement of dealing with a legal case. Realizing what Cao was about to do, the others left Xun where he was and moved to hustle Cao into the car.

"It's just a peasant woman, Chief Justice, nothing to concern yourself about. Your health is what's important, and you need to go home to rest. Chief Justice Xun can handle this."

They picked Cao up and carried him to the car. Still struggling, he rolled down the window, pointed at Xun, who was standing by the second car, and, in an official tone of voice, said, "Zhengyi, you to investigate this case. I've said in the past that any official who doesn't stand up for the common people might as well go home and sell sweet potatoes."

Zhengyi stumbled up to Cao's car.

"Leave it to me, Sir," he said. "I haven't forgotten all you taught me over the years. I'll get to the bottom of this and report to you tomorrow."

The car drove off with Cao muttering in the back seat. Xun did not climb into his car as a result of what Cao had said to him, not out of a fear of what Li Xuelian might do if she had heard it, but because the next day, after Cao had sobered up, his mentor might recall what he'd said and would expect Xun to carry out his promise, even though he hadn't really meant it. It would not look good to agree to things that were said sober, but not things said drunk. He could lose a lot by trying to save a little. A retired official might be in no position to offer help, but he could still make things hard on people. He would have IOUs from those above and below over many years in a position of power, and rain from the next passing cloud could pour down on someone's head. So even though he was fairly drunk at the time, Xun Zhengyi knew that he had to deal with Li Xuelian; but precisely because he was fairly drunk, there was a testy quality to the questions he asked:

"What's with you?"

"I want to lodge a complaint against somebody."

"Who?"

"Dong Xianfa."

Actually, as we know, her first target had been Qin Yuhe; she had then moved on to Wang Gongdao, for it was he who had ruled against her. But that was then; now the object of her complaint was Dong Xianfa, with whom she'd had no quarrels before their one and only meeting, where he had turned down a request to reexamine her case; that would have put an end to the matter if only they had not engaged in a conversation in front of the courthouse that had become increasingly acrimonious and drawn a crowd. That had been more than he could stand. "Get out of here, you troublemaker!" he'd bellowed. And that was too offensive for Li to let pass. I'm suing to right a wrong, she was thinking, and that's the business you're in, so how dare you call me a troublemaker and tell me to get out of here! So she went looking for Chief Justice Xun, Dong Xianfa's boss, to take Dong to court before carrying out her complaint against Qin Yuhe and Wang Gongdao. Poor Xun Zhengyi could not make heads or tails out of what she was telling him.

"What did Dong Xianfa do to you?"

Dong hadn't done anything to Li, except to call her a troublemaker and tell her to get out of there, hardly actionable offenses. But she was pressed to say something, and so:

"Dong Xianfa is on the take!"

Obviously, this was a groundless accusation. While he might have been on the take sometime, somewhere, definitely not in regard to Li Xuelian's case. Granted, Dong's wife had accepted the gift of cotton and a couple of hens, and though that did not rise to the level of bribery, Dong himself had accused his wife of accepting a bribe when he'd seen the chickens stewing in a pot at home.

A gust of cold wind swept past at that moment, eliciting a shudder from Xun Zhengyi. If he hadn't been drunk before that gust of wind, he was now. A prudent man when sober, he had an explosive temper after drinking; alcohol made him a different man, and that was one of the reasons he avoided the stuff most of the time, the underlying cause of his five proscriptions.

"You can say anything else about him," he reacted impatiently, "and I'd look into it. But not accusing him of being on the take."

"Then who will look into it?"

"The Public Prosecutor's office."

He was telling the truth. As a public servant, if Dong Xianfa had ruled incorrectly on a case, it was a matter for the chief justice. If, however, he was accused of being on the take, that was out of the chief justice's jurisdiction, and became a matter for the Public Prosecutor. This was all unfamiliar territory for Li Xuelian, and was beginning to take its toll on her.

"Everyone I talk to sends me to somebody else. I want to know who I'm supposed to talk to!"

What she said next really set Xun Zhengyi off:

"As chief justice, you should not be on the take like Dong Xianfa."

Now Chief Justice Xun could have been on the take sometime, somewhere, but definitely not in regard to Li Xuelian's case. Sober, he might have let this comment pass. But he wasn't, and he didn't.

"You and I have just met!" he shouted into Li Xuelian's face. "How dare you accuse me of being on the take! You really are a troublemaker, so get out of here!"

Even the words were the same as Dong Xianfa's.

8

Li Xuelian met County Chief Shi Weimin—For the People Shi—
in front of the government office building. Shi was in the back seat
of his car enjoying a bowl of rice porridge when a woman suddenly
appeared in front of his car. His driver slammed on the brakes, sending Shi lurching forward, where his head collided with the back of
the seat in front, spraying porridge all over him. He rubbed his forehead, sat back, and looked up, only to see a woman kneeling in the
road directly ahead, holding up a cardboard sign with a single word
scrawled on it: 冤 INJUSTICE.

A county chief would not be expected to go to his office on a
Sunday, but Shi never took a Sunday off, not with the multifarious
affairs and daily lives of a population of more than a million, including workers, farmers, merchants, and intellectuals, to look after.
Every day more than a hundred directives from the Central Government, provincial officials, and municipal authorities arrived on Shi's
desk, demanding his attention. Workers put in an eight-hour day; Shi
Weimin logged fourteen or fifteen, not counting the nightly meet-
ings. Hardly a day passed without someone from the provincial or
municipal level coming to inspect county work, and he was responsible for entertaining the members of at least eight senior inspection
teams from the more than one hundred provincial and municipal
departments on a daily basis, which meant sixteen lunches and dinners. And since they were all functional departments, he had to steer
clear of the slightest hint of offense. Shi Weimin's stomach suffered
grievously from all that food and drink. He was often heard to grum-
ble to his subordinates, hands pressed against his belly:

"County chief is no job for a human being."

And yet, ascending to the position of a county boss had not been easy. It was a dream shared by a million residents of the county, but wormwood does not grow on all ancestral tombs. The main reason was the ease in which a person can fall into the trap of government work. A township boss strives to become a county chief, who then strives to become a municipal or provincial boss. A man in that position has no one to blame but himself. This did not escape the attention of Shi Weimin, who had no regrets, despite his grumbles. If liquor was ruining his health, it was up to him to nurse himself back to health. Lunch and dinner invariably involved liquor, but for breakfast he ate rice porridge, to which he added pumpkin and yam, coarse grains that were a boon to his ailing stomach. There were times when the previous night's meeting did not end till very late and he overslept the next morning, forcing him to eat his porridge in the car on the way to the office.

Li Xuelian's experience with Xun Zhengyi, the chief justice, had taught her an important lesson: rather than meet the county chief at lunch or dinner, she'd confront him first thing in the morning. Important people tend to drink during the lunch and dinner hours, but their heads are clear in the mornings. So she accosted him in front of the government office building early that morning.

Shi Weimin was on his way to a ribbon-cutting ceremony for a new restaurant called Peach Blossom Heaven. This so-called "heaven" was very much earthbound, located amid a grove of trees some twenty li southwest of town, with an occasional bird and a few spotted deer that belonged to the owner. What added splendor to the restaurant was the spa and bathing facility directly behind it, equipped with a sauna, massage rooms, and everything normally associated with such a place. Enterprises of this nature sometimes dealt in illicit activities, and that should have kept the county chief from attending the ceremony. But the owner happened to be the brother-in-law of a provincial bigwig, and since the rented land fell within Shi Weimin's county, as "landlord" he had no choice but to attend. Besides, once Peach Blossom Heaven was open for business, there would be taxes to pay, and generating revenue was one of his important responsibilities. The ceremony had been planned for a Sunday morning in order to attract as many people as possible. But last night's meeting had dragged on so late that the county chief had overslept and was eating his porridge in the car. It was already 8:30, half an hour before the scheduled ceremony, and Shi was getting anxious. That anxiety intensified when his car was stopped almost as soon as it left the government compound. But Shi was a paragon of serenity compared to his driver, whose anger stemmed not from a concern that they would be late or that his boss had banged his head against the back of his seat or even that the county chief was now covered in porridge; no, it resulted from the sudden appearance of a woman kneeling in front of his car, which had made him slam on the brakes and break out in a cold sweat. He rolled down his window.

"You got a death wish?" he barked.

This was not the first such incident experienced by Shi Weimin, a man with more self control than his driver; in fact, for county chiefs, these things came with the territory. He reined in the driver, opened his door, and stepped out of the car. After brushing off the porridge that clung to him, he went up and helped the woman to her feet.

"Come on, get up and tell me what this is about."

Li Xuelian stood up.

"Who are you looking for?" Shi asked her.

"The county chief."

He knew that a woman like this could not own a TV set and so would not have seen local news programming, which made him a stranger in her eyes.

"What do you want with him?"

Li Xuelian raised her "Injustice" cardboard sign.

"To bring legal action."

"Against which person?"

"Persons, not person."

Shi Weimin chuckled.

"How many altogether?"

"First against Chief Justice Xun Zhengyi, second against Judicial Committee Member Dong Xianfa, third against Justice Wang Gongdao, fourth against my husband, Qin Yuhe, and fifth against myself."

What confused Shi Weimin was not that she wanted to bring legal action against all those other people, but that she ended her indictment with "myself." First time he'd ever heard anything like that, and he knew this was going to be no easy case, and was probably going to take more time than he had at the moment. He looked at his watch—already 8:40.

"I'll go find the county chief for you."

He turned to run back to the office building with two goals in mind: one, to be on his way to the Peach Blossom Heaven ribbon-cutting, and two, since he couldn't attend spattered with porridge, to change clothes in his office. Li Xuelian reached out and grabbed his sleeve.

"Stop," she said. "I think you're the county chief."

Shi Weimin flicked bits of porridge off his clothes.

"Do I look like a county chief?" he said, staring her in the eye.

"I asked around for your car license number, and this is it. That makes you the county chief."

"Just being in the county chief's car doesn't make me the county chief," Shi replied. "I'm his secretary, and a case like yours is way too big for me. I'll go find him."

Li Xuelian was forced to let go of his sleeve, freeing Shi to run back to his office, where he changed into clean clothes and had someone call up the County Complaint Department Head to handle a complaint by a woman at the building entrance. He also called for another car to meet him out back to take him to the ceremony.

The rest of the day passed with no news, but that night, when he went to the county guesthouse to join visitors from the provincial government, he was met at the front steps by his Complaint Department Head, a man named Lü. By that time, Shi Weimin had forgotten about the woman with a complaint that morning. Department Head Lü happily came up as he stepped from his car:

"I need your support, County Chief."

"What for?"

"The head of the Municipal Letters and Complaints Bureau, Chief Zhang, is on his way. He's booked into Room 888. You need to go see him as soon as he arrives."

"I didn't know he was coming."

"He phoned a while ago. Normally I wouldn't bother you with something so trivial, but it's special this time. The first quarter appraisal of letters and complaints departments is underway."

Shi Weimin counted on his fingers.

"Yours will be the ninth banquet for me today."

"Three drinks with him and you can leave. If you'll do that, I can be in the top three. This involves stability. If a county has trouble maintaining stability, it won't be the department head who loses his official cap."

"All right, I'll go see him in a little while, how's that? But why try to scare me with talk about official caps?"

Lü smiled, as Shi Weimin was reminded of the woman who had blocked his way that morning.

"Oh, right, what about the woman who stopped me this morning?"

Lü waved his arm dismissively.

"I sent the shrew packing."

The news displeased Shi Weimin.

"How can you call a woman who risked her life to block my way with a big sign with the word 'Injustice' on it a shrew?"

"Her sign may have been big, but the affair is peanut size."

"Tell me about it."

"She was divorced last year, and now she's having second thoughts, insisting it was a sham divorce."

"She's suing all those people over *that*?" Shi remarked. "And all of them in the court system. Did she take her case to court and get turned away?"

"I checked. They didn't turn her away. She's suing them because they all did their jobs. She insists that the divorce was a sham, but the court said it was perfectly legal. They can't be expected to break the law and invalidate a divorce just because she wants them to, can they?"

But Shi Weimin was sympathetic to Li Xuelian's situation.

"Did she say why she has second thoughts?"

"If she has," Lü replied, "she should take them up with her ex. That's who she divorced, not the government."

Shi Weimin chuckled. "You shouldn't make jokes like that about someone with a bellyful of anger," he said.

As he was speaking, the vice chief of the Provincial Water Department walked up to the guesthouse entrance in the company of a deputy county chief. With a smile, Shi Weimin left Lü's side and went up to greet his visitor. They shook hands and went inside.

9

Li Xuelian sat in front of the Municipal Office Building, her "Injustice" sign prominently displayed, for three days before the mayor, Cai Fubang, was aware of it. He could never be blamed for callous disregard of someone prepared to do what she was doing, since he was off in Beijing the whole time. As soon as he returned he learned of the sit-in. A crowd of curious bystanders had gathered, forcing city workers to give them a wide berth when they showed up for work on their bicycles. Mayor Cai flew into a rage, not over Li Xuelian's public protest, but over his executive vice-mayor, Diao Chengxin, for letting the situation persist for three days without taking action, waiting instead for Mayor Cai to return from Beijing.

Everyone knew there was friction between the mayor and his executive vice-mayor. That friction was a particularly bitter pill for Mayor Cai to swallow, since it was not of his creation. No, it was an historical accident. Ten years earlier, as party secretaries of county committees, the two men had gotten along reasonably well, sharing a drink from time to time when they visited one another's county. Eventually, both were promoted to serve as vice-mayors, listed in order of stroke count in their surnames, which put Diao ahead of Cai. Their next promotions were as directors of the Municipal Propaganda and Municipal Organization Departments, after which Cai surged ahead of Diao as Party Secretary of the Municipal Committee, while Diao was assigned as executive vice-mayor, a position he retained when Cai was promoted over him as mayor. They had moved together, first one and then the other, until one came out ahead in the end; unhappiness was born where there should have been none, a grudge was created when one was not called for. They saw one another as rivals, without being obvious about it. Though courtesy required certain behavior in public, Diao did everything he could to trip up Cai in secret. Allowing a three-day sit-in in front of the government office building without lifting a finger to resolve the protester's complaint, waiting instead for Cai to do so upon his return, was but one of Diao's many underhanded tactics. But it was not the tactic itself that caused Cai to blow up; rather it was the stupidity of his subordinate, the man's brainlessness. Provincial authorities, not Cai Fubang, had determined the rate of promotion for the two men, and the best hope Diao had of becoming mayor one day was to get behind Cai and help him rise to a new position at the provincial level. Constant squabbles and open warfare that kept the mayor from doing his job was a guarantee that he would go nowhere and Diao would be stuck in the job of executive vice-mayor in perpetuity. Corruption is narrowly defined as bribery, lawlessness, graft, degeneration, and philandering. But at its worst, corruption is the neglect of one's official responsibilities or, as in the case of Diao Chengxin, the obstruction of those duties. Worse still was that there was nothing Cai could do to Diao in regard to his open defiance, since the decision to appoint him as executive vice-mayor rested not with him, but with provincial authorities. What bothered Cai most was the timing of Diao's attempt to trip him up, for it occurred in the midst of a "cultured city" campaign. Nationwide, only a few dozen cities would be designated "cultured," and the image of those fortunate few would be transformed, with enhanced access to funds to improve both hard and soft environments, and a bargaining chip to attract overseas investments. Cai Fubang had invested a year of hard work in creating a cultured city, with park renovations, street improvements, sewer upgrades, and the modernization of schools, farmers' markets, and shantytowns. The exteriors of all buildings facing city streets had received a fresh coat of paint. A year's preparation for a day three days hence, when a team of dignitaries from the Central and Provincial governments would descend on the city to inspect the results of Cai's work. A month before the planned visit, Mayor Cai had launched a campaign to rid the city of flies, involving officials and ordinary residents; cadres in all government offices were required to bring in a minimum of ten dead houseflies every day as part of their year-end assessment. The campaign was so successful that in two weeks, cadres complained that they were unable to fulfill their quota. But in the midst of those complaints, the city was freed of houseflies. Cai was aware of the complaints, but he knew that rectification can require overcorrection. After the elimination of flies, school children were told to sing and old ladies to dance.

Cai had traveled to Beijing to report on the success of his work on creating a cultured city, and now he returned home to receive the team of dignitaries. The last thing he'd expected to find was a woman sitting in front of the government office building for three days, and no one had come out to see to her complaint. One way to put it: the city's houseflies had been eradicated, only to have a gigantic fly show up right in front of him. If this wasn't a blatant attempt to undermine the cultured city prospect, what was it? The first thing Cai Fubang did when he walked into his office was send for his chief secretary, point out the window at the entrance, and demand angrily:

"What's with that?"

Cai's chief secretary, a beanpole of a man with a face yellowed by chain-smoking, sputtered:

"She's lodging a formal complaint."

"I can see that. They say she's been there for three days, so why is no one dealing with her?"

"They've tried, but she's not listening."

"Hasn't Diao Chengxin come to work these past three days?"

Afraid of stirring up friction between his superiors, the secretary hastened to reply, "Vice-Mayor Diao personally went down to talk to her, but she refused to listen to him. Since it's a woman, one who's drawn a crowd, sending for the police would only have made things worse."

Cai had calmed down a bit, but the look on his face was anything but calm.

"Are you saying you can't manage a piddling affair like this? It's not like it's murder or arson."

"No," the secretary assured him, "none of those. Hardly anything at all. She got a divorce, but has had second thoughts. Probably looking for monetary compensation. A small matter, but a tricky one. Murder and arson would be easier to deal with."

"Which county is she from? Why wasn't it taken care of it there?"

"They tried, but failed. She's set her sights on more than one person, a lot more, in fact."

"Like who?"

"Since no one could help her, she took that as indifference, so she's suing her county chief, the chief justice, a member of the Judicial Committee, and the presiding judge at her trial. Then there's her husband and probably others I can't recall at the moment."

Cai Fubang got a laugh out of that.

"It takes guts to turn a minor affair into something like this," he said.

"She's a stubborn broad, no doubt about that," his secretary said as he nodded his agreement. "What do you plan to do, Mayor Cai?"

"You say people up and down the line have tried their hand," he fumed, "but all anyone can do is dump the problem on me! What do *I* plan to do? In three days the cultured city dignitaries will be here, which leaves me no choice. I want you to get rid of her. If there's a problem, we'll deal with it in a week."

This conversation took place in the morning, when Li Xuelian was sitting in front of the government office building, holding her "Injustice" sign over her head. She was still there that afternoon, still being officially ignored. As night fell, her curious entourage broke up and went home, leaving her alone. She took a piece of hardtack from her bag and was about to take a bite when a band of plainclothes policemen surrounded her and unceremoniously spirited her away. Mayor Cai had ordered only that she be removed, not where she was to be removed to; he had other things on his mind. His order had made its way down the chain of command, from the government office to security headquarters, and from there to the district police station, and finally to the local substation on Dongda Avenue, near the government office building. All that movement produced significant changes in the mayor's order, culminating in a seething demand to lock Li Xuelian up. Which the accommodating police did, charging her for being a public nuisance.

10

Three days later, the city qualified as a cultured city. A week after that, Li Xuelian was released from detention. There should have been no direct link between the two occurrences, but since she had been locked up in furtherance of acquiring the cultured city designation, a link was established. After her release from detention, she made no inquiries regarding the establishment of the cultured city designation. Everyone in the city knew that Mayor Cai had ordered her arrest; that included Xuelian herself. But instead of going to see him or continuing her sit-in, she returned to her hometown, where she went to see Old Hu, the pig butcher. He was still selling pork at market, displaying some of his meat on a butcher block and hanging some from hooks.

"Come here, Old Hu," Xuelian called out before she even reached his stall. "I want to talk to you."

He was cutting slabs of meat when he heard his name called. He looked up and was surprised to see Li Xuelian. He laid down his cleaver and followed her to the abandoned mill behind the market.

"I heard you were in jail, Babe."

"I'm here now, aren't I?" she said with a smile.

"You don't look like someone who's just gotten out of jail," he said, astonished by her appearance. "You're the picture of health."

He moved closer to her. "And you also smell like perfume."

"I had a good time in jail," Xuelian said. "Not a care in the world. Three meals a day, brought right to my cell."

There was not a word of truth in what she said. She'd suffered terribly during her week in jail, locked up in a dark room with no fewer than ten other women and barely enough room to turn around in. Three meals a day: one steamed corn bun and a chunk of salted turnip, not nearly enough. As for toilet visits, they were restricted to exercise periods. If you couldn't wait, you peed on the floor, and many did, Xuelian included. No mystery over what the cell smelled like. But the worst aspect of being locked up was the prohibition against talking. Going hungry or living with toilet smells were tolerable; not being allowed to talk was suffocating. The first thing Li Xuelian did after her release was run into a wheat field to breathe in the fresh air, turn to face the mountains, and yell, "Fuck you!"

She then went to the town's public bath, after which she returned home to change clothes and powder her face; that done, she rouged her cheeks and went looking for Old Hu. A man not given to close examination, he detected none of what she'd been through.

"Do you still remember what you said a month ago, Old Hu?"

"What was that?"

"You said you'd help me kill someone."

"I did," he said with a sense of astonishment, "I said that. But you said no, you wanted me to beat someone up for you."

"That was then, this is now. And it's murder I want."

Old Hu had a shifty look in his eyes.

"If that's what you want, okay, but first there's something you and I have to do."

"It's a deal."

Suddenly wild with delight, he reached out to fondle Xuelian's breasts.

"When do we do it? How about today?"

She grabbed his hands. "Do you know who I want you to kill?"

"I thought it was Qin Yuhe."

"Qin Yuhe, sure. But that's not all."

He was confused. "Who else?"

Li Xuelian took a slip of paper out of her pocket. It was a list:

Mayor Cai Fubang
County Chief Shi Weimin
Chief Judge Xun Zhengyi
Judicial Committeeman Dong Xianfa
Presiding Justice Wang Gongdao
That bastard Qin Yuhe

Old Hu couldn't believe his eyes.

"One stopover in the clink has made you dotty, my dear."

"Every one on that list is hateful," she said.

Old Hu stammered his next comment:

"How am I, one, you know, person, going to kill all them? And that's not the end of it," he added. "Except for Qin Yuhe, everyone on that list is an official, surrounded by people, morning, noon, and night. That would make it virtually impossible."

"Just kill as many as you can. You don't know how bad I feel."

Old Hu suddenly went weak in the knees. Wrapping his arms around his head, he squatted down in the rut formed around the millstone and showed the whites of his eyes.

"This is no bargain," he said. "For one roll in the hay with you I've got to kill six people." He held his head tighter. "Am I some kind of mobster?"

Li Xuelian spat out her contempt:

"I always knew you were lying."

As tears gathered in her eyes, she gave him a swift kick, turned, and walked off.

11

After leaving Old Hu, Li Xuelian decided she wouldn't kill anyone after all, wouldn't even subject them to a beating. In fact, putting herself through so much trouble and anguish, trying to bring action against them, had been a waste of time. The torment she'd wanted to heap upon those people had, instead, come crashing down on her head. But she wasn't about to give up, not until she'd had her say. The whole world believed that Li Xuelian was in the wrong, all but one person; the whole world believed that her divorce the year before was legitimate, all but one person, someone who knew the whole story. And it was that person who had driven Xuelian to the point that her version of events convinced no one and had culminated in her spending seven days in jail. Who was that person? None other than her ex husband, Qin Yuhe. It was time to ask him to his face if the divorce was real or fake. But her goal in asking this question had changed. Up till now it had been what had thrust her into the judicial system. Now legal action no longer concerned her; gone, once the issue of real versus fake was settled, was her desire to remarry and then re-divorce Qin Yuhe and to have him divorce his present wife, for her to torment all concerned until, as they say, the fish dies or the net breaks. Now all she wanted was a simple affirmation by that one person that she was right in order to call a halt to her quest. She would put aside all thoughts of the grief she had suffered. Powerless to prove the truth to others, Li Xuelian would prove it to herself. Putting an end to it this way also created a new beginning.

Twenty-nine was neither particularly young nor noticeably old, and Li Xuelian was not unattractive. She had large eyes, an oval face, and was slim-waisted with a nice bust; why else would pig butcher Hu be attracted to her like a fly to blood? She mustn't sacrifice her youth to pointless matters. So she made up her mind to abandon past grievances and find another husband. Once she'd managed that, she and her daughter could settle into a new life.

The first step in putting an end to the past and opening a new page in her life was to go see Qin Yuhe at the fertilizer plant in town. Her purpose in going the last time had been to trick him into coming back home to kill him. She'd even carried her two-month-old baby girl with her; but when she got there she'd been told that he'd driven to Heilongjiang with a load of fertilizer. Then her younger brother had taken off to Shandong so he wouldn't have to kill Qin for his sister. Going off like that had likely saved Qin's life. And if she'd managed to have him killed, where would she be now? Probably in prison awaiting execution, and she wouldn't have been here today to look him up.

Unlike the previous trip, when she hadn't succeeded in finding him, this time she spotted him before she entered the plant. He was enjoying a leisurely beer with half a dozen other men around a table at an outdoor diner next to the plant entrance. She recognized one of them, a bearded fellow named Zhang who also drove for the plant. They were having a spirited conversation as they nursed their beers. To the left of the plant entrance was the pay toilet; the diner where the men were sitting was to the right. Only a few dozen feet separated the two, and both were busy with people relieving themselves, eating a meal, or drinking beer. After Wang Gongdao had thrown out Li Xuelian's case at court, Qin Yuhe had stopped avoiding her. He was free to once again live life out in the open, no longer finding it necessary to travel to Heilongjiang with a load of fertilizer, free to enjoy a leisurely beer with friends in front of the plant. As far as he was concerned, his troubles were all in the past. No one at the table spotted Xuelian until she walked up and called out:

"Qin Yuhe."

Qin gulped in surprise when he turned around and was face to face with Li Xuelian. So did the other men. But Qin quickly regained his composure.

"What do you want?"

"Come here, I want to talk to you."

Qin glanced around the table but made no move to get up. He thought for a moment. "Whatever you have to say you can say it here."

"What I have to say is meant for you and me, nobody else."

Having no clue what she'd come for, he stayed put.

"I said, whatever you have to say you can say it here. Everybody in the county and in the city know what's going on with us, so there are no secrets."

She thought that over, and made up her mind.

"All right, I'll say it here."

"Well?"

"Since there are others here," Xuelian said, "I want them to hear you tell the truth. Our divorce last year, was it real or was it a fake?"

Qin was not pleased to hear her bring that up again, unaware that she'd done so in order to bring the matter to an end. All she wanted was a truthful answer, but he assumed she hadn't given up her original plan of tormenting him.

"Real or fake," he said, keeping his head down, "what did the judge say when you went to court?"

"I lost the case, but now I don't care what anyone thinks, including the court. I just want to ask if you think the judge made the right decision. Our divorce last year, was it real or fake?"

Qin was more convinced than ever that she wanted to make things hard on him again. And who could say she wasn't secretly recording this conversation? His face darkened.

"I'm not going to go round and round with you. The court made its ruling, so what could you possibly have to say? Go back and sue me again."

"Qin Yuhe," Xuelian sobbed, "you're a man without a conscience. How can you look me in the eye and lie like that? Are you a man of your word or aren't you? Last year we agreed to a sham divorce, you know that, so what made you change? And not only change, but team up with others to fabricate charges against me. Why can't you admit it was a sham?"

Seeing Xuelian cry really angered Qin Yuhe.

"What do you mean, fabricate charges? When did I do that? Did the court and all the way up the government ladder fabricate charges against you too? Take my advice, Li Xuelian, and quit pestering me. Keep it up, and things could turn ugly. Even if I had wronged you, did everyone up the line wrong you as well, from the court to the Judicial Committee, the chief justice, the county chief, even the mayor? If you stop this nonsense now, you could get away with having been briefly detained, but keep it up, and you could wind up in prison." He added, "Are you looking for a fight with me? Or with the others up the line? If you are, do you really expect things to go your way in the end?"

Li Xuelian had not come looking for a fight. All she'd wanted was a simple statement. But what he said made her blood boil. This was not the Qin Yuhe she'd married. No, he'd changed. Back when she and her truck-driving husband were together, he'd had his faults, but he'd been a reasonable man who'd let her have her way some of the time. But in a single year they'd become bitter enemies, and he'd turned into someone who was hard to deal with. Why else would he be on the lookout for another wife? It was also what made him insist that their private talk go public. To make matters worse, he'd dragged the court, the Judicial Committee, the chief justice, the county chief, and the mayor over to his side, as if they were family, leaving her on the other side all alone. The truth was, what had happened over the past month proved that they had indeed taken his side. If Xuelian wasn't angry enough by now, Qin Yuhe underscored his comment by spitting on the ground, picking up his bottle, and chug-a-lugging the beer inside. Had she brought a knife along with her, this would have been the moment she really did kill him. Qin's friend Zhang stood up to make peace.

"Xuelian, this is going to take time to work out, so why don't you go home for now?"

She stayed put and started crying again.

"Qin Yuhe, we were once husband and wife, how could you be so cruel?"

She sobbed some more.

"I'm not interested in courts or lawsuits, and I don't care about any county chief or mayor. All I want to ask is how you could have the heart to hook up with another woman while I was pregnant?"

Mention of his hooking up with another woman both embarrassed and angered Qin. He tipped his head back, chug-a-lugged what was left in his bottle, and spit on the ground again.

"You should be asking yourself that, not me," he said.

"What does that mean?"

"Where fooling around is concerned, I'm the one who should complain."

"What do you mean by *that*?"

"Were you a virgin when you married me? On our wedding night you said you'd slept with someone before me. Are you Li Xuelian, or are you Pan Jinlian, China's most famous adulteress?"

That remark thudded into Li Xuelian's head like a thunderbolt, and if she hadn't braced herself against the wall, she'd have fallen to the ground. That was the last thing she thought she'd hear. Up till this moment, what had tormented her had been the question of whether their divorce had been real or a sham, but all that seemed to have gotten her was a comparison to the notorious Pan Jinlian. Her attempt to torment Qin Yuhe had backfired.

She'd been quite pretty as a young woman, and had caught the eye of many men, several of whom she had dated before marrying Qin. Two of her romances had gone beyond the level of a casual relationship, but for a variety of reasons, neither had worked out, and she'd married Qin. On their wedding night, he'd discovered that she was not a virgin, and she'd admitted that truthfully. These days, how many eighteen-year-olds were? But Qin was obviously unhappy, and it took several awkward days for them to put the matter to rest. Or so it seemed. Eight years later, by bringing it up, Qin showed that it still rankled. The problem was, the fictional Pan Jinlian had had relations with Ximen Qing *after* she'd married Wu Dalang, while Li Xuelian's sexual initiation had occurred *before* her marriage to Qin Yuhe, before she even knew him. And, unlike, Pan Jinlian, she did not conspire with a lover to kill her husband, but was herself a victim, when her husband took up with another woman. It was obvious to her that his spur-of-the-moment outburst had been a way to vent anger and cover his embarrassment, not a desire to reveal a secret; either that, or a way of freeing him from an entanglement. But whatever the impulse, she sensed that things had taken an ugly turn. Why? Because it was not a conversation involving only the two of them; his beer-drinking friends had heard every word. The saying "good news never leaves the home; bad news travels far" had it right. By the next morning, word of Li Xuelian as a modern-day Pan Jinlian would spread throughout the county, and by the day after, all over the city. She already had a reputation in both places, thanks to her lawsuit over the validity of her divorce. But Pan Jinlian? That would be a lot more interesting to them. The validity of her divorce was no longer an important issue. What would matter to people now was whether or not Xuelian was Pan Jinlian incarnate. For if she was, then Qin Yuhe had every right to divorce her—real or sham—since no man would be willing to share his life with a Pan Jinlian. Put another way, if Xuelian was, in essence, a Pan Jinlian, then Qin Yuhe was justi- fied in doing what he wished, and she went from being a plaintiff to being the prime defendant. And that was what made his comment so toxic. She had come to put the past behind her and find a man with whom she could start a new life, but had wound up being smeared as a modern Pan Jinlian. Her hopes for a new life were dashed. Who in his right mind would want to marry a Pan Jinlian? As she stood there looking wobbly, supporting herself against the wall, Old Zhang rebuked Qin Yuhe:

"That's going too far, Old Qin. That's not what this is about. Don't forget the saying, 'Don't hit people in the face and don't point out a weakness in an argument.'"

He turned to Li Xuelian.

"Xuelian," he said, "this is getting out of hand. Why don't you go home?"

Li Xuelian blew her nose and walked off, not in response to Zhang's urging, but because she had an idea. If the future was now closed to her, then she'd have to revise her past. Her earlier revision of the past had been tied up with the question of the validity of her divorce; this new revision had to deal with proof that she was no Pan Jinlian. Up till this moment she'd wanted to punish Qin Yuhe; now she needed to demonstrate her chastity. That was what made it a complex problem: the question of whether or not Li Xuelian was a Pan Jinlian evolved out of the validity of her divorce from Qin Yuhe, and so to prove that she was not a Pan Jinlian, it was necessary to resolve the divorce issue. Two unrelated issues had been twisted, cruller-style, into one by Qin's comment. Old Zhang's mention of the saying "Don't hit people in the face and don't point out a weak- ness in an argument" resonated with her, for the other men clearly believed Qin, thus exposing her weakness; in their eyes she was already a Pan Jinlian. She'd come with no intention of causing a scene or tormenting anyone, but that had all changed; the question was, where could she take her cause now? She'd already caused scenes in all the appropriate places—every relevant office in the county and city, where she had offended just about everyone. Bring- ing legal action had failed her once and would surely fail her again, could even end in her imprisonment. At that point in her thoughts, she made a decision: she'd take her case directly to Beijing. Getting through the days from now on would be nearly impossible if she could not satisfactorily resolve this issue. Here she was surrounded by simpleminded people, but Beijing, the nation's capital, had to be home to the clear-minded. Every official she'd encountered locally, from Judicial Committee member to chief justice, county chief, and mayor, had turned the real into the sham, the true into false. People in Beijing ought to be able to keep them separate—the real as real and the sham as sham. But real or sham was secondary in importance to the fact that she was Li Xuelian, not Pan Jinlian. Even better, she was the martyred heroine Dou E in the yuan drama *Snow in Midsummer*.

12

Li Xuelian chose the wrong time to go to Beijing. She had no understanding of the capital, nor it of her. She traveled there while the National People's Congress was in session. The two should have had no bearing upon one another, but because they occurred at the same time, they did. So-called redundant people were prohibited from entering the city when the NPC was in session. Just how "redundant people" was defined no one could say for sure, but was generally interpreted as anyone who might somehow bring harm to the Congress. Trash pickers, beggars, thieves, prostitutes who worked out of hair salons, and people who had come to lodge protests, disappeared from the city streets overnight.

Xuelian had ridden a bus to Beijing; she'd originally planned to take the train, until she learned that it cost fifteen yuan more than a bus. After a day and a half of bumpy travel, she arrived at the toll station where Hebei province bordered Beijing, which is where she learned that the Congress was in session. A dozen police vehicles with flashing lights stopped every vehicle entering the city to check its occupants; the roadway was cluttered with buses, delivery trucks, minivans, and sedans that had been stopped for inspection. Li Xuelian's bus fell in at the end of the long queue. Two hours later a pair of policemen finally boarded her bus to check the identity papers and luggage of all passengers; they asked why the visitors were coming to Beijing and demanded to see authorizing documents. The reasons were diverse and colorful: company or official business, commerce, family visit, illness, even someone looking for a missing child . . .

A few of the passengers were allowed to continue on, the others were told to get off the bus, which they did without a murmur of protest. Li Xuelian watched carefully to detect selection standards, but failed. Finally, a policeman stepped up and asked to see her ID card.

"What's your purpose in going to Beijing?" he asked.

She knew she looked nothing like someone on a business trip, a traveling salesman, or a woman looking for a missing child. And since telling the truth was out of the question, she took her cue from a passenger up front:

"Medical," she said as she leaned her head against the window, trying to look as sick as possible.

"What's the problem?" the policeman asked, his eyes boring into her.

"A descended uterus."

The policeman's cheeks twitched.

"Which hospital in Beijing?"

Xuelian was momentarily stuck for an answer. She'd never been in the city, let alone seek medical treatment there, and knew the names of none of its hospitals or what they were noted for.

"Beijing Hospital," she ventured.

She'd taken a chance on the obvious. The policeman gave her a long look, and when he asked his next question, she knew there must be a Beijing Hospital in the city, and breathed a sigh of relief.

"Your medical record?"

That was unexpected. "What do you mean, my medical record?"

"If you're going to a hospital," he said impatiently, "you have to have a medical record."

"This is my third visit," she said. "I left my records at the Beijing Hospital the last time."

This time he gave her a very long look before moving on to his next question.

"Where's your proof?"

"Proof? Proof of what?"

The policeman's patience was wearing thin.

"Don't you know anything? The National People's Congress is in session, and anyone wanting to enter Beijing must have a letter of introduction from a county or higher government office. You say you're coming to town to see a doctor, but what proof do I have?"

Poor, foolish Li Xuelian had no idea that she needed such a letter to come to Beijing when the Congress was in session; even had she known, no county office would have given her one.

"I forgot that the Congress was in session," she said.

At last the policeman got what he wanted. He relaxed.

"I can't let you into Beijing without a letter."

"But I'll miss my treatment."

"The People's Congress is in session only for two weeks," he said. "You can come back after that. Now off the bus."

Li Xuelian's stubborn streak surfaced.

"I'm not getting off."

"Why not? Other people do as they're told."

"My uterus is in danger of rupturing. I need my treatment now."

Again the policeman's cheeks twitched.

"That's not my problem," he barked. "Don't cause a scene. It's only two weeks."

"I'll get off if I have to," she said as she stood up. "But it's on your head."

"What's that supposed to mean?"

"I'm not sure I want to go to Beijing anyway. My money's gone and I'm not any better. Why go on living. You want me to get off and wait two weeks? No, I'll get off and go hang myself from the nearest tree."

Li Xuelian read the identification on the tongue-tied policeman's badge.

"I've got your number. In my suicide note, I'll say you drove me to this."

He stood there, mouth open, dumbstruck. In the end, he spat out the window and grumbled, "Women like you are nothing but headaches." He shook his head. "Troublemakers, you're all troublemakers."

With a frown he moved on to the seat behind Li Xuelian.

As night fell, she breathed a sigh of relief out the window.

13

Li Xuelian's entry into Beijing was a dizzying experience. Her first sensation was wonder at the size of the place—bigger than her village, the town, the county seat, and the city back home, unimaginably huge. She boarded a bus that took her past tall buildings, and more tall buildings, under flyovers, and more flyovers. Her sense of direction betrayed her. Back in school she'd learned that Tiananmen Square was on the northern edge of Chang'an Avenue, but as her bus passed by the square, she discovered that it was on the southern edge. The north-south orientation of her village was no help in clearing up her confusion, no matter how hard she tried. While she was in Beijing, it seemed, she'd have to turn north into south, east into west. But that was the least of her worries. She'd come to lodge a protest, but now that she was here, she had no idea where to go or whom to see. Where did the people who could receive her complaint live? It was, she figured, her good fortune that the National People's Congress was in session. She knew they would be meeting in the Great Hall of the People, which was on the western edge of Tiananmen Square—naturally, to her that meant the eastern edge—and that was where anyone who was anyone would be found; and important anyones at that. She had a sudden brainstorm: once she'd settled in, she'd take advantage of the Congress to stage a sit-in in Tiananmen Square. That was her best shot at gaining the attention of important members of the Congress.

But first she needed a place to stay, and for that she turned to a classmate named Zhao Jingli, a boy who'd sat behind her for six years at school. Zhao had a big head with an indentation in the middle of his skull that gave it the appearance of a gourd. At school, everyone in class called him Big Head Zhao. That had replaced his name to such an extent that if someone called out Zhao Jingli, even he might not realize they were talking to him. For the first three years as classmates they never exchanged a word. But during the first year of high school, Li Xuelian could tell that he'd gotten interested in her. Big Head's mother had died, his father was a tailor in town, and he had three younger brothers. Life was tough for a tailor with four sons, but every few days Big Head slipped her a "Big White Rabbit" nougat candy from the seat behind. Where the money had come from was a mystery. But in two years it never went beyond gifts of candy, until one day just before graduation, Zhao was waiting for her at the classroom door when she returned from the toilet during a study session.

"Li Xuelian," he said as he looked around, "I have something to say to you."

"Go ahead," she said.

"Not here."

"Where then?"

Zhao led her to a threshing ground behind the school. The night sky was black as ink.

"What do you want to say to me?" she asked him.

Without a word, he stepped up, wrapped his arms around her, and tried to kiss her. His movements were so abrupt and so unexpected she wasn't sure what to do. So she shoved him back and tripped him with her leg; he thudded to the ground. Any other boy would have jumped up and tried again. He'd have groped her, even if she'd said "You're getting me mad" or "I'm going to scream," ripped off her clothes and done the deed. Big Head surprised her by getting up off the ground, looking at her, and, like an idiot, saying, "I thought we liked each other." He added, "Don't tell anyone."

With that he ran off. Xuelian stood there, following his departure with angry laughter, not because he'd wrapped his arms around her and tried to kiss her, but because he'd run away. When they met the next day, Zhao kept his big head low and turned red. He couldn't look Xuelian in the eye, and she knew that he was too naïve for his own good. Out of spite, she ignored him from then on. After high school, neither of them passed the college entrance exam, so Xuelian went back to her village, while Big Head went to the county seat to apprentice himself to an uncle who was a cook. When the uncle was transferred to the Beijing office of the provincial administration, Big Head went along, and when his uncle retired, he stayed behind.

Li Xuelian had no one in Beijing to turn to, no one but Big Head Zhao. But she was worried that after taking his nougats for two years and then frightening him on the threshing floor he'd bear a grudge. If he didn't, she'd found a place to stay; if he did, she'd try somewhere else, and that somewhere else, she already knew, would be the train station. Though she'd never been to Beijing Station, she knew that train stations all over the country offered eaves under which people slept at night.

Xuelian arrived with the knowledge that Big Head worked in the Beijing branch of the province's administrative office, but finding the place was not easy. She asked for directions time and again, took eight different buses, and wound up in the wrong place or down the wrong road more times than she could count. After arriving in Beijing in the early morning hours, it wasn't until just before nightfall that she finally found the building she was looking for, the place where Big Head Zhao worked as a cook. It was a thirty-story high rise, and she was denied entrance. A courtyard with an arched gateway, sealed off with police tape, fronted the building, where half a dozen gate guards kept people from entering. A hundred or more provincial delegates to the Congress were housed in the building, she learned, and when she walked up, the guards at first thought she might be was one of them; but one look at her clothing left doubts. Nonetheless, she was greeted politely:

"You'll have to find somewhere else to stay. This place is reserved for Congress delegates."

For the second time, Xuelian felt the impact of the National People's Congress. But she would not be deterred.

"I'm not looking for a place to stay, I'm here to see a relative."

"You have a relative here for the Congress?" another guard asked.

She shook her head.

"No, not a delegate, he's a cook. His name is Zhao Jingli."

The man grew pensive.

"I know all the cooks here, and there's no one named Zhao Jingli."

"Everyone in the county knows he works here," she said, starting to get anxious. "You must be wrong. I've traveled more than two thousand li to get here."

Noting her distress, one of the other guards stepped up.

"We know everyone who works in the kitchen," he assured her, "and take my word for it, there's no one named Zhao Jingli."

Then it hit her:

"I forgot, he's got another name, we called him Big Head Zhao."

They laughed when they heard that.

"Oh, Big Head. Why didn't you say so?" one of them said. "Wait here, I'll go get him."

Five minutes later, Big Head Zhao walked out in his white uniform and chef's hat. He hadn't changed much since leaving school, except that he was a lot bigger around the middle. Skinny as a stalk of hemp supporting a big head back then, now he was just plain fat, which made his head seem smaller, especially under the chef's hat. Xuelian would have passed him on the street without recognizing him. But after a brief, head-scratching pause, he knew who she was and clapped his hands excitedly.

"My word!" he exclaimed. "What are you doing here?"

Xuelian relaxed the moment she saw the broad smile on his face, confident that what had happened in school had been forgotten.

"I was visiting my aunt in the northeast and stopped to say hello on my way home."

Zhao stepped up and took her travel bag.

"Come on in, I'll get you a glass of water."

One of the guards surprised them both by blocking their way.

"Big Head," he said, "you can talk out here. With the Congress in session, strangers aren't allowed inside."

Big Head was stumped; so was Xuelian. But only for a moment.

"Fuck off!" Big Head said as he pushed the guard out of his way. "She's my sister and that makes her no stranger."

"We have our orders," the man said.

Big Head spat on the ground.

"Are you a guard dog, treating advice like an order, a mere token of authority? Or is your old man inside? Has he just had a baby and is afraid of catching cold?"

The guard's face reddened. He was on the verge of losing his cool.

"Why do you have to talk to me like that, Big Head?"

"Not because you won't let my sister in, but because of your ingratitude. You never miss a day coming to the kitchen to enjoy freebies. Just yesterday I cut off a chunk of beef tendon for you. Talk to you like that? I ought to slug you, you bastard!"

He raised his fist. The red on the man's face deepened.

"You just wait," he said. "I'll report you for this."

With his hands over his head, the man ran to hide behind a stone lion in front of the gate. The others had a good laugh over that. Xuelian saw that Big Head Zhao, a wimp in school, was one no longer.

He led her past the police tape into the compound, but instead of going to the front entrance, he took a path around to the rear, up to a two-story building where a sign proclaimed: Kitchen Staff. She followed him into a storeroom with a bed. This, obviously, was where Big Head Zhao slept.

"I watch the storeroom, and they let me bed down here."

After she washed up, Zhao poured her a cup of tea and then went to the kitchen, returning with a bowl of steaming noodles in thick sauce. By the time she'd finished, it was nine o'clock.

"So what are you doing in Beijing?" Big Head asked.

Afraid to tell him the truth, she said:

"Like I said, I stopped to say hello on my way home from visiting my aunt in the northeast. I thought I'd see the sights of Beijing."

"Good idea, enjoy some sightseeing. You can sleep here tonight."

"Me? What about you?"

"Don't worry, I know a dozen places around here where I can bed down."

Before leaving, he said:

"Get some sleep. I have to prepare midnight snacks for the delegates."

So Xuelian slept in Big Head Zhao's bed that night; where he slept she did not know. Early the next morning, before she was up, there was a knock at the door. She draped something over her shoulders and opened the door. It was Big Head, looking anxious.

"Hurry," he said, "hurry."

"What is it?" She thought they were found out and she had to leave.

"Didn't you say you wanted to see Beijing? Well, I have a day off to take you to the Great Wall. We need to get a head start to catch a bus at Front Gate."

Xuelian breathed a sigh of relief, but then she paused. She'd come to Beijing to protest, not see the sights, but that is what she'd said the night before, and Big Head had taken it to heart. She did not want to seem ungrateful, nor was she willing to change her story about why she'd come to the city; she mustn't let him know the story behind her protest. She surely could not finish what she'd come to do in one day, not when the National People's Congress would be in session for two weeks, and a day would not be enough to get things done, nor would losing one day make any difference. So she brushed her teeth, washed her face, and went with Big Head Zhao to Front Gate, where they boarded a sightseeing bus to the Great Wall. It was a day filled with sights, but for Xuelian one filled with so many worries she could not enjoy the outing. Big Head, on the other hand, had a raring good time. The next day he took her to the Forbidden City and the Temple of Heaven. He even accompanied her to a beauty salon near the Temple of Heaven to get a permanent wave. That done, he looked her over.

"Much better," he said. "Now you look like a local. A woman's hairstyle tells people where she's from."

He chuckled, and she had to smile when she looked in the mirror.

Now that she was spruced up, it was time to try Beijing's famous lamb hot pot. As they sat in front of the steaming pot, she tried to express her gratitude.

"Big Head," she said, her words carrying through the steam that separated them, "you've wasted two whole days and spent a lot of money showing me around the city."

Big Head did not like hearing that.

"What does that mean? Am I a stranger?"

"No. I'm just saying . . ."

Happy again, he slapped the tabletop.

"We're not finished."

"How's that?"

"Tomorrow it's the Summer Palace, where we can go rowing."

That night, as she lay on Big Head Zhao's bed, Xuelian had trouble falling asleep, unlike the previous two nights, when sleep had come easily. All the changes that had occurred in her life over the past year and the legal experiences crowded her mind. She never thought it would be so hard, nor had she imagined the difficulty in convincing people of the truth in a truthful comment. Conversely, she had not been able to convince them that her divorce from Qin

Yuhe had been a sham. Most disturbing of all was how she had been branded a Pan Jinlian over something she had said; all this had brought her to Beijing to lodge her protest. Stumped by questions of how to go about doing that, she'd settled on a sit-in in Tiananmen Square, but to what effect she could not hazard a guess.

Big Head was a good man; he knew Beijing far better than she, and was someone with whom she could talk about anything, anything but this. She sighed. Then thoughts of her daughter, who had been cared for by her classmate since the quest for justice began, entered her head. Two months old when she'd been handed over, she was now more than three months old, and it was hard for her mother to imagine what she looked like now. Almost from the day the baby was born, Xuelian had been caught up in dealing with Qin Yuhe and making her appeal for justice, so busy the child didn't yet have a name. She'd come to Beijing to seek justice, not to see the sights, and she could no longer take time away from what she'd come to do by traveling around the city with Big Head. Though she had no idea about how to lodge her protest, she knew that, like anything else, getting an early start was much better than being late. Just then she heard the heart-stopping sound of a key in the lock. A bit of light filtered into the darkness through a door that opened to admit a rotund figure. Big Head Zhao. Xuelian knew that the time to pay for the guided tour had arrived. She closed her eyes and lay perfectly still as Big Head tiptoed up to her bed and bent over until his face was nearly touching hers. Nothing moved for several minutes, until her eyes snapped open and she said:

"You don't have to look, Big Head. Just do what you came to do."

Blurting that out in the darkness threw a fright into him. She reached over and switched on the lamp. Zhao was standing there, looking awkward, wearing a tank top and a pair of underpants, over which his big belly flopped. When Xuelian said for him to "do what you came to do," he suddenly didn't know what to do. Maybe it was how she said it that made him feel so awkward. His face turned beet red.

"The way you said that," he said as he wrung his hands, "I wonder what kind of man you take me for."

He turned and began a search for something in the pantry.

"All I came in for was some yeast. I need to start the dough at night so I can steam crullers in the morning. I tell you, our governor loves the things."

Xuelian draped a jacket over her shoulders and sat up.

"I said you could do it. Don't blame me if you don't."

Big Head stood there tongue-tied.

"You'd have wasted two days otherwise."

That embarrassed him further.

"Li Xuelian," he said, gesturing wildly, "what do you mean by that? It was just sightseeing. We were classmates for six years."

"Big Head, I don't want to go to the Summer Palace tomorrow."

"Where do you want to go?"

Unwilling to tell him she wanted to stage a sit-in in Tiananmen Square, she said, "I want to go shopping for my baby."

"That sounds good, I'll go with you." He perked up.

"I don't want to waste any more of your time."

"I told you, I asked for time off. While you're in Beijing, where you go, I go."

Xuelian took her jacket off.

"Big Head, forget about the yeast. It's not too late to do what you want."

He stared at her, and stared some more, before crouching down next to her bed and lighting a cigarette.

"Listen to you! If I want to do it, well, you need to give me time."

That made Xuelian laugh. Ten years had changed Big Head's appearance, but he was still the same innocent kid.

"Big Head," she said, "I want to go out on my own tomorrow, just me, how's that? As they like to say these days, I need my space."

He didn't put up a fight. He laughed too.

"If you want to be alone, then that's what you should do. To be honest, the senior chef has been hinting that two days to show you around is enough."

Xuelian laughed again. She planted a kiss on the top of his head.

Early the next morning, Li Xuelian put on her new clothes, walked out of Big Head Zhao's room and left the Kitchen Staff store-room, heading for Tiananmen Square to stage a sit-in. The clothes were a nod to the square itself. If she had the slovenly appearance of a petitioner, she might be stopped by guards from even making it onto the square. A month earlier, after deciding to make a formal complaint, she'd bought a set of new clothes. A month had passed without putting them on; now was their time. What she had not been able to do back home she was going to do in the capital. But she had barely made it around the building and reached the flower pond when she was called to a halt:

"Where do you think you're going?"

She almost jumped out of her skin. She turned and saw a thickset, middle-aged man in a suit and tie, with a brass official badge pinned to his coat. He looked like an office bigwig, and Xuelian thought she was being stopped for sneaking into Big Head Zhao's room and spending the night there. But he'd asked her where she was going, not where she'd been, and she relaxed a bit. What should she say? She couldn't tell him the truth. Her mind was a blank. All she could come up with was:

"Just out to take a walk."

"No you're not," he said angrily. "Get that stuff loaded right now."

"What stuff?"

The man pointed to some cardboard boxes on the steps, then to the gate.

"Those boxes. Load them onto the bus. Have you forgotten that we have to make our Government Work Report today? Hurry up, the delegates will be leaving for the Great Hall in a minute."

Xuelian looked from the stacked boxes to the gate, where seven or eight large sedans were parked, their engines running, filled with passengers who were talking and laughing among themselves. Seeing Xuelian walk out in neat clothes, with her hair done in the latest Beijing style, the man must have assumed that she worked in the building. Knowing what he was thinking, she didn't dare ignore his instruction to load the boxes for fear of being found out for spending the night there without permission. Besides, how hard could moving a few boxes be? She picked them up; they hadn't looked heavy, but they were. She carried them to the bus at the rear, where someone inside said:

"Put them in the back."

Li Xuelian glanced at her province's delegates—they were all wearing People's Congress badges—who were engaged in lively conversations. No one paid her any attention. From outside, the bus had looked full, but once she was inside, she saw that the back was empty. She finished loading just as the door shut behind her and the bus took off. The driver must have taken her for a member of the official party. Scared silly, she felt like shouting "Stop the bus!" but quickly changed her mind. They were going to the Great Hall of the People, which was on the west edge of Tiananmen Square—east edge to her, of course—so she'd be foolish to get off and squeeze aboard a bus heading to the same place; she'd also save the money. When they reached their destination, the delegates would walk to the Great Hall of the People to attend the Congress, while Li Xuelian would walk onto Tiananmen Square to stage her sit-in. This put no one out, so she sat back and enjoyed the ride.

Since it was rush hour, any space not occupied by a vehicle was taken over by people. But her convoy sailed down the street, their way cleared by a police car. Every red light along the way turned green before they reached the intersection, while all other traffic was stopped to let them pass. The trip to Tiananmen took fifteen minutes. And when she looked around, she was immediately aware of the solemnity surrounding the National People's Congress. Hers was not the only line of vehicles that had driven up. Cars and buses from more than thirty provinces, municipalities, and autonomous regions drove up from all directions. Dozens of policemen directed traffic around the hall. Their experience showed: in less than two hours, hundreds of vehicles were neatly parked just beyond the hall's eastern gate. Then thousands of delegates, briefcases tucked under their arms, poured from the parked cars and happily made their way to the steps of the Great Hall of the People. Astounded, speechless, Li Xuelian remained on the bus after everyone else had piled out and the boxes had been removed. She looked around until the driver, still thinking she was one of the delegates, turned and said:

"Why aren't you going in?"

That woke her up. If she could get inside the hall with the delegates, this protest would be a snap. Since it was the day for making reports on government work, the presence at the Congress of national leaders was assured. How much better than sitting alone in Tiananmen Square if she could personally plead her case to those people. And so, without a second thought, she jumped out of the bus and fell in behind the line of delegates. As a passenger in an official bus that had been waved through several police check points, she made her way up the steps to the Great Hall entrance without drawing any attention.

But to actually enter the Hall, every person was required to pass a security inspection carried out by personnel with batons they brushed across everyone's body. Thousands of people crammed into a small space made for plenty of pushing and shoving, and the staff was too concerned over security to pay much attention to each individual delegate. Jammed in the midst of the other delegates, Xuelian made it past security and followed the crowd toward the auditorium. At the entrance a middle-aged security guard in civilian clothes stopped her, smiled, and pointed to her chest.

"Welcome, Madame Delegate," he said politely. Please pin on your delegate badge."

He too had mistaken her for a delegate. Since striding through the door, she had been bowled over by the splendor of the auditorium. Festooned around the interior were magnificent floral bouquets in honor of the delegates, a sight the likes of which she'd never seen. Her heart was thumping against her chest. The spell was broken when another man came up to her. Nervous beyond imagining, she managed to control herself.

"My delegate badge, I left it at the guesthouse."

The man had a gentle look.

"Don't worry about that. Which group are you with?"

She had her wits about her and gave him the name of her province.

"May I ask your name?"

For that she had no answer. She could tell him, of course, but she knew that wouldn't help. And she didn't know the names of any other of the delegates she'd come with. She stood there frozen.

"So, may I ask your name?" he asked a second time.

She needed to tough it out. Maybe she'd be all right.

"Li Xuelian."

She stammered a bit—a case of nerves. She might not have done that if she'd given another name, but she was done in by her real name.

"Thank you, Delegate Li Xuelian. Would you come with me, please. I need to check your name against the list. It's nothing to worry about. We need to keep everyone safe."

Li Xuelian had no choice but to go with him into a passageway on the left side of the auditorium. He spoke softly into his walkie-talkie as they made a turn onto a long hallway that appeared to be deserted. Suddenly, Xuelian saw four or five young men in suits walking toward her, and she knew her cover had been blown.

Hurriedly digging in her bag to take out her protest sign, she held it over her head, and shouted:

"Injustice!"

They were on her like beasts of prey before she could shout a second time and wrestled her to the floor. One of them clapped his hand over her mouth, other hands pinned her arms and legs to the floor. She couldn't move.

It was over in less than five seconds. Meanwhile, delegates engaged in lively conversations poured into the auditorium, not one of whom saw what had happened. A bell rang—it was nine o'clock. The hall burst into thunderous applause. The government work reports were called for.

14

The day's schedule for the National People's Congress:

Morning, Government Work Reports.

Afternoon, Group Delegate Discussions.

The delegate group from Li Xuelian's province was assigned an assembly room in the Great Hall. The decision to have both morning and afternoon sessions held in the same building was not made to save the delegates travel time, since they had to return to their lodgings for the noonday meal, where they would normally stay for the discussion session. It was intended to accommodate the schedule of one of the national leaders, who would attend the discussions of several delegations that afternoon. What that meant was, all the afternoon sessions for discussions attended by one of the national leaders would take place in the Great Hall of the People for his convenience.

The results of a discussion in which a national leader participated differed from those in which none did, for they made that night's TV news. And, like the results, the format differed. Most of the time, the leader would first listen to the delegates' reports and then give a speech to summarize what he heard. In order for everything to go smoothly, the discussion for this delegation was carefully orchestrated: A dozen delegates representing a broad range of fields, from mayors and village chiefs to railway workers, entrepreneurs, and university professors, had been selected to speak. The length of the reports was limited to ten minutes or less.

The session was to begin at two in the afternoon, and the delegates were to arrive at the Hall no later than 1:30. Those from ethnic minorities were dressed in national costume. Casual conversations and occasional laughter typified the discussion site until 1:50, when everyone silently awaited the arrival of the national leader. Such dignitaries were seldom late, but, given the myriad of affairs they must attend to, sometimes that was unavoidable. By 2:30 on this afternoon, there was still no sign of the leader, and the delegates began to grow restless. The provincial governor, Chu Qinglian, tapped his teacup to demand patience. At 2:45, the door opened to admit the expected personage, whose entry would have been greeted by applause. But it was not him; a representative of the Congress Secretariat walked briskly up to Governor Chu and whispered something. Somewhat unnerved by the news, Chu waited till the visitor had left to announce:

"The national leader had to attend to an urgent matter and will not be with us today. We will proceed on our own."

Since nothing could be done to alter the leader's schedule, the discussion began without him, though the scenario underwent a significant change: as residents of the same province, the delegates knew one another well, and if the speakers put on a show of formality and engaged in high-sounding speech, they would appear affected. So Governor Chu suggested opening the discussion to anyone who wanted to address the delegation. Enlivened by the change, more than a dozen delegates raised their hands. The eagerness with which they volunteered to speak belied the substance of their offerings, which was essentially the same: support the government work reports, combine the demands raised in the government work reports, coordinate local work, or coordinate departmental and corporate work, find gaps, list ways to correct problems, and strive to catch up. After six delegates had spoken, Governor Chu was about to announce a mid-session rest break when the door opened and, to everyone's surprise, in walked a different national leader on an unplanned visit, followed by a bevy of TV cameramen, lights on. This particular individual had not planned to observe this delegation's discussion, but here he was, to everyone's surprise. Applause erupted as soon as the moment passed. The ruddy-faced visitor waved to the gathering and then lowered his hands to stop the applause.

"I just left the discussion of another delegation, and thought I'd drop in to say hello."

That triggered another round of thunderous applause.

The leader strode confidently into the midst of the delegates and sat in an easy chair next to Chu Qinglian, where he accepted a hot towel from an attendant and said to the governor:

"Go on with what you were doing, Qinglian. I'd like to hear what everyone has to say." Then he pointed to the people. "Before you start, I want you to know that today I brought only my ears, not my mouth. I'll have nothing to say."

Chu Qinglian laughed. So did the others. The meeting began again—no rest break—but, thanks to the leader's presence, the format returned to that originally planned for the session. The meeting pretty much started over, as the designated speakers were again required to perform. The leader took a notebook out of the briefcase his secretary handed him and readied himself to take notes. The speakers also took out notebooks, even though their speeches were prepared and ready to go—lofty speech was more spirited than extemporaneous talk.

Some of the presenters left their prepared speeches in mid-report to give details on work in their particular region or department or field of endeavor. The leader listened with keen interest equaling or exceeding that of the prepared parts of the reports; he nodded frequently and took notes. His obvious interest kept Governor Chu from breaking in on the unscripted presentations, and when the last of the appointed delegates had finished, he announced:

"I now invite our distinguished leader to honor us with his instructions."

TV camera lights snapped on. Applause filled the room. The national leader began with a laugh:

"Qinglian, didn't I tell you I wouldn't say anything today?"

The applause grew louder. The leader laughed again.

"Well, it looks like I'm going to have to eat my words."

That was greeted with laughter, as he shifted in his seat and sat up to make comments on the presentations, sharing his agreement with the successes, accomplishments, and failures mentioned in the reports, and plans for the year to come. With gravity befitting his status, he urged the delegates to hold firmly to the central issues of growing the economy, advancing reform in the economic system, methodically promoting reforms in the political system, improving Party leadership, increasing work on democracy and law, reinforcing unity, mobilizing all elements subject to mobilization, increasing initiative and a sense of urgency, and reaping a bountiful harvest from socialist material and spiritual civilization. Like the delegates before him, once he had rattled off his list, he departed from the government work reports and moved on to other matters, beginning with the international situation. His talk ranged from North America and Europe to the South American and African continents, spending a bit more time on Africa, since he had recently returned from a visit to the continent. Then it was on to Asia and a return from the international to the domestic, focusing on the realities of the current people's economy. From the cities he turned to the countryside and from industry to agriculture. He talked about tertiary industries and technology . . . spoken of as extemporaneous, it was anything but. Throughout the room the only sounds were the voice of the leader and the scratching of delegate pens on notebook paper. A needle falling to the floor would have been inaudible. Now that this was behind him, he said:

"Of course, the beneficial state of affairs overall is indisputable. Now let me speak of shortcomings."

And that is exactly what he did, with no let up in candor, and as they continued taking notes, the delegates shared a feeling that their leader was being both frank and down to earth. After dealing with deficiencies in work in general, he spoke of cadre behavior, including corruption and degeneration. Finally he turned to the cameramen.

"Now I'll speak off the record."

They lowered their cameras.

"Corruption, degeneration, and malpractice are problems that cause me the biggest headaches and have elicited the strongest reactions among the public. These problems are getting worse by the day, Comrades, and they have become a major topic of conversation. Water can float a boat, it can also swamp it. If we do not root out and destroy these cancerous growths, sooner or later our Party and our nation will come to grief."

The somber nature of the leader's speech affected everyone in the room.

"As the ruling party, our primary aim is to work unstintingly for the benefit of the people. But not everyone furthers that aim. By their very nature, corruption, degeneration, and malpractice serve only self-interest, placing it above party and the general public. Why does someone like that become an official? Not to be a public servant, but to set himself up as a powerful bureaucrat, to get rich, to take on a mistress. The details of these cases are horrific and shocking. I advise anyone walking down that path to stop before it is too late. Chairman Mao said it best: Countless revolutionary martyrs shed their blood for the good of the people, made the ultimate sacrifice, so is there any form of self-interest we cannot forego? Am I right, Comrades?"

"Yes," they cried out in unison.

The leader stopped to take a drink of tea.

"Qinglian," he said, turning to Governor Chu, "is such-and-such County in your province?"

Not knowing where the leader was going with this question, Chu looked up from his notebook with a perplexed expression. Since such-and-such County was indeed in his province, he nodded hastily.

"Yes," he said, "yes, it is."

The leader laid down his teacup.

"Something strange occurred this morning. A woman lodged a protest right here in the Great Hall. My secretary tells me she is a resident of that county. Do you know what this is all about, Qinglian?"

Governor Chu broke out in a cold sweat. His province, his county, a resident who actually lodged a protest in the Great Hall of the People in the midst of the National People's Congress. Without doubt a major political incident. Having heard nothing about such an incident, he shook his head animatedly.

"Neither did I. She was arrested and interrogated as a possible terrorist, but it turned out to be a simple divorce case. A divorced woman from the countryside bringing her case to the Great Hall is nothing less than bizarre. How could something so minor have come to this? Did she blow it out of proportion? No. Officials at every layer of government failed to attend to the people's well being. Officials at every level refused to get involved, they passed the buck, they threw up obstacles. In line with what I was saying just now, she was driven to despair, and just like that, a sesame seed had turned into a watermelon, an ant became an elephant. The woman's divorce should have been a matter between her and her husband. And now? Now she wants to bring charges against seven or eight individuals, from the mayor of the responsible city to her county chief, the chief justice, judges, and others. She is a modern-day 'Little Cabbage.' No, even stranger than the Qing dynasty Little Cabbage, because she is even pressing charges against herself. I admire the woman's courage.

I've been told that because of her protest, the local security bureau placed her under arrest. Who drove this woman to despair? Not us members of the Communist Party. No, it was people who suck the blood of the laboring masses, tyrants who ride roughshod over the laboring masses . . ."

The leader's face darkened from rage. He banged his hand on the table. No one present dared look up. Governor Chu's clothes were soaked.

"The wrongs this Little Cabbage has suffered do not stop there," he continued. "She brought her complaint to the Great Hall to get out from under the smear of being a Pan Jinlian. In order to stop her from staging her protest, many local individuals changed course to confuse the issue and tried to ruin her good name by fabricating a rumor that she lived an unchaste life. For her being a Little Cabbage was bad enough, but how was she supposed to live besmirched with the label Pan Jinlian? If denied the right to bring her case to the Great Hall, where was she supposed to go? The UN? Who made it necessary for her to come to the Great Hall? Not us members of the Communist Party. No, again it was people who suck the blood of the laboring masses, tyrants who ride roughshod over the laboring masses . . ."

The national leader turned to Chu Qinglian.

"Qinglian, do we or do we not want to have officials who become oppressive bureaucrats?"

Chu Qinglian too was pale with rage. "No," he said, nodding like a pecking chicken, "we do not."

The national leader heaved a sigh.

"My secretary is a good man, at least he was today. He happened to walk by when the security personnel arrested the woman as a potential terrorist, so he asked them what was going on, and made them let her go. I was told she had left a three-month-old baby in the care of someone else back home, and so my secretary performed a remarkable kindness. This is not an issue of properly treating an ordinary countrywoman alone, but all the people. We are engaged in a People's Congress, aren't we? Who do we represent? And whom do we arrest as potential terrorists? Who dispenses terror? Not a laboring woman, that's for sure. It's the corrupt, degenerate people who become officials to oppress the common people and refuse to lift a hand for their benefit!"

The leader's growing anger was interrupted by the entrance of a worker who quick-stepped up and whispered something in his ear. "Oh, I see," he muttered as he regained his poise and said mildly:

"Of course I was speaking of extreme cases and might be wrong. I just offer this for your consideration."

He stood, smiled. "I'm told a foreign VIP is waiting for me, so I'll stop here for today."

With a wave to the delegates, he walked out, leaving Governor Chu in a perplexed void. The delegates exchanged looks of incomprehension, suddenly aware that they had forgotten to applaud when the leader finished his wrap-up. And Governor Chu realized that he'd forgotten to make a statement in response. Of course, even if he'd wanted to make his thoughts known, the leader would not have had time to hear them anyway.

Governor Chu could not sleep that night. At 4:30 he summoned his secretary to his room, where he found Chu pacing, which he knew was the governor's habit. He dealt with major problems by pacing, back and forth, back and forth, a habit he shared with Lin Biao, but in this case minus a military map. Chu Qinglian was a man of few words, and such people are given to deep thought. When drafting a document or making an important policy decision, he could pace the floor for hours, blurting out a phrase every so often and leaving people who did not know him far behind as he leaped from thought to thought. He would not explain what his thoughts meant; that was the responsibility of the listener. No one had trouble understanding him when he read a prepared talk, but one on one, as he paced the floor, releasing a single utterance from time to time, the listener was often left in a fog, as if sailing through clouds. Fortunately, this secretary had been with him for more than a decade and had no trouble following the rhythm of his leapfrogging thoughts. Normally, a few hours of pacing was the limit for Chu, but this time he kept it up from evening till early in the morning—a first for the secretary, who did not have to be told that something big was up. Chu had not said a word or taken a break in his pacing when his secretary first walked in. A quarter of an hour later, he stopped in front of the window, gazed into the darkness, and said:

"What happened yesterday afternoon presents some thorny issues."

His secretary knew he was referring to the discussion session.

Chu resumed his pacing and glanced at his secretary.

"He came prepared."

The secretary knew he was referring to the national leader's illustration of the woman who had managed to get into the Great Hall with her protest.

More pacing, then a pause.

"He came looking to find fault with us."

The secretary broke out in a cold sweat, for he knew exactly what Chu was getting at. While it may have seemed as if the national leader were making casual remarks about the woman from the country-side, they were in truth anything but casual. He had not been scheduled to attend this discussion session, and though his arrival may have appeared unscripted, a sudden impulse to "greet the delegates," he had actually come with an ulterior motive. The secretary's thoughts turned to Governor Chu, whose prospects for promotion had, in recent days, reached a critical stage, with word that he was to be transferred to another province as the new provincial Party Secretary; rumor had it that there were varying opinions regarding his case at the Central Government level. From that to what they now faced left the secretary speechless.

Chu Qinglian paced some more and stopped again at the window, where early light was beginning to show in the Beijing sky.

"Suggest to the provincial Party committee that they sack the lot of them," he said.

The secretary's first layer of cold sweat had not dried before it was joined by a second. He knew that his boss was referring to the individuals who had mishandled the woman's complaint, which had led to her bringing it into the Great Hall of the People, the ones the national leader had referred to by position, men who had turned a sesame seed into a watermelon, an ant into an elephant; that is the mayor, the county chief, and the chief justice.

"Governor Chu," the secretary stammered, "do you think one woman's divorce is a valid reason to sack all those cadres?"

Back to the window Chu Qinglian paced.

"I had someone look into the matter. Although one or two of the details differ, what the national leader said was accurate."

He turned and paced his way over to his secretary, anger filling his eyes.

"The way those people mishandled the case is a black mark for the whole province."

He ground his teeth.

"Our leader was right on target yesterday. Who are these people? They're not Communists and they're not public servants. They are people who suck the blood of the laboring masses, tyrants who ride roughshod over the laboring masses, and they must be punished for their sins. They are the criminal Pan Jinlians!"

15

Seven days later, the following directive was issued from the provincial office:

Cai Fubang is hereby relieved of duties as mayor of such-and-such City. Members of the Municipal Standing Committee of the People's Congress are advised to affirm this at their next meeting.

Shi Weimin is hereby relieved of his duties as chief of such-and-such County. Members of the County Standing Committee of the People's Congress are advised to affirm this at their next meeting.

Xun Zhengyi is hereby relieved of his duties as chief justice of such-and-such County. Members of the County Standing Committee of the People's Congress are advised to affirm this at their next meeting.

Dong Xianfa is hereby relieved of his duties as Member of the Judicial Committee. Members of the County Standing Committee of the People's Congress are advised to affirm this at their next meeting.

The County Court is advised to record a major demerit for Justice Wang Gongdao.

Mayor Cai Fubang was at a loss when he received the directive, and did not know what had caused this startling development. He soon discovered that a single comment, passed on during the recent Cultured City campaign, had turned out to be a huge mistake, for it had resulted in the incarceration of a local woman for staging a sit-in in front of the government building. The path from the woman's protest to his official sacking had been tortuous, and the results both saddened and rattled him. As mayor, he knew there was more to this than met the eye, but there was nothing he could do to change the outcome. Anything he attempted now would be wasted effort.

Provincial decisions were always the last word. He could only sigh and exclaim:

"Where malpractice is concerned, this is the most egregious example."

Another sigh.

"Who's the 'Little Cabbage'? That would be me."

County Chief Shi Weimin and Chief Justice Xun Zhengyi both protested an "injustice." County Chief Shi, experiencing a stomachache, fulminated:

"Where's the logic in that damned directive? Tomorrow I'm lodging my own complaint!"

Chief Justice Xun Zhengyi lamented tearfully:

"If I'd known this would happen, I wouldn't have gone out drinking that day."

He was referring to the day he'd encountered Li Xuelian. Well on his way to being drunk, he had scolded her as a "troublemaker" and angrily sent her on her way. Sober, he'd have handled it differently.

Justice Wang Gongdao had escaped with the lightest punishment, largely because he had no duties from which he could be relieved. And yet a demerit was more than he could stomach.

"Are we or are we not expected to follow the law here?" he thundered. "You demand that of us, but not of yourselves, apparently!"

The only one among them who neither raised an uproar nor bemoaned his fate was Member of the Judicial Committee Dong Xianfa, who walked out after hearing what the directive had to say.

"Screw you," he said. "I've wanted to quit for a long time. I'm going to the market to sell livestock."

16

On her way home from Beijing, Li Xuelian stopped first at the home of Meng Lanzhi to pick up her child. She then went to the Mt. Jietai Temple, where she bought a ticket, lit incense, and knelt before the Bodhisattva.

"Great Merciful Bodhisattva," she said as she touched her head to the floor, "you get things done with your ruthless hand. Thanks to you, many greedy, corrupt officials were removed from office, to them a fate worse than death, and I was allowed to vent my anger."

That done, she rose, burned another incense stick and knelt a second time, once again touching her head to the floor.

"While attending to important affairs, Bodhisattva, you cannot ignore trivial ones. You have punished the greedy and the corrupt, but that bastard Qin Yuhe remains blissfully free of the law. You have yet to comment on the matter of whether or not I am Pan Jinlian."

Appendix

As a result of one woman's public protest in a certain county, several individuals, from a municipal mayor and county chief to officials in the county courthouse, were removed from their jobs, news of which appeared in *Domestic Trends*. A representative of the Central Committee who had attended the discussion meeting of NPC delegates from that province saw the news one morning and summoned his secretary.

"What's this all about?" he asked.

This document secretary had also seen the news.

"Delegates from that province must have gone into action right after you voiced your displeasure over the incident at the discussion meeting during the Congress."

"What idiots!" he snapped as he smacked the publication down on his desk. "I was just critical of what the incident represented and never meant they should fire all those cadres. They've overreacted."

"Shall I phone them so you can put things back the way they were?"

The man thought for a moment.

"Then I'd be overreacting if I did that," he said with a wave of his hand.

He sighed.

"There's nothing easier than adopting organization measures. So why do people always take shortcuts? Why can't they stop to figure out what makes something important and judge the whole of it by its parts?"

He paused.

"If I'd known this was going to happen, I'd never have attended that discussion meeting. You recall that I was scheduled to meet a foreign VIP at four that afternoon, but that he had some sort of stomach incident on the way over and was taken to the hospital, which opened up that time slot. When I heard about that woman I only used her as an example."

He began pacing the floor. After several trips back and forth, he stopped and said:

"That Chu Qinglian is too calculating."

Now that he'd gotten that off his chest, he sat down and turned his attention to other matters.

The man in charge of the province, Governor Chu Qinglian, had been scheduled for reassignment as Provincial Party Secretary of another province. But a month later an inside candidate from Li Xuelian's province was chosen, and Chu remained in his position as governor. Three years later he was appointed Chairman of the Provincial Political Consultative Conference. Five years after that he retired from public life.

Chapter Two

Prologue: Twenty Years Later

1

Wang Gongdao pounded on Li Xuelian's gate for fifteen minutes. No one in the compound responded.

"It's me, Cousin, Wang Gongdao," shouted as he continued pounding.

Still no response from inside.

"Open the gate," he shouted. "I can see a light in the window."

No response.

"It's pitch black out here, and I haven't had dinner. I've brought a ham hock. We have to cook it soon."

And still no response.

Early the next morning, Li Xuelian came out to open the gate. Wang Gongdao was standing there in the company of several courthouse employees. She could not believe her eyes.

"Did you people stand out here all night?"

"Of course," Wang said, pointing to his head. "See the frost here?"

Li Xuelian examined his head. Not a thing. Wang Gongdao chuckled.

"Do you think I'm stupid? I pounded on the gate last night, but you pretended you didn't hear me. So I went home and got up early this morning. I was determined to catch you at home."

Li Xuelian could only invite the contingent inside. Wang Gongdao, a youngster twenty years earlier, was now a rather bloated middle-aged man; the thin brows he'd sported back then were gone without a trace. No hair sprouted on his chin, which could have hidden the skin tags on his face. And the fair-skinned young man of twenty years earlier was now dark and had rough skin. But he wasn't the only one who had changed. Twenty years earlier, Li Xuelian had been a young woman; she was now forty-nine and middle-aged. A head of lush black hair was now graying. Back then she had been favored with delicate features, a full bust, and a thin waist; twenty years had not only introduced wrinkles onto her face, but had thickened her bust and her waist. She and Wang Gongdao sat in the yard.

"Cousin," Wang said, "I just dropped by to see if there's anything I can do for you. Nothing special."

One of the members of the party laid a ham hock down on a stone bench beneath the jujube tree.

"If that's what you came for, then you're free to go, since everything's fine here. And take that with you. I'm a Buddhist and a vegetarian."

She stood up and put her broom to work. Wang Gongdao jumped off his bench and scurried out of the way. He grabbed the broom to help sweep.

"I'm glad to hear that, Cousin, but as family, can't I drop by to say hello?"

"Please stop calling me 'cousin.' It unsettles me to hear that from a chief justice."

Wang stopped the movement of the broom.

"Well, let's see about that. Big Face Ma from Ma Family Village, who died a couple of years ago, was my uncle. Did you know that?"

"Why ask me?" Xuelian said. "Go ask your mother."

"The younger sister of Ma's wife married someone in Hu Family Bend, while a cousin in your aunt's family married the nephew of her mother-in-law's uncle. Which makes you and me only slightly distant cousins."

"Justice Wang, if there's nothing on your mind, there's no need for us to jaw back and forth. I have to go see my daughter. Their cow calved last night."

Wang let go of the broom handle and sat down again.

"Since you and I are family, I'll give it to you straight. You know, Cousin, that another National People's Congress begins in ten days, and I'd like to know when you plan to stage your protest."

"So that's why you're here. Well, you'll be pleased to know I'm not going to do it this year."

Wang's initial look of surprise was quickly supplanted by a smile.

"I said I'd give it to you straight, Cousin, so why won't you do the same? You've lodged your protest every year for the past twenty. Now you say not this year. I find that hard to believe."

"Things are different this year," she said.

"How's that?" Wang said. "I can't wait to hear."

"I always held out hope in the past, but no more."

"I'm not convinced, Cousin. I know how you've suffered these twenty years, but you have to understand that it's no longer only about you. What began as a matter no bigger than a sesame seed has now grown to the size of a watermelon. What was once an ant has wound up as an elephant. A simple divorce led to the removal of a mayor, a county chief, a chief justice, and a member of the Judicial Committee. Nothing like that has happened since the fall of the Qing Dynasty. But tell me in all good conscience, could the mayor or the county chief have decided whether or not your divorce from Qin Yuhe was legitimate or whether or not you could remarry and then re-divorce him? Was it their fault you were denied that permission? You claim injustice for yourself. Well, everyone else could make the same claim. The principal in your case is Qin Yuhe, not the mayor, not the county chief, not the chief justice, and not the courtroom judge. If that prick Qin Yuhe had lived in the Qing Dynasty, I'd have had him shot. Too bad we have laws against that these days. I tell you, he's a bad person. Getting a divorce and remarrying caused enough trouble, but he made things worse by calling you a modern-day Pan Jinlian, and together those acts drove you into a blind alley. Officials at every level of government can understand why you've staged a protest every year for the past twenty. Leading officials in the previous government and the courts worked on Qin Yuhe as much as they could, but nothing could make that stubborn ass change his mind. His refusal to be reasonable has been the cause of all this trouble, don't you agree? We share the same view, so can't we talk this out and convince you not to do it this year? We'll focus on the real cause of the problem, and I'll keep working on Qin Yuhe. Time can be unforgiving, but it can also be all forgiving. The son you had with Qin Yuhe is not quite thirty this year and he already has a son who's in the third grade. Twenty years have passed, and Qin Yuhe isn't made of iron. Even if he were a stone, if you held him against you he'd warm up.

I've mapped out a strategy. When we work on Qin this year, instead of tackling him straight on, why not go about it through your son or through his wife? Let them work on Qin. Blood is thicker than water, after all. And don't forget your grandchild. As a third-grader he knows a thing or two, and we can get him to talk some sense into his grand-dad. Who knows, something he says might hit Qin smack in the heart. Then there's your daughter, who's not a little girl any more. Whether for your sake or for her own, she should try to talk some sense into her dad. Her parents wrangling over remarrying and re-divorcing for twenty years can't make her the proudest person alive. With people coming at him from all sides, something will get through, and he'll divorce his present wife. Then you two can remarry and all that Pan Jinlian nonsense will collapse on its own . . ."

Li Xuelian broke in on Wang's long-winded oration:

"You can stop working on Qin Yuhe. Even if you talk him around, I won't marry him a second time."

"If not, how will you prove that your divorce was a sham? And how will you prove you're not a Pan Jinlian?"

"I no longer want to prove those things," Xuelian said.

"You've been trying to do that for twenty years, and now this year you've changed your mind? Who do you think will believe that?"

"I told you. I've seen the light."

"How can you be so stubborn, Cousin? What you just said shows that you still plan to stage your protest. I'm telling you, forget about everyone else, just do it for me. Twenty years I've slaved away at this, you've seen that with your own eyes. I've done things I shouldn't have done, all because of you; I've fallen down and picked myself up. Becoming a chief justice was not easy. If you don't protest, I'll keep my job. But if you go on this way, I could be fired, just like Chief justice Xun twenty years ago. My future lies in your hands."

"If that's the case, then you can stuff your heart back into your stomach. I'll tell you again, no protest this year."

"Cousin," Wang said, on the verge of tears, "how can you look me in the eye and lie like that? We're like brother and sister, and we ought to be able to have an honest, open conversation, don't you think?"

"Who are you calling a liar?" Xuelian tensed. "I'm telling you the truth. Believe me or not, it's up to you." She picked up her bag from the step under the jujube tree. "You're not going to believe me, no matter what I say, so I'm through talking. I'm going to my daughter's. You can hang around here if you want, just be sure to shut the gate when you leave."

She walked out the gate. Wang Gongdao ran after her.

"Wait up. What's your hurry? I can drive you there, even if it's only for a family visit."

2

The new county chief, Zheng Zhong, had been in office only three months. He alone, among all the leading cadres, was unaware of how formidable Li Xuelian could be. That did not mean he'd come to office ignorant of the fact that she was a modern-day Little Cabbage, that classic thorn in the side of officials. By staging a protest, she had been responsible for the sacking of a string of officials, but the effect of this knowledge on Zheng was a feeling that the local officials were too timid, like the person who sees a snake once and has a fear of ropes for a decade. How, he wondered, could a simple peasant woman strike fear in and hold such sway over the lives of so many high officials? Allowing someone access to your weaknesses closes off all routes of escape and no one knows peace any longer. Stability is a good thing, as is harmony, but that is not the way to achieve either, just as concessions must not be made to terrorists, since they'll keep upping the ante. Negotiations are not foolproof. In his eyes, the local officials had been too soft; they should not have backed down when firm measures were called for. There's nothing wrong with letting an incident occur; if the terrorists want to open fire, let 'em. Granted, a mayor, a county chief, and a chief justice had been sacked when an incident occurred twenty years earlier. But that was precisely the reason not to be fearful now. Where the sacking of officials was concerned, history would not repeat itself, and the world's most dangerous spots often turn out to be the safest.

Not only was Zheng Zhong aware of all this, he had personally dealt with a grievance as executive deputy chief in another county, and that experience had taught him a lesson. The situation back then had been far more serious than Li Xuelian's protest. When the government and peasants were unable to reach agreement on compensation for two hundred acres of village land on which the county planned to build an industrial park, more than a thousand peasants, men and women, had staged a sit-in in front of the government offices. Ten rounds of talks with the peasants by County Chief Xiong had produced no agreement, as the ranks of protesters swelled. Xiong asked the mayor, Ma Wenbin, to send in the police. Ma's response came in the form of three words:

"Resolve it peacefully."

Under assault from above and below, a worried Chief Xiong was hospitalized, which shifted the responsibility for resolving the matter to Zheng Zhong, who knew that his boss was faking an illness to keep from getting stung. But Zheng also knew what to do. Seeking no instructions from above, he summoned the protest leaders to the government compound to open an eleventh round of talks. As soon as they entered the conference room, they were surrounded by a phalanx of police who, without a word, spun them around, snapped on handcuffs, put gags in their mouths, and manhandled them out a back door. When news reached the protesters that their leaders had been arrested, more than a thousand of them stormed the government compound, smashing windows and overturning three cars, which they torched. This was the moment Zheng Zhong had been waiting for. Without warning, the ransacking peasants discovered a massing of security forces on all sides, eventually numbering as many as four hundred uniformed policemen, some armed with loaded weapons, others with police batons. Zheng had mobilized all the police in the county. When the unavoidable clash broke out, he ordered the police to fire into the air; the protesters scattered like frightened birds and beasts at the sound of gunfire. Two retreating peasants were injured by stray bullets, but the revolt was quashed. The detained representatives were released, seven or eight of the leaders of the rampage were arrested and ultimately sentenced to three to five years in prison for "public disturbance," "preventing the carrying out of official duties," and "destruction of public and private property." The government then paid the original price to the farmers for their land; the villagers accepted the amount offered, no one caused a stir, and work on the industrial park got underway. Injuries caused by the stray bullets led to a reprimand for Zheng Zhong. Mayor Ma was not well acquainted with Zheng before this incident, but he now found a lot to appreciate in his subordinate. Not, of course, the fact that gunfire had resulted in injuries, but that he'd had the guts to deal with the problem on his own initiative, without instructions from above. In other words, he had fearlessly taken on the responsibility. A year later, the chief of Li Xuelian's county was reassigned, and Mayor Ma appointed Zheng Zhong to the post, despite the black mark on his record. When Justice Wang informed Zheng of the situation with Li Xuelian, he wondered glumly if Li was planning to stage another protest this year; Zheng was not concerned.

"Over twenty years," Wang said, "that broad has become impossible to handle. The more she denies her desire to protest, the less I believe her. I can't figure her out."

"Then stop trying. Let her protest."

Wang waved his arms frantically. "You're new here. You can't let her do that."

"Where does the Constitution say you can't protest?"

"She's not lodging it in our county courts," Wang explained. "That wouldn't bother me. No, she's taking her complaint to Beijing. Even that wouldn't bother me, in most cases. But the National People's Congress is about to take place. If she crashes her way into the Great Hall of the People again, everyone, from the mayor to you and down to me will be out of a job."

Zheng Zhong smiled and repeated his theory that the sacking of a string of officials twenty years precluded its happening a second time. Wang disagreed:

"You may not want to hear what I'm about to say, Chief Zheng. I understand that things are different now, but that only means we can no sooner fathom what our superiors are thinking these day than what Li Xuelian is thinking. Are you one who believes that senior leaders feel bad about sacking cadres? China may lack a great many things, but not party cadres. The leaders can sack a slew of cadres and replace them with their own people."

This was something Zheng hadn't thought of. He sat back in his chair.

"They can sack me if they want," he said. "I'm not crazy about this job anyway."

"It's not you who makes these decisions," Wang said anxiously. "You may not like your job, but what about the mayor?" He lowered his head. "And I'd like to keep mine."

Seeing that Wang was not a devious man, Zheng could only laugh.

"Are you telling me that a countrywoman can effectively hamstring people at all levels of government?"

"That's what I'm saying," Wang said, "and she's done it for twenty years. The problem is, we could deal with her if she were only one person. But she's actually three."

"How's that?"

"We see her as a 'Little Cabbage,' her husband has labeled her a 'Pan Jinlian,' and she calls herself 'Doue,' after the wronged heroine in the famous play. See what I mean? Three people. All capable of making trouble, and none that can easily be separated from the others, which makes her superhuman. Like the legendary Madame White Snake, who perfected her martial arts skills, she's been refining hers for twenty years, to a point where she's almost supernatural.

"To pacify her," he continued, "we've given her everything she wanted. I've personally given her seventeen or eighteen ham hocks. People give officials gifts all the time, but when was the last time you saw an official give a gift to a village woman? There are too many NPCs," he groused, "a small one every year and a big one every five. This year's special, a fifth-year congress where a new slate will be elected. She can't be allowed to interfere with that. We must be careful."

He sighed. "Everything's turned upside down. If you'd told me that a countrywoman could one day become a matter of national interest, I'd never have believed you."

"That's because of how you people handled it," Zheng Zhong said. "She is what you made her."

"I'm just telling you where things stand, Chief Zheng. I'm a minor official. She won't listen to anything I say. But you're in a position to talk some sense into her."

Zheng smiled. He knew that Wang was hoping to dump the problem on him to keep from getting stung himself. He may not appear devious, Zheng was thinking, but there's larceny in his heart. But he didn't let that bother him. Better to attack from another angle.

"Can we take a closer look at the woman to see if there are skeletons in her closet? Theft, for instance, or fighting, or gambling, anything like that."

Wang saw where Zheng was going with this.

"I wish she did, but anything like that would have gotten her arrested long ago. That would have taken me off the hook, since it would have been the security people who had to deal with her." He stopped and scratched his head. "We've watched her for twenty years. A countrywoman wouldn't have the guts to commit a crime and she certainly doesn't have money to gamble with."

That was not Zheng's view, however:

"Based on your description, it's not that she wouldn't have the guts, but that she has good character. Let's look at it from a different angle. What if we work on the ex-husband, see if he'll consider remarrying her. That way there'd be no need for her to protest any longer."

"We've also tried that for twenty years; I've personally tried hundreds of times, but her ex is too pig-headed. He said he might have considered it if she hadn't raised such a stink all these years, but not now, not if she was the last woman on earth. Besides, he found another woman, and they have a child who's nearly twenty. To remarry Li Xuelian he'd have to first get a divorce. Not only that, Li Xuelian doesn't want to live with him again. She wants to marry him so she can divorce him. In a word, she wants to hound him into proving that she isn't a Pan Jinlian. Well, she hasn't been able to hound her ex," he said with a sigh, "but she sure has managed to hound us. Twenty years, Chief Zheng, there are times when I'm so depressed all I want to do is to quit this job and open a shop."

Zheng Zhong laughed.

"If that's what she's done to you, I guess I ought to meet the woman."

Wang jumped to his feet.

"That's the ticket, Chief Zheng. Tell her whatever you have to in order to get through this month. Once the NPC has ended, she can protest anywhere she pleases. We can rest easy as soon as this critical moment has passed."

Zheng Zhong shook his head.

"How in the world did this county produce a Pan Jinlian?"

"By accident," Wang replied, "purely by accident."

The next morning County Chief Zheng traveled to Li Xuelian's village to meet her. Justice Wang went with him. Zheng wanted to have a talk with her not only as a result of Wang's persuasive arguments, but also because Mayor Ma Wenbin had phoned after Wang had left to inform him that he'd be leaving for Beijing in ten days to participate in the National People's Congress, and to remind him of a woman named Li Xuelian from Zheng's county who had caused a commotion at the congress twenty years before and kept it up every year since.

"I'll be in Beijing for the Congress," Ma had said, "so let's see that Li Xuelian won't be."

Zheng could have taken Wang Gongdao's spirited warning to heart or not, but he could not and dared not ignore Mayor Ma's phoned message. In any case, he wanted to meet Li Xuelian to see if she impressed him as supernatural in her ability to successfully hound every official in the chain of command for twenty years. But then he met her: an ordinary gray-haired, thick-waisted, soft-spoken woman from the countryside. She was surprised to see Wang Gongdao.

"Weren't you here yesterday?" she asked. "Why are you back today?"

"That was yesterday, Cousin. Today's different."

He pointed to Zheng Zhong.

"This is County Chief Zheng. I didn't have the standing to talk you around yesterday, so I've invited the county chief to come try."

They sat beneath the jujube tree in her yard.

"Dear Sister-in-law," Zheng began, "I'm someone who prefers to get right to the point, and so, to make a long story short, since the National People's Congress will open in a few days, tell me if you plan to lodge a protest this year."

Li Xuelian pointed to Wang Gongdao. "I told him yesterday I don't."

Zheng Zhong's next question did not differ from those Wang had asked.

"And why is that?"

Xuelian's answer also did not differ. "I hadn't seen the light in the past. Now I have."

Wang Gongdao smacked his palms together.

"The more you say things like that, the less assured I am. You say you're not going to do it means you are."

Zheng Zhong stopped Wang with his hand.

"Justice Wang doesn't believe you," he said to Li Xuelian, "but I do. Since you say you've seen the light, you can prove it with a letter of guarantee, what do you say?"

She hadn't seen that coming.

"What's a letter of guarantee?"

"You sign your name as a guarantee that you won't stage a protest."

"What good will that do?"

"If you go ahead and stage a protest, you'll be in violation of the law."

"Then I won't do it."

That gave Zheng paused. "You say you're not going to protest, so why are you afraid to put it in writing?"

"I'm not afraid. It's about more than this, and so was my reason. I don't have to make an appeal for justice if I don't want to, but I'm not going to put that in writing. Writing a guarantee is like an admission that I've been in the wrong. It's no big deal to be wrong once, but that would mean that I've been wrong for twenty years."

That too gave Zheng pause. This was no ordinary woman he was up against. What she said had not occurred to him.

"Dear Sister-in-law," he was quick to respond, "it's not as serious as you make it out to be. It's just a formality."

"A formality now," she said, shaking her head, "but in the future, if anything happens, you could use that piece of paper to come after me."

Zheng Zhong now realized that handling the woman was not going to be easy. She was everything others said she was. She'd seen through his strategy.

"That's not how it's meant to be used," he hastened to explain. "It's intended to put people's minds at ease. How are we supposed to come to an agreement if you're free to say anything you feel like?"

Wang Gongdao took a form out of his briefcase; it had been filled in.

"We've written out the agreement. All you have to do is sign it in front of County Chief Zheng."

He took a fountain pen from his coat pocket. "Sign this and I won't bother you anymore."

She shocked them by knocking the pen to the ground.

"I hadn't planned on staging a protest this year, but you won't leave well enough alone. So listen to me, I've changed my mind. I'm taking my protest to Beijing again this year."

Zheng Zhong froze. Wang Gongdao picked his pen up off the ground and smacked it against the agreement in his hand.

"There, you see, the truth is out."

3

Mayor Ma Wenbin censured County Chief Zheng to his face for exacerbating the dispute between the government and Li Xuelian. During his tenure as executive deputy chief in a neighboring county, Zheng had exacerbated the volatile situation of a mass demonstration at the government office building by farmers. He'd been correct in doing so then, but not this time. A countrywoman had staged a protest twenty years in a row, then surprised people by stating she would not do so this year. Whether she was being truthful or not, it was the first time in all those years that she'd taken the positive step of saying there would be no more protest. Even if she wasn't telling the truth, she hinted at a desire to change the method and momentous nature of the protest, an incentive for them to lead her in a positive direction. But everyone, from the chief justice to the county chief had thrown cold water on that possibility by insisting that she was lying, and in order to turn her lie into the truth, insisting that she sign a pledge and bind herself legally to it. So what happened? They ruined something that had started out as positive, a desire to do the right thing. And how had it all started? By not trusting her. How do you expect someone to trust you if you won't trust her? A dog will jump a wall if it has no choice. Their tactic backfired; they got the opposite of what they'd hoped for. The woman had told them there'd be no protest this year, but was forced to change her mind. Now they knew it would be harder than ever to turn her around. When a person wants something constructive, you are all working toward the same goal. But when that person digresses from you, then you must start from the difference, working from a divergent direction toward the same goal, and that means more work. More because of whom? Not because of the countrywoman. No, because of the people trying to work on her. The approach was flawed, and not just in its appearance, but in its essence, in its attitude toward the people. They won't trust you if you don't trust them. The way you approached the matter shows that you did not consider yourself a civil servant but a bureaucratic official. An even greater mistake in trying to resolve this matter was Zheng's inability to see the big picture. In two weeks the National People's Congress would convene, and once the countrywoman and an event of national importance came together, she would no longer be an ordinary countrywoman, though in our work we had treated her as one. After crashing the People's Congress twenty years ago, she had witnessed the sacking of a string of officials who had dealt with her just as we are doing. Wouldn't you think we'd have learned something after all that time? But politics is what really counts here. This year's congress will differ from those that have preceded it, since it is time to vote in a new administration; the eyes of China and the rest of the world are on it. In previous years the woman disrupted an ordinary congress, but if she tries again this year and is successful, the political impact and ramifications will be extraordinary. In a word, it will be big news, especially given the Internet and the blogosphere. The whole world could know about it within a day, and we, like our predecessors, can count on being sacked, or worse, since China's prestige will suffer in the eyes of people all around the world.

Ma Wenbin's censure of Zheng Zhong was severe, though Ma wore a smile the whole time. That was a personal trait of a man who stood barely five-feet-two. Sometimes when scheduled to give a speech he had to stand in the wings until the previous speaker had finished, then walked to the podium, where workers had speedily lowered the microphone for him. Short, skinny, and never without his gold-rimmed glasses, he looked like a meek scholar. He spoke softly and always began and ended comments with a slight laugh. But being in the right is not reliant upon elevated speech; if others could explain one level of reasoning on any given matter, he could manage three. He appreciated good work, but met shoddy labor with bruising condemnation. Soft-spoken most of the time, when it came time to examining the work of cadres, he raised the volume substantially. His stand was always clear-cut regarding who to promote and who to sack. Few people dared question his promotion decisions, and those who did never had a chance in the debate. He always had the final word, as he was able to present three levels of reasoning. Municipal and county cadres were in awe of him. Ma's censure of Zheng Zhong did not deviate from a fixed routine, in that the comments were interrupted by slight smiles, until Zheng's skin was wet with cold sweat, not out of fear of Ma's criticism, but because he knew that in every respect Ma was more talented than he. The difference between the two men? That was it. Ma was mayor, Zheng was county chief, and that was attributable to Ma's higher level of achievement and ability.

Once Ma had wrapped up what needed to be said, Zheng responded with heartfelt gratitude:

"You are absolutely right, Mayor Ma. I underestimated the complexity of the problem and underestimated its severity. I didn't see the big picture or the political ramifications. I lost sight of the times. I'll go and write a self-criticism."

With a smile, Ma Wenbin waved him off.

"That won't be necessary. Your knowing what you did is enough for me."

He moved on.

"Sometimes I find myself contemplating classical idioms, many of which are worth pondering, since they are so profound. Take 'a tiny ant hole can ruin a dike,' for instance. Or 'attend to the small to ward off the big.' Then there's 'save a little and lose a lot.' Notice that they all deal with the idea of something 'small.' Many people stumble not over the 'big,' but over the 'small.' They can't grasp its profound significance."

Zheng Zhong nodded in agreement.

"I'm one of those who tried to save a little and lost a lot. The small was my undoing."

"There's another idiom," Ma said, "that goes, 'the loss of a horse may not be a bad thing.' Stumble once, and the next time you'll think twice. Draw inferences from one instance. I believe you've learned your lesson."

"When I'm back home," Zheng Zhong said, "I'll do things differently, starting with having a talk with the woman."

Ma Wenbin smiled, pointed a finger at Zheng.

"You pushed her to the point of no return, and bringing her back won't be easy."

He rapped the sofa arm.

"The Congress will convene in nine days, so you'd better leave that to me. Go back and extend a dinner invitation to the woman on my behalf."

Knowing that the mayor's invitation stemmed from his own inability to resolve the matter made Zheng Zhong uneasy.

"My failed attempt has made trouble for you, Mayor Ma."

"Meeting the people is part of my job," Ma said with a wave of his hand.

He smiled and added:

"I've been in this job for three years and haven't had the pleasure of meeting the 'Little Cabbage.' Oh, that's right, I haven't met this 'Pan Jinlian,' or the one you just called 'Doue,' this supernatural demon-queen. I should have. I've been guilty of bureaucratic behavior."

Taking advantage of a lightening of the mood, Zheng smiled unctuously.

"The female characters in all three works are lovely young women. Ours is a gray-haired middle-aged one."

Before Mayor Ma fulfilled his promise to treat Li to a meal, he had reason to be critical again, this time of his secretary and—back for seconds—Zheng Zhong, over the location. Ma hosted dinners at his three favorite spots. For provincial-level officials or municipal colleagues, he reserved tables at the Municipal Government Guesthouse; for foreign investors, it was at the upscale Regal Hotel; and for old classmates and friends, he had food catered from the Guesthouse to his home. His secretary, assuming that an invitation to a countrywoman made it work related, reserved a table at the Municipal Guesthouse and arranged for a car to pick her up. When he reported to the mayor, Ma frowned.

"I'm not unhappy with you, but one meal can make your attitude toward the masses crystal clear. Are you having a commoner call on you or are you calling on her?"

The secretary realized his mistake at once.

"Yes, of course, we should go to her."

He left the mayor's office and placed a call to County Chief Zheng Zhong, who reserved a table at Peach Blossom Heaven, the finest restaurant in the county. Though located in an inland province, the restaurant took pride in its seafood offerings from all over the world. In the past, whenever Ma Wenbin went down to the county on an inspection tour, if he stayed for dinner, he ate at Peach Blossom Heaven. Zheng Zhong informed the secretary, who made his report to Mayor Ma. Another frown.

"Didn't I caution you to draw inferences from one instance? That should not be hard to get your head around. If you take a guest from the masses to Peach Blossom Heaven, with its fancy décor, bright lights, and seafood menu, you'll intimidate her before she even sits down to eat. She'll assume that this is how you dine every day, which will only upset her more and make your job harder than ever. So, since I'm inviting her to dinner, do you think you could find a place where she'd be comfortable and relaxed? A place like a lamb stew diner in her township, where we could each enjoy some flatbreads and a bowl of steaming hot, sweat-inducing lamb stew, and quickly find common ground."

Once again, his secretary realized his mistake.

"Yes, of course," he said, nodding enthusiastically. "We'll go to her township and all have a bowl of lamb stew."

"But," he added with a worried look, "how sanitary could a little diner like that be?"

"I grew up in a peasant household," Ma Wenbin replied. "I'll eat what she eats. If you don't feel comfortable doing that, don't go."

More enthusiastic nodding.

"No, I'm fine with that. I'll go."

He scooted back to his office and phoned Zheng Zhong, who also realized his error and immediately made arrangements for the mayor and his guest at a local lamb stew diner. His admiration for Ma Wenbin rose even higher. No matter was too small for him to grasp its full significance. Zheng knew he had yet to thoroughly comprehend the importance of the word "small." If you're looking for a gap in talent, that's where you'll find it.

The following night, Mayor Ma Wenbin treated Li Xuelian to a meal of lamb stew at the Lao Bai Lamb Stew Diner on the western end of Round the Bend Township. Most of the time, Lao Bai was a filthy eating place, inside and out. But not tonight. A hovel that morning, it was spotless by that afternoon. The floor had been swept, the tables scrubbed with hot water, sheets of newspaper had patched holes in the overhead canopy, and caked-on grease in kitchen nooks and crannies had been scraped clean with a spatula. Lao Bai Lamb Stew

Diner looked brighter after the extensive cleaning job. A roadside
stall to the left of the diner that sold sheep's entrails was open for
business that morning and had been cleared away by the township
head, Lai Xiaomao, by that afternoon. The owner of the stall to the
right of the café, Lao Yu, pulled teeth and sold odds and ends; he too
was sent away by the township head. Now swept clean, the entrance
to the Lao Bai Lamb Stew Diner presented a more expansive façade.
The mayor would be accompanied to the diner by his secretary, the
county chief Zheng Zhong, and Chief Justice Wang Gongdao; a table
for five awaited them. The remainder of the Mayor's entourage—
employees of the municipal and county governments and the county
courthouse—were to be taken to the Round the Bend government
canteen for a meal hosted by the township head. That too was out
of a fear that too many people would scare Li Xuelian away. Zheng
Zhong dithered when it came time to send someone to collect her.
He and Wang Gongdao had both recently sparred with her, pushing
her nearly to the point of no return, and didn't dare chance setting
her off again, so Zheng shifted the responsibility onto the shoulders
of Township Head Lai, a short, fat man in his forties who couldn't
say three words without cursing, and wasn't above getting into a fight
when he'd had too much to drink. He owned a VW Santana 3000,
and when he was drunk, he sat behind his driver and turned into a
volatile back-seat driver. If his man drove too fast, he'd wave his arms
excitedly, smack the back of the man's head, and curse:

"Where's the fucking funeral? Your old man will wait for you!"

If the driver was going too slow, he'd go through the same
routine:

"Who's driving this fucking thing? Your dad? And when did it
turn into an oxcart?"

The current driver was his sixth. None of the dozens of local
cadres had escaped being cursed at one time or another, and none
of the heads of the township's twenty villages had missed being
kicked. But during his five years as township head, he had treated
Li Xuelian, who lived in one of his villages, with respect, though
he kept his distance, since she'd staged a protest every one of those
years. And because of those protests, Round the Bend Township was
publicly censured at every year-end county meeting over a lack of
stability, which kept it from being labeled a progressive township.

But every year, Lai returned from the meeting to tell his subordinates that it was better to forego the progressive township label than to try to stop Li Xuelian from staging a protest. They were staged for higher authorities, and if he did not try to stop them, she'd cause no trouble for the township. If he did, turning her protests into local events, the hornets' nest would fall on his head.

"We work in Round the Bend Township," Lai would say, "so we have to round a mental bend every so often."

Normally a slapdash individual, Lai sometimes surprised people by being calculating. As the person chosen by Zheng for the unpleasant job of inviting Li Xuelian to the diner, he was powerless to refuse. So, profane, violent Lai Xiaomao was all smiles when he met Li, befuddling her when he called her "Aunt."

My protests are bringing relatives out of the woodwork, she mused.

"Township Head," she said, "I can, with some difficulty, tolerate Chief Justice Wang Gongdao calling me 'Cousin,' but you put yourself a generation behind me, and calling me that makes me break out in hives."

Lai glared at her.

"Justice Wang may call you cousin, but he has no family claim to back it up. I, however, am perfectly justified in calling you Aunt. Hear me out. My mother's hometown is Yan Family Village. Her brother is my uncle, and he married the niece of Old Chai from Chai Family Village . . ."

He began counting on his pudgy fingers.

"Township Head," Xuelian interrupted his account, "can we not beat around the bush? What is it you want? If you're here about my protests, we stop right here."

"This has nothing to do with that," he said. "I've worked in the township for five years, Aunt, and in all that time have I ever mentioned those protests to you?"

After a thoughtful pause, she said, "No, you haven't."

"You see," Lai said as he clapped his hands. "Settling scores and redressing injustices has been a guiding principle since the Three Kingdoms period. I'm not one to interfere with protests. I'm here today to invite you to dinner. Actually, I'm not the host, that would be our Mayor Ma. He is giving you much face, Aunt."

Li said, with an angry look, "I don't care who invites me to dinner, the mayor or the county chief, it can't be good news. They might even be hatching a plot against me."

She paused, then continued:

"He's never invited me to dinner before. Why now all of a sudden? It couldn't have anything to do with the upcoming People's Congress, could it?"

She turned and started walking out of her yard. Lai Xiaomao ran ahead of her and held his arms out.

"I completely agree, Aunt," he said. "Nobody that important extends a dinner invitation without a reason, especially not at such a special time. But even if it's a trap, you have to go."

"What does that mean?" Li Xuelian said with a gulp. "Are you going to tie me up and drag me there?"

"I wouldn't dare. I've come to beg you, not for them, for me."

He added:

"None of this had anything to do with me, not flesh and not blood, at first. But I should have known to expect the unexpected, and the job of getting you to dinner has fallen to me."

He wasn't finished:

"I know the mayor wants to ask you not to stage a protest. You think he's wrong to ask, so do I. What you think is your business, but whether or not you accept his invitation is my business. Just so long as you go, you can raise a mighty stink for all I care."

There was still more:

"This is big, Aunt, real big, too big for a minor functionary like me. All along you've been dealing with high-ranking people, so please don't get me in trouble over a dinner invitation. A little pissant township head with a future like dewdrops. If you don't take pity on me, I'll just evaporate."

And finally:

"I have family responsibilities, too, old and young. My eighty-year-old father, an elder cousin of yours, is confined to bed after a stroke that left his face all twisted. He might only have days to live. If you won't take pity on me, Aunt, then take pity on my father."

He filled up the doorway and shifted his body to bow with his hands clasped in front. That made Li Xuelian laugh. She rapped him on the head.

"You're more scalawag than township head," she said. "It's only one meal. I'll go even if there's a mountain of knives waiting for me."

Lai Xiaomao was the one who hit people, not the other way around. To hit him would have taken the courage of a leopard. But there he stood, rubbing his head and smiling.

"That's the ticket, dear Aunt. Like everyone says, lay down the butcher knife and take the path to Buddha."

He gleefully drove Li Xuelian into town in his VW.

Xuelian was the model of decorum when she was introduced to Mayor Ma, not because he was mayor, but because he wore gold-rimmed glasses, like a gentleman, and because he spoke politely, preceding and ending each utterance with a little laugh that made her feel welcomed. In such a cordial atmosphere, causing a scene seemed inappropriate. But more than cordial, he impressed her as being a sensible man. Others might approach a matter from one side, and still get it wrong; he could approach it from three sides, and be right in every respect. He spoke only of common, everyday things, not of protests, and he never talked down to her. He asked personal questions, like how big her family was and what everyone did, private matters she found it hard to answer and hard not to. Then he began talking about himself, pointing to the diner décor and telling her that he was born in a peasant village, to a family so poor he could only dream of eating lamb stew. After school each day he'd run up to a lamb stew diner in his hometown, lean against the door, and gaze inside. One day he saw a big man order three bowlfuls of stew, one after the other. He left a bit in the bottom of the third bowl and signaled for Ma Wenbin to come inside. Ma edged in slowly.

"If you can bark three times like a dog, you can have what's left in this bowl," the man said.

"Arf arf arf," Ma barked three times, and the man pushed the bowl over to him. He licked it clean. Everyone around the table laughed, including Li Xuelian. Then they turned their attention to the flatbreads and bowls of stew in front of them, crunching and slurping until their faces were sweaty, and the mood congenial. There was more Ma Wenbin wanted to say. As a gullible little boy who couldn't tell a lie, he said, he was easily and often taken advantage of by a kid brother who was much cleverer than he was. If this brother stole something to eat at home, he got the blame and suffered the beating, since his brother could outtalk him any day of the week. He was even blamed once for a lost goat. What bothered him the most was, he always told the truth and was punished for lying, while his brother was always lying, and everyone still believe him. By this time, Li Xuelian was drawn into the conversation, given the tone and the topic.

"That's precisely why I'm protesting," she blurted out. "How could something so patently false be considered true? And why does no one believe me when I'm telling the truth?"

Now that she had broached the subject, it was time for Ma to confront the matter at hand, but in a roundabout manner. He began by criticizing County Chief Zheng Zhong and Chief Justice Wang Gongdao. That was why they were there. He had censured them for their simplistic approach to work, for placing themselves in opposition to the masses. Forgetting that they are public servants, they acted like officious bureaucrats. An even greater mistake was always assuming that the masses were lying, rather than putting themselves in the people's shoes. Here you had someone who had been lodging the same protest for twenty years, sacrificing her youth to principle. Would she have persisted until her hair turned gray if there was nothing to her claim of injustice? Would you two have been capable of doing what she did? Li Xuelian was moved by what she was hearing, as if for the first time she had found a true friend. Who said there were no decent cadres in the government? There's one right here. Zheng and Wang, their faces red from the verbal thrashing, nodded over and over.

"I'll write a self-criticism when I'm back home," they promised.

Li Xuelian felt as if the criticism had been too harsh.

"It's not all their fault," she said to Ma. "As officials, this hasn't been easy for them."

"You see," Ma said as he smacked the tabletop with the palm of his hand, "a countrywoman has greater awareness than either of you two."

More head nodding by Zheng and Wang.

"Greater than ours, much greater."

Ma Wenbin smiled and forged ahead:

"Let me ask you something, dear Sister-in-law. Don't answer me if you don't feel like it. They didn't believe you when you said you weren't interested in protesting this time, and forced you into saying something extreme. Can you repeat what you said? Or can we take back what we said?"

He added:

"I won't force you if you'd rather not."

Once again, Li Xuelian was moved by what Ma Wenbin was saying.

"I can when you say it like that, Mayor. I can repeat myself."

She pointed to Zheng Zhong and Wang Gongdao.

"I told them twice I wasn't going to protest this year, but they refused to believe me."

Ma Wenbin also pointed to Zheng Zhong and Wang Gongdao.

"Just like I told the truth when I was a kid and powerful people wouldn't believe me."

Everyone laughed.

"We're only talking now, dear Sister-in-law, so let me ask another question. Why would you decide to stop protesting after twenty years?"

That was the same question Zheng Zhong and Wang Gongdao had asked on two separate occasions. She supplied the same answer as before:

"Because I finally saw the light."

Ma laughed. "Why this year and not before? Did something happen to change your mind? I want to remind you that you don't have to answer if you don't want to."

It was a question Wang and Zheng had overlooked both times. They had been so focused on finding out the "what" that they'd neglected to investigate the "why." Of course they wouldn't believe her. But Ma knew that a physician doesn't dispense medicine without asking about symptoms, which is what he was doing. The other two were no match for him. This is where the "small" came in, and was why the mayor was a cut above. They nodded out of admiration.

"No," Li replied, "nothing happened. I just listened to what my cow said."

That was the last thing any of them expected to hear and they did not know how to deal with this strange and sudden turn of events. Even Ma Wenbin was so bewildered he stammered his reaction:

"C . . . cow? What cow is that?"

Zheng Zhong regained his composure in time to ask:

"How does a cow come into a conversation about people?"

"For twenty years, not a single person has believed me, but my cow did. And that's why I made up my mind. In the past, every time

I asked my cow if I should protest, it said 'Yes,' so I did. But this year, my cow would not go along with it, so I decided not to protest."

The question they all wanted to ask stumbled out of the bewildered secretary's mouth:

"Is this a real cow you're talking about, or are you teasing us?"

"I'm not teasing anybody. It's a cow I raised myself."

Ma Wenbin had recaptured his presence of mind.

"Can I see this cow?" he asked her. "Will it speak to me?"

"No."

"Why not?"

"It died a few days ago."

The men did not know whether to laugh or cry.

"Sister-in-law, Mayor Ma has traveled quite a distance to meet with you," Zheng Zhong said indignantly, "and with the best of intentions. You should not be playing games with him when he's trying to help you resolve your problem. That is a sign of disrespect."

Zheng's indignation fueled her anger.

"You see," she said as she smacked her palms together, "this is what's been happening all along. I try to tell the truth and nobody believes me."

Ma stopped Zheng from saying more and, with a smile, said to Xuelian:

"I believe you, Sister-in-law, I'm sure the cow is real."

Then he said:

"Let's all take the cow's advice and have no protest this year, how's that?"

"There's a difference," Xuelian said.

"What difference," Ma asked.

"The difference is, I'd listen to what the cow said but not to what you say."

"How's that?" Ma was confused.

"My cow said not to protest because it was a waste of time. You want me not to protest and let the injustice stand. Those are two different things."

"Sister-in-law," an utterly confused Ma said, "didn't we come to help you resolve your problem?"

Li Xuelian was now in tears.

"Don't try to trick me," she said. "If you thought I was being unjustly treated, there'd have been no need for you to come see me. All you had to do is right the wrong."

She pointed a finger at Zheng Zhong and Wang Gongdao.

"You're all the same. You came here to confuse me so I won't go to Beijing to protest and cost you your jobs.

"If you're so interested in helping me," she continued, "how come you've only come to see me just before the National People's Congress meets? And one after the other. Your plan is to deceive me for a few days, then go away and forget about me."

Ma Wenbin frowned. He now knew that Li Xuelian was a force to be reckoned with. He'd come to see her in order to resolve a problem, never dreaming that she would show such disrespect—a talking cow! As both sides vied to outwit the other, he had fallen into her trap. Had he known this could happen, he'd never have asked what had changed her mind, and there'd have been no mention of a cow. And yet, how could he dispense medicine without asking about the symptoms? To be sure, Ma Wenbin wasn't frightened off by falling into her talking cow trap, since he'd come expressly to see where things stood. Now, with the arrival of the cow, he saw that there was nothing he could do. She said she wasn't going to protest, but she was. Either that, or she was having fun at their expense. Zheng and Wang's view of the situation had been proven right. And yet Ma wasn't frightened off by knowing there was nothing he could do either. In dealing with cadres under his supervision who screwed up, he first determined if there was something he could do about it. If there was, he called the person in for a talk. If not, there was no need for that.

Seeing the frown on Ma's face, his secretary got up and announced:

"That'll do it for today's conversation. Mayor Ma has business in the city."

Ma stood up, a broad smile on his face, and said:

"Sister-in-law, I have to leave to take care of some business. You do as you see fit."

He left the diner, his secretary and County Chief Zheng hard on his heels, leaving Chief Justice Wang to pick up the pieces. His hand shook as he said:

"Just what were you doing, Cousin? Instead of talking about your case, you brought your cow into the discussion. Why abuse people like that?"

"I didn't abuse anybody," Xuelian said as she dried her tears.

"Comparing somebody to an animal isn't abuse?"

He walked in circles, his hand trembling.

"You'll listen to an animal before you'll listen to what the government has to say, which means none of the officials, all the way up, aren't even the equal of a farm animal."

"No matter what I say," Xuelian said, getting angry, "none of you will believe me. You only think the worst of me."

She paused.

"Since that's how it is, I've decided to protest again this year."

Wang Gongdao clapped his hands.

"Well, now, you've finally told the truth."

4

Li Xuelian's large compound included a three-room house with a tile roof to the north, a kitchen to the east, and two cow pens to the west. The house had been built twenty-two years earlier, when she and Qin Yuhe had been married six years and their son was five. She raised cows and three old sows to make it possible to knock down a thatched cottage and build their three-room house. Half of the money for wood and bricks came from the sale of calves and piglets; the other half came from her husband's overtime earnings as a truck driver for the fertilizer plant, nighttime work that left him bleary-eyed. He regularly dozed off at the wheel late at night, and one night ran into a roadside scholar tree. Repairs to the truck cost two thousand yuan, so he had to start over. He and Xuelian argued a lot, but never enough to cause a rupture in their marriage. But then, a year after the house was completed, Qin Yuhe changed, and Xuelian began to regret her decision to talk to him about a sham divorce when she discovered she was pregnant again. They spent as much time apart as they did together, and what began as a sham became a reality. Arguments gave way to court proceedings, which continued for twenty years, until their hair had nearly turned white, and still no resolution in sight. What she regretted most was that the sham divorce had been her lousy brainstorm, and had been for the benefit of the daughter she would give birth to, and with whom she would later have an unexpected falling out.

Twenty-two years of being buffeted by wind and rain had taken their toll on the house. The northern wall had collapsed under the onslaught of summer and autumn rains, bricks on the other three sides had fallen off and crumbled into dust at an alarming rate. Large sections of the interior wall plaster were disintegrating, and the roof had sprung leaks ten years before. Anyone else during those twenty years of protest would not have cared about house repairs. For the first ten years, she too had neglected house repairs and housekeeping, and the place had turned into a sty. She'd also neglected her own appearance, seldom changing out of dirty clothes and letting her hair start to look like a rat's nest. Out on the street, from a distance she looked like a beggar, or the apt picture of a protester. After ten years, her protests had become routine, and she'd gotten used to it. She'd gotten used not to all the annual travel, but to when it was disrupted on the rare occasion when she was ill and confined to her bed at home. When she could not carry out her protest, she did not know what to do with herself. It had evolved into such a habitual event that it became the essence of her daily life, and that was the stimulus for her to start taking care of herself and her house. She cut her hair short, washed her clothes on schedule, and would not go out to protest unless she was presentable. Repairing walls, inside and out, was too big a job, but she had to deal with her leaky roof, so she hired someone to replace the old tiles and seal the gaps with lime that effectively kept the rain out. She swept up the flakes that had peeled from the walls in the house, which spruced the place up considerably, even though the walls had a mottled appearance. She made sure the rooms were neat and tidy, lining the base of compound walls with scarlet sage and cockscomb. Anyone coming inside would not think this was the house of a perennial petitioner.

The three rooms were divided by partitions. The one on the left served as a pantry and storeroom; the center room was essentially a hallway, and the room to the right was their bedroom. Twenty-one years before it had been the room in which Li Xuelian and Qin Yuhe slept together; now she slept there alone. A student's math booklet hung on the wall beside the bedroom window; it was where she recorded her twenty-year protest history. Time had not been kind to the notebook, which was falling apart and as dirty as an old rag. But an old rag that recorded the locations of all her protests and whom she'd met at each one. As her hair turned from jet black to gray and her once slender waist thickened, she hoped that her booklet would one day help her make the false false and the true true. But after twenty years, the false was still true and the true remained false. At the same time, she had not been able to shed the title of Pan Jinlian. Ten years earlier, this had nearly driven her mad. But as one year led into the next, she'd gotten used to it, just as she'd gotten used to carrying out her protests.

Everyone at the provincial, municipal, and county levels knew she did that every year, but what was remembered was the protest, not the frequency. Even she could not recall all the details of her protest history. It was all there in her notebook. In addition to the recorded details, it included a tally, according to which she had gone to Beijing to protest at the National People's Congress nineteen times in twenty years and had been stopped by local police eleven of those times. She had been detained three times by the Hebei police before she even reached Beijing, and on five trips, she had been visited in her hotel room by county police, who had "advised" her to return home three of those times. She'd been arrested by Beijing police on the two other trips, once on Chang'an Street and once in Tiananmen Square. What it added up to was that not once in twenty years had her protest been successful, and not once, after the first time, had she managed to make it as far as the Great Hall of the People. Reason enough for her to keep at it. What puzzled her was why people at all government levels—province, municipality, county—remained apprehensive of her after twenty years of failed protests. It had gotten so bad that she was called "Cousin" by the chief justice and "Aunt" by the township head. Maybe she hadn't considered the possibility that her failures had put everyone even more on guard against the possibility of one success.

But no protest this year, not because anything had been resolved or because she had been frightened off by the officials or even because she had lost heart after so many failures, but because the one person who actually believed her had died. And that person wasn't a person at all, it was her cow. Twenty-one years earlier, Xuelian and her husband had discussed a sham divorce in the cowshed, whose only other occupants were a cow and her nursing calf. No one else in the world overheard the conversation. That worked to Qin Yuhe's advantage, for six months later he took up with another woman, telling people that the divorce was real and making it possible to marry the other woman. It was also the reason nothing had come of Li Xuelian's protests after twenty years. That had nearly driven her mad ten years before, when she'd carried on until people on the street thought she was mentally disturbed. Her ten-year-old daughter felt the same way, and wouldn't sleep in the same bed with her, preferring to stay at a neighbor's house. Xuelian herself thought that something must be wrong with her, greeting people with broad smiles during the day and running off to the cowshed at night to try to teach her cow to speak, hoping that one day it would help her get justice. But a cow speak? Really now! Then one day the cow died, leaving its daughter behind, an eleven-year-old calf, one year older than Xuelian's daughter. Ten years had passed since the calf had arrived with its mother, and it was now a middle-aged cow. It had cried when its mother died, earning a kick from Li Xuelian.

"You cry when your mother dies, but not for me and my ten years of fruitless protest"

The cow looked into Xuelian's face.

"I know you can't talk, but you ought to be able to nod and shake your head, can't you? You were there when we talked about divorcing eleven years ago, so tell me, was it real or was it a sham?"

Imagine her surprise when the cow shook its head. Li Xuelian threw her arms around its neck and wailed:

"My darling little one, finally, someone who believes me!"

Hearing Xuelian's tearful howl, her neighbor assumed it was a moment of madness, and ran over, thinking she was crying over the death of her cow. Once the neighbor had left, Xuelian said to the cow:

"Tell me, should I or shouldn't I keep protesting?"

The cow nodded. The courage to continue swelled inside Xuelian. Her mental problems were abruptly a thing of the past. Then ten more years passed, and the cow reached the age of twenty-one. One night, as it lay dying, it looked up at Xuelian, who said:

"Please don't die, little one. You are the only one in the whole world who believes me."

Tears filled the cow's eyes.

"Before you die," Xuelian said, "tell me if I should keep protesting?"

The cow shook its head, breathed its last and shut its eyes. Xuelian threw herself on its body and wept.

"You shit, even you stopped thinking I can win my case!"

She cried on:

"No one on earth believes me, so why the fuck keep at it!"

Most people whose cows die simply sell the carcass to the town's knacker, but Li Xuelian did not do that for either of the two cows that died during that ten-year period. She had them buried them on the riverbank instead, the daughter next to her mother.

After the cow shook her head, Li Xuelian decided to take the dying animal's advice to stop. In truth, the cow's response to her question was not the sole deciding factor. Twenty years of protests had worn her down to the point where though her body managed to hold on, her heart could not. So she buried her impulse to torment people along with the younger cow. But then she told Mayor Ma Wenbin and the others about her cow, and they didn't believe her, accusing her not only of telling a lie, but also of humiliating the officials with a rebuke so strong they stormed off. Her actions had nearly made Chief Justice Wang Gongdao explode from anger. Xuelian found it hard to blame them, for if they told people they'd run into a woman whose cow could talk, no one would believe them. What angered her was the fact that not a soul on earth ever believed her. How come no one was the equal of a cow?

Of greater significance in Xuelian's decision not to protest this year than what the cow told her was something her classmate Big Head Zhao said. Zhao, who'd cooked for the Beijing resident representatives of the province twenty years before, had put her up in his room on her first trip to Beijing. There, as we recall, she had caused a political firestorm by crashing the National People's Congress in the Great Hall of the People, for which Zhao should have shouldered some of the responsibility. But one of the national leaders had made a case for Xuelian's action, which had then led to an investigation of local officials who had created the conditions for the protest. No one else dared launch a similar investigation on this angle of the case, and Zhao worked on in his kitchen for another eighteen years without incident. He retired at the age of fifty and returned to his home, where he got a job in the kitchen of the Hongyun lou Restaurant, where he could earn a bit of extra money. His wife had died of breast cancer the year before and their son had married and moved out, leaving him all alone. He regularly rode his bicycle from the county town to visit Xuelian, and was there the day after her cow died. As they sat under the jujube tree in her yard, she told him the story of her cow and then asked him:

"Do you believe me that my cow talked to me?"

He did not.

"I know how bitter you must be, but don't think crazy thoughts."

Li Xuelian glared at him.

"I knew you wouldn't believe me. So tell me this: I don't plan to protest this year. Do you believe that?"

Suddenly bringing a halt to her protest after twenty years came as a shock to him. When that wore off, he asked the same question the chief justice and county chief had asked:

"Why stop now?"

"Because my cow said so. Just before she died she told me not to keep at it."

With a clap of his hands, Zhao said:

"I don't care if your cow talked or not, that's something I've wanted to talk to you about for a long time. I just didn't want to upset you."

"What sort of talk?"

"The same as the cow. You can't keep protesting forever. After twenty years, what good has come of it?"

"But that's why I keep doing it, because nothing good has come of it."

"That's not what I'm getting at. Twenty years of torment, initially intended for someone else, has now come back to you. Let me ask you this: who planted the seeds of your protest?"

"That bastard Qin Yuhe."

Again Zhao clapped his hands.

"There, you see, twenty years of protesting have had no effect on him. Despite the constant harassment campaign, he continues to sleep with his wife and child, leaving you as the only victim of harassment. Look at you, your hair has turned gray."

"That's exactly why this sticks in my craw."

"Then let me ask you this: You say your divorce was a sham, but Qin Yuhe says it was real. Why would he say that?"

"He found himself a willing whore."

More hand clapping.

"There's your answer. He's got a new life with his whore, but you're stuck on harassing something belonging to the past, so of course he won't admit that the divorce was a sham. Unless he relents one day, you cannot win."

"That bastard has done this to me. I should have killed him when I had the chance."

"As I see it," Zhao said, "instead of killing him back then, you should have done what he did."

"Like what?" a surprised Li Xuelian asked.

"Found a man and gotten married. If he could do it, so could you. You know, what's good for the goose . . . Wouldn't that have been a lot better than fighting over who's right and who's wrong? If you'd done that back then, you could have enjoyed a happy life these past twenty years instead of growing old on the path of protest."

Li Xuelian just stood there. Not only had Big Head Zhao been a social outcast in school, but he'd spent his adult life as a cook, and yet at this critical moment, he spoke with the sort of good judgment no one else had managed. He might not have said it as a high school student, but as a cook he did. He might not have said it twenty years before, but he did now. Back then Li Xuelian had had a similar thought. She'd gone to the fertilizer plant to get Qin Yuhe to say honestly that the divorce had been a sham. If he'd done that, she would not have pestered people the way she did and could have put her grudge aside to start a new life. But he had called her a Pan Jinlian and given her no choice but to protest for the next twenty years. Regrets crept in: if she'd simply ignored Qin and looked for another man with whom she could start anew, she might now have a wonderful life instead of winding up as empty as a bamboo basket used to fetch water.

"What good does it do to talk about that now?"

"Plenty," Big Head said. "There's still time to find a man."

With a look of disdain, she said:

"Who would want a forty-nine-year-old, gray-haired woman like me?"

"I would," Zhao said without a second's hesitation.

Li Xueilian froze on the spot. She thought he was joking, but he looked dead serious. And yet it was a corner she could not turn, not the idea of marrying Big Head Zhao, but because in twenty years of lodging her protest, unwilling to stop until she remarried and then re-divorced Qin Yuhe, the thought of marrying someone else had never occurred to her. To have it brought up as a proposal put a scowl on her face. She gave Zhao a little kick.

"How could you make fun of me in the midst of all my troubles?"

"I'm not. You and I are both single and would make a perfect match."

"But everybody knows me as Pan Jinlian."

"I'm a fan of Pan Jinlian. I love a woman with spice."

She kicked him a second time.

"See, you're making fun of me."

Zhao moved out of kicking distance.

"Okay," he said with a laugh, "I don't believe your name is Pan, how's that?"

He turned serious.

"Think it over. It's a lot better than protesting."

After Zhao left, Li Xuelian did think it over, thought about it all night. By morning she was convinced that Zhao had been right, that he made more sense than the cow had. What good had it done to tell her not to protest with no idea as to how she was supposed to get by afterward? Big Head had told her what he thought she could do when she stopped protesting. Remarry. Then there'd be no need. And if Pan Jinlian remarried, she'd no longer be Pan Jinlian. Or so she figured. The problem was Zhao's unexpected proposal. Unexpected, maybe, but he was no stranger. Thirty years earlier they'd been schoolmates, and he was interested in her enough even then to hand her candy from the desk behind hers. Thirty years earlier, Zhao had been a coward; ten years after that he was still a coward. But not now, not if he could stand there and propose marriage. Pan Jinlian couldn't scare him off now; he was a different man, and she was tempted. But a proposal alone could not make her leap from protest to a second marriage. It was a hairpin curve that required time to get used to. She had told Mayor Ma Wenbin only part of the reason she planned not to protest this year, the part about the cow; she hadn't said anything about the possibility of remarrying, and not just anybody, but someone who had already proposed, a hotel cook, Big Head Zhao by name. Talk of the cow and not of Zhao had sent Ma and his entourage off in anger, thinking she was playing games with them. Their anger had fueled hers. If the chief justice, county chief, and mayor had not come to talk to her individually, she'd have listened first to her cow, and next to Big Head Zhao, and there'd be no talk of protest this year. But when they pressed her to stop her campaign, she saw through their scheme to fool her enough to get past this year's National People's Congress, and knew that they didn't care one iota about her. They were only worried about themselves, afraid that if she went to Beijing again, they could lose their jobs. That was all the reason she needed to decide to go after all. She could put the situation between her and Big Head on hold for the time being; after twenty years, a little more time couldn't hurt. If she decided to accept his proposal, before they married she had to get something off her chest, and one last protest could do that. The difference this time would be the addition of a bit of spite, and would no longer resemble those that had gone before. The target would no longer be Qin Yuhe. This year, she'd take aim at the chief justice, the county chief, and the mayor.

5

In the wake of the disaster at the Lamb Stew Diner, Mayor Ma Wenbin rode silently out of Round the Bend Township. County Chief Zheng Zhong sat beside him, Ma's secretary was up front next to the driver. Since Ma didn't say a word, neither did the other two. All they could see in the darkness was the up and down movement of their headlights on the bumpy, twisting country road, which did not smooth out until they were on the open highway; the inside of the car was quiet as death. Ma was heading back to the city, Zheng and his people to the county, so at the intersection where the roads split, Zheng got out of Ma's car and waited for his car to pull up behind them. Zheng and his retinue then stood on the side of the road to see Mayor Ma off. But when Ma's car reached the toll station, it stopped and began backing up. Zheng Zhong rushed up in time for Ma to roll down his window and gaze into the night, still without saying a word. Zheng was forced to stand there as Ma's gaze turned toward the highway up ahead, where he could see the headlights of speeding vehicles. After a long moment, he said:

"That countrywoman has really disappointed me."

That simple comment made Zheng Zhong shudder. The words "really disappointed" from Ma in regard to a cadre would have been a clear indication that the individual's political life had come to an end. But Li Xuelian was not a cadre, just a simple countrywoman with a protest, someone no local official could abide. Ma drew back his gaze and sighed.

"I think we all underestimated her," he said.

Zheng did not know how to respond to that. If he echoed the other man's comment, by belittling himself, he would also be doing the same to Ma Wenbin. Everyone present at the Lamb Stew Diner could see that the woman had ridiculed Ma, or offended him, something none of them could have predicted. But he could not come up with a good reason to disagree? Best to merely open his mouth and shut it right away. Ma glanced at him, adjusted his gold-framed glasses, and said:

"So we'll do it your way."

What did that mean? Zheng did not know. If he had a "way" he wasn't aware of it. Of course, he didn't dare ask for an explanation. But then he recalled how he had handled the government office siege when he was Executive Deputy Chief in that neighboring county. He'd waged a tit-for-tat struggle. So that was what Ma meant.

"I'll go back and arrest her," he said. "I'll find an excuse."

Too bad he'd misunderstood Ma's meaning.

"I don't want you to arrest her," Ma said with a frown. "You can't go around arresting anybody you want. Without a good cause, it can come back to bite you—hard. Why do you think all those people were sacked twenty years ago? They tossed her in jail, that's why. You can't lock her up forever. And she's definitely no ordinary countrywoman." He was getting hotter by the minute, and Zheng was beginning to sweat. He'd misunderstood what his superior said and spoken too fast, bringing the night's wrath down on his head. Lucky for him, Ma was a self-possessed man who could keep his anger in check.

"When you were Deputy County Chief you had to deal with a siege, but not here. You can't paint a melon with a calabash model, understand?"

Normally quick on the uptake, Zheng didn't have an answer now. Did he understand or didn't he? He was terrified of saying the wrong thing a second time and really setting the mayor off. Ma's secretary saved the day by sticking his head out the window and saying:

"Mayor Ma is right, all matters need to be dealt with in their own way."

Then, in a more jocular tone, he said:

"Since she didn't lay siege to our government building, I guess we'll have to find a way to lay siege to her."

Finally, Zheng understood what Ma wanted him to know, which was to have someone from the county keep her under surveillance to prevent her from taking her protest to Beijing. Nothing new there, since officials at all levels of government regularly did that to stop people from airing grievances. Zheng realized that Ma Wenbin's anger had not been directed at him, after all; it was directed at himself. He had been pestered by a countrywoman with a protest, and had not been able to come up with a means of dealing with her. Not only had he wasted a whole evening, but now he needed to devise a strategy to keep her home. As someone who took pleasure in trying out new things, things others hadn't thought of and could not manage, Ma was angered by the knowledge that this was something he could not manage. Zheng Zhong tried to help him out of his predicament.

"The problem originated in my county," he said, "so the responsibility is mine. You can rest assured, Mayor Ma, you and your secretary, that I'll do whatever it takes to convince her to stay home and not go to Beijing to disrupt the Congress this year."

6

From the next day on, a policeman was stationed outside Li Xuelian's house, day and night, one at each corner. Dressed in civilian clothes, they just smoked and moved around. This was not the first time she'd been under police surveillance. Over the past twenty years, three or four police had taken up positions around her house each year at NPC time. There were also two or three during county and municipal elections, and it had become a habitual occurrence both for Li Xuelian and for the police, who greeted one another amicably. Since she was not a criminal and bore no grudge against the police, they treated her with deference, smiling and calling her "Aunty." Some were even returnees.

"Nice to see you again," she'd say.

"Back to serve as your bodyguard, Aunty," they'd reply with a little laugh.

As long as she stayed in the yard, they left her alone, but the minute she left her home, they fell in behind her.

"How could I be so lucky as to deserve all you footmen?" she'd remark.

"You and the American president," they'd joke.

At home, when her handlers were thirsty, she gave them water.

This year's force was made up of two regulars and two new policemen, one of whom, the son of the town's one-time butcher, was an auxiliary worker. Twenty years before, Li Xuelian had gone first to her younger brother for help in killing Qin Yuhe; but when she learned that he had gone to Shandong, she had turned to Old Hu, the butcher, telling him—untruthfully—that she only wanted to beat Qin, not kill him. But when he'd heard that it was about killing, and not just one person, but several, he'd nearly wet himself. Now he was confined to bed, the victim of a paralytic stroke, and could no longer sell meat in the market. Xuelian was surprised to learn that one of her new "bodyguards" was butcher Hu's son, a slim, handsome young man, nothing like his squat, dark-skinned father. She struck up a conversation with him, and quickly sensed that the kid could be a problem.

"So you're Hu's son. How's he doing?"

"Not so good. Confined to bed. Probably not long for this world."

"How come they sent you here today?"

"To get even. I had an argument with the station chief last month, and he paid me back by dumping this shitty job on me."

"Isn't watching people better than arresting them?"

"That's easy for you to say, since you sleep warm and toasty in your bed at night, while we have to stand out here in the cold. They say spring is right around the corner, but you wouldn't know it by the temperatures."

"Who said I had to be watched?"

"Aunty, let's not talk about that. It's not your fault and it's not mine. Let's blame it on the NPC."

She laughed.

Laughter and chatting, however, did nothing to change her decision to lodge her protest. And to get to Beijing she had to escape the surveillance. But not yet, since the Congress would not start for a week. There had been escape attempts in the past, some successful, some not, and all at night. On this particular day, Big Head had ridden his bicycle over, and when he saw the cordon around her house, he greeted one of the cops, whom he knew. Inside the house, he said to Xuelian:

"There's only one other place in China as well guarded as this."

"Where's that?"

"Zhongnan hai, where the national leaders live."

They went out and sat under the jujube tree.

"Have you been thinking about what I said last time?" Zhao asked.

"What was that?"

"About you and me getting married."

"No matter what I might think about that, Big Head, it'll have to wait."

"Why?"

"Because I have to protest first."

"Didn't you say the cow told you not to? And forget the cow, do what I said."

She told him what had happened at the Lamb Stew Diner with the Mayor, how the gathering had ended in rancor. "They were bullies," she said angrily. "I hadn't planned to protest this year, and I said so, but they wouldn't believe me. So I told them what the cow had said, and they thought I was being insolent. You understood me when I told you about the cow, why couldn't they? And why do they think the worst of me, no matter what I say? They wouldn't have police out there if they didn't think I was a troublemaker. Little by little they're driving me to despair. I decided not to protest for my own sake, but now, if I don't do it, I'm pathetic. They'll think the police surveillance worked. In the beginning, my target was Qin Yuhe. Now it's all those corrupt officials. Since they think I'm a troublemaker, I won't let them have a moment's peace. Can you believe it? Inferior to a mere cow."

Big Head had to agree that by distrusting her vow not to protest, the mayor and his crowd had made things worse. And worst of all, they'd put a crimp in his plan. He scratched his head.

"Instead of lowering yourself, do as we talked about. Put aside your plan to protest and live a peaceful life with me."

"No," she insisted. "They've backed me up against a wall, and I won't take it. Even if we got married, I couldn't be happy as long as I had this anger inside."

Worried that there was no way to save the situation, Big Head carped:

"Everything seemed to be going so well, and then it changed."

"Big Head," Xuelian said, "there's something I'd like you to do for me."

"What's that?"

"There are four men out there keeping an eye on me. If I'm going to lodge my protest, I need to slip out of the house, but I can't do that alone. Can you help me?"

He hadn't expected that.

"You want me to get physical with them?"

"That's one way. I don't care how you do it, just help me get away."

But Big Head saw a daunting downside.

"It'd be me against four of them, and I wouldn't stand a chance. Besides, I'd be going up against the government, and the consequences would be severe."

"I've gone up against the government for twenty years," she replied indignantly, "and here you are refusing to square off against them even once. And you want me to marry you. If we can't be together on this, there's no way we could live together!"

"Now hold on, I'm thinking. Can't I even think it over?"

Li Xuelian was still angry, but she had to laugh.

"Big Head, this is a test, and we'll see if you're up to it. Twenty years ago, I tested butcher Hu in town. He failed the test. Don't be like him."

"I'm no butcher Hu, I just haven't figured out how we can do it."

"Then go home and see what you can come up with. The NPC starts in a week. Come back in three days and help me slip away."

Three days later, no Big Head, and Xuelian knew that he too had failed the test, just like butcher Hu. He wanted her for the good times, but wouldn't stick around for the bad. He'd run at the first sign of trouble. But she was going to get away, with or without him. And it had to be at night. Unfortunately, it was the fifteenth day of the lunar month, with a full moon lighting up the ground all around. The first watch, the third, the fifth, Xuelian looked over the latrine wall and spotted the four policemen, smoking as they patrolled the area; no chance. If she made a break for it, they'd catch her for sure, a forty-nine-year-old woman on her own trying to outrun four twenty- or thirty-year-olds. If she tried and failed, they'd be even more vigilant. They might increase the number to seven or eight the next time, making escape impossible. She had suffered her share of setbacks over the years, and learned from the experiences. She put off trying until the sun came up, after which escaping was out of the question.

That day passed uneventfully, and night began to fall. Xuelian had hoped it would be a dark night, but the full moon ended that. Even the heavens are against me, she cursed inwardly. Then came a knock at the gate. She assumed it was one of the policemen wanting a drink of water. But, no, it was Big Head, who walked in with his bicycle, a big cardboard box on the rear rack.

"I thought you weren't coming," Xuelian said unkindly. "What changed your mind?"

Big Head dragged her into the yard and began emptying the box of its three barbecued chickens, four cooked pigs' feet, and five stewed rabbit heads. Next out were six bottles of strong liquor. Puzzled at first, she quickly caught on to his plan and planted a kiss on his big head.

"Good old Big Head. I thought you'd lost your nerve, while all along you were working up a scheme. A man I thought was wooden-headed actually has a devilish mind."

"Get a fire going," he said, waving off her compliment, "and cook some food."

When the table was set in the house, Big Head invited the police inside. Though it was early spring, the nights were cold, and the watchers were huddled around a bonfire to keep warm.

"You're going to freeze out here, Old Xing," Big Head called out. "Come inside to warm up with a drink."

Xing stood up and smiled. "We're on duty," he said. "That means no booze."

"You're supposed to watch her, aren't you?" Big Head said. "Well, she's inside, and if you've got eyes, you can do your job. Better, even, than outside." The four men exchanged looks.

"Besides," Big Head continued, "there's really no need to watch her."

"Meaning?" Xing asked.

"What's been your goal all along, if not to keep her from lodging her protest? Well, she doesn't plan to do that this year."

Xing showed his surprise before saying with a sarcastic laugh:

"Who do you expect to believe that?"

"Li Xuelian has agreed to marry me. That's what tonight is all about, an engagement party. Why would she be out protesting about a divorce if she's going to marry me?"

The four exchanged more looks.

"Is that true?"

"Would I joke about something as serious as that? Even if I wanted to, the prim and proper woman inside would not let me. You're wasting your time here this year."

Xing scratched his head.

"Sounds reasonable to me," he said. "But if the station chief knew we'd been drinking, he'd give us hell when we got back."

To everyone's astonishment, butcher Hu's son stood up and walked from the bonfire into the yard. "We're crazy to keep freezing out here while they're inside about to get hitched."

The other three exchanged doubtful glances, but got up and followed him into the yard.

The men feasted from eight at night till three in the morning. At first they were withdrawn, and Xing was wary of the wisdom of what they were doing. But they were treated to the sight of Li Xuelian happily cooking at the stove, then placing food on the table, and sitting down beside Big Head Zhao, leaning up against him to let him place a morsel of pig's foot tendon into her mouth. That convinced them that everything was on the up and up. They started toasting one another and moved from there to drinking games. Before anyone knew it, the three chickens, four pigs' feet, and five rabbit heads had been consumed, as had all the side dishes Xuelian had prepared for them, wetted down with six bottles of strong white liquor. Thanks to a lifetime of kitchen work, Big Head was able to drink as much as the others with no effect. Xing and Hu's son passed out, heads on the table. One of the other men went to the latrine and fell down next to it, out like a light. The fourth man needed to answer nature's call, but couldn't get his legs working. So, with no need to rush, Xuelian and Big Head packed up her things, collected the policemen's cell phones, put them into a sack, and tossed it onto the roof. They pushed his bicycle out the gate, locked it behind them, and got on the moonlit road. Back inside, the only policeman who had not passed out realized what had just happened and tried to get up and go after them; his legs still weren't working. So he crawled out the door and up to the gate, pounding on it and shouting at the top of his lungs:

"Come back here, get back here right now!"

By that time Big Head and Xuelian had ridden a couple of li, him in front and her in back, her arms around his waist.

7

Li Xuelian's escape threw first the county and then the city administration into pandemonium. On the morning after she disappeared, County Chief Zheng Zhong received the news with horror. Hoping to fix the problem locally and keep the news from spreading to the city, he sent county law enforcement teams to look for her and bring her back. Since she had to be on her way to Beijing to protest, he sent teams to all the bus stops and the one and only county train station, where local, but not express trains stopped. He also set up roadblocks on all roads heading north—large, medium, and small. By the time news of the escape reached Mayor Ma in the city, a mobilized force of more than four hundred had turned up nothing. Ma immediately phoned Zheng.

"I hear you've been busy today, Chief Zheng," he said to open the conversation.

Zheng did not have to be told that paper cannot contain a fire, that the cat, as they say, was out of the bag.

"I was just about to make my report," Zheng sputtered.

"What the hell good would a report do?" Ma replied. "What I want to know is, have you managed to catch her in your dragnet or haven't you?"

"Not yet." What good would it do to lie?

"How many times do I have to remind you," Ma said as his anger rose, "that 'a tiny ant hole can ruin a dike'? You must 'nip things in the bud,' do not 'save a little to lose a lot.' Time after time it's been the little things that have gotten you into trouble. Why is that? With all the police you have there, how does a single woman get away?

They may be the ones who lost her, but where are the seeds of their failure? I'm looking at the leading cadres for that. Was it a problem of underestimating the importance of the matter or the lack of a sense of responsibility? Whatever it was, I'm a little disappointed."

As we have already seen, Ma Wenbin's use of the word "disappointed" in regard to a Party cadre usually spelled the end of a career. Even the words "a little" had no effect on Zheng's cold-sweat fears, perhaps because of the existence of the phrase a "lack of a sense of responsibility."

"We did fail to carry out our responsibility, we came up short there," Zheng admitted. "But don't worry, Mayor Ma, we've learned our lesson this time. I guarantee you we'll find her within two days."

Two days, the amount of time remaining before the opening of the NPC. Ma Wenbin laughed. A cynical laugh.

"What you're guaranteeing is the one thing you cannot guarantee. That woman isn't a rock waiting for you to move it down the mountain. She's got a pair of feet at the bottom of two usable legs, and you have no idea where those legs have taken her. So how do you expect to find her in two days?"

Zheng had no answer. He'd said his piece to show a positive attitude. When an official catches an inferior in a misstatement, it's like a snake being struck in the heart. That was Zheng Zhong at that moment: standing open-mouthed, holding the phone to his ear, no answer forthcoming. For Ma Wenbin, the conversation had reached its end.

"I'm off to Beijing the day after tomorrow to attend the Congress. I do not want to run into Little Cabbage there. Whether or not the city or Yours Truly are humiliated is all up to Chief Zheng. Help me out here, please, Chief Zheng."

Ma hung up, leaving Zheng holding the handset, clueless as to what to do next. He discovered that his underwear was sweat-soaked. The sarcasm in Mayor Ma's final comment constituted very bad news. He smashed his teacup on the floor, then picked up his phone and summoned his police chief, who had been so busy he'd missed lunch *and* dinner.

Chief Zheng did not mince words:

"Have you located that woman after a day of running around?"

About the same question Mayor Ma had asked him.

"Not yet," the police chief stammered.

The exact same answer he'd given Mayor Ma. Zheng's anger finally found an outlet. Flames seemed to shoot from his eyes as he glared at his police chief.

"Raising a dog is easier than training the likes of you people. You can't even keep tabs on one person. I want you to find her by tomorrow and bring her to me. If you can't manage that, bring me your resignation letter."

Not a peep from the police chief, who immediately ran off to beef up the search team. He summoned the four policemen who'd been assigned to watch Li Xuelian—Xing, Hu, and the others—and the township station chief, to send them to jail, not as criminals, since losing a detainee is not a crime, but as guards for the real prisoners, considered by all to be the worst job possible.

"Raising a dog is easier than training the likes of you people. You can't even keep tabs on one person," he berated them, word for word what Zheng had said to him. "Since you've forgotten how to keep tabs on people, you can start all over by guarding prisoners. Ten years ought to be enough to help you remember how."

It was then the aggrieved township station chief's turn to rail, ripping the four policemen up one side and down the other. All the time the chief was sounding off, Xing and his men bemoaned their fate, though it would have been worse if they hadn't been able to hide the fact that they'd been drunk. They confessed to sloppy police work and concealed the far more serious charge of neglecting their duty.

While all was in disarray, Chief Justice Wang was the picture of calmness. Li Xuelian's case had been his, but her escape had not. That was a police matter. Public security and court were two different systems.

8

After escaping on bicycle, instead of heading north to Beijing to protest, Xuelian and Big Head went east, a long detour to throw the police off her trail. After twenty years of battling the local police, she knew she would be safe from their clutches *only* when she was out of the village. And the shortest route out was to head east. They started out in an upbeat mood, but before too long that gave way to nerves, worried that the drunken policemen would sober up enough to report to their superiors; once they were informed, a dragnet would spread throughout the county. Big Head pedaled hard, working up a sweat by the time they'd gone twenty li. Xuelian offered to spell him, but he would have none of it, so she jumped off the bicycle, forcing him to stop. Then, with him on the back, she rode the next fifteen li so he could regain his strength. After that it was his turn again, and by sunrise they had made it past the county line. They stopped after another five or six li to rest beside a bridge.

"Amita Buddha," Xuelian exclaimed. "We made it this far."

"Thanks to your quick thinking, Xuelian, heading east instead of north. We'll still make it to Beijing in plenty of time."

"I couldn't have done it without your help, Big Head," she said. "You can go back now. I'll continue on alone."

"No, I'm not going back."

"What does that mean?"

"I can't go back. By now the county officials know I helped you escape by getting the policemen drunk. They'll grab me as soon as I get home and throw the book at me."

That hadn't occurred to Li Xuelian.

"I planned all along to burn my bridges behind me," Big Head said, with a smile. "And don't forget, you can take your protest to Beijing, but I lived there for thirty years and know the city a lot better than you do."

What he said was beyond Xuelian's expectations. She was moved to throw her arms around him.

"I'll marry you, Big Head, as soon as we get home after this year's protest."

The embrace roused Big Head to exclaim:

"I'm in this all the way. Once we're married, if you want to do this every year, I'll be right with you."

Fully rested, they got back on the road, reaching the county seat by noon. They were exhausted after traveling through the night and all morning. They were also afraid that the police back home would expand their search into neighboring counties. Since they'd be easy to spot in broad daylight, they found a restaurant on the edge of town, where they shared a meal, after which they checked into a small, out-of-the-way inn, planning to stay until nighttime, when they'd set out again. Both for the sake of economy and because they were far from being strangers, they took one room. Intimacy had not been the plan, but the moment they were in the room, Big Head grabbed her in a bear hug. On the road, it had been Xuelian who'd thrown her arms around him, but Big Head's embrace wound up on the bed, where he began clawing at Xuelian's clothes. She shoved him away and sat up.

"Not so fast, Big Head. Take it easy, don't get me mad."

"I've waited thirty years for this," he said, undaunted. He pressed her down onto the bed again and continued taking off her clothes.

All that travel had exhausted Xuelian, who hadn't the strength to fight him. But he'd traveled all night and morning, too; where had he gotten all that vigor? she wondered. Since he was accompanying her to Beijing and they had, after all, decided to get married, after a bit of symbolic struggling, she stopped and let him strip her naked, after which he took off his clothes. Big Head Zhao then steamed right into the harbor. After twenty-one celibate years, Xuelian was understandably nervous, but he was barely in the harbor when she discovered to her surprise that he was an experienced sailor, and she relaxed. Once there, he didn't move, except to kiss her on the ears, the eyebrows, the mouth, and finally the breasts. Then the movement began, unhurriedly, fast and slow, this way and that, a technique that aroused Xuelian, something she hadn't felt in all those years. Faster and faster, and rougher, and stronger until, all of a sudden—climax! While she shouted and moaned, Big Head Zhao kept at it, never slowing, and—another climax! More shouts. Never once, while she was married to Qin Yuhe, had she experienced anything like this. Big Head Zhao might have looked like a big lummox, but he had a bagful of tricks in bed, and not even a day and a half of travel could quench his fire. When it was over and the shouting had died out, they lay on the bed, naked.

"Big Head," Xuelian said tearfully, "that was rape, and don't you forget it."

Zhao dried her tears and patted her on the thigh.

"We wasted thirty good years," he said. Then he lowered his voice. "Well, how was it?"

"In the middle of the day," she said, embarrassed. "You should be ashamed of yourself."

Then she laid her head on his chest and whispered:

"That was the first time in my life."

This most intimate of events altered both the direction and the destination of their trek. Big Head covered them both with the quilt, exposing only their heads, and held her hand.

"Let me ask you something, my love. Do people prefer to be with those they like or those they have nothing to do with?"

"That's a dumb question," Xuelian answered. "That's obvious."

"Do people prefer to be with loved ones or with enemies?"

"That's another dumb question."

"Okay, saying that I ask dumb questions just proves how dumb you are."

"What makes you say that?"

"Since you know the difference between loved ones and enemies, I think you ought to forget about your protest. Protesting takes you away from loved ones and into the arms of enemies. If you succeed in bringing down your enemies, then the protest has been worth it. But it's been twenty years, and you have nothing to show for it. And there's no guarantee that this year will be any different. You'll be the same as always, and so will your enemies."

"I've finally come around to your way of thinking," Xuelian admitted. "I didn't want to protest at first, just as the cow said, but those rotten officials backed me into a corner and forced me to change my mind. When they turned everything I said against me, they became my target instead of Qin Yuhe."

"You don't have to tell me how bad they are," Big Head said. "But just because they're worse than Qin Yuhe, tormenting them will take even more out of you, and still you'll come away with nothing."

Xuelian sat up with a bounce.

"But I've got all this anger inside me."

"That's precisely what I'm talking about," he said with a clap of his hands. "It's that anger that has caught you up in this struggle for twenty years, and you and I aren't getting any younger. There's nothing wrong with fighting them except that it stands in the way of our future."

He touched her down below. She lay back.

"There's a saying," he said, "that you have to step back to see the vastness of the ocean and the sky. You are one person against many levels of officialdom. You are fighting with your bare hands, but they have the power to call in the police anytime they want. We're running away from them, aren't we? That's because we can't beat them. The issue isn't whether or not you'll eventually come out of this with something, but that you've been throwing your life away, one year at a time. How long do you want to keep jumping into this mud hole? Why don't we rescue ourselves and enjoy a happy life?"

"Tell me," he whispered, "was that fun or wasn't it?

They were having this talk only because of what they'd just done. In the past, she had refused to listen. Now things were different. What he said now made sense, and if she put her happiness aside to keep battling corrupt officials, she was indeed doing what he said. At the age of twenty-nine, she'd had plenty of time, but at forty-nine, there wasn't that much life left to throw away. He was right when he said there was no one she could ask for help, that she'd have to save herself. But maybe, just maybe, she was saved today by what he said. Quietly, her eyes filled with tears, tears of bitterness for wasting twenty years of her life. He dried her tears for her.

"If you want to put an end to this, you and I can go back and get married. Then we won't have to deal with people like that or any other enemies ever again. If they know you've decided to stop tormenting them, they'll forget about getting the police drunk—they know their priorities."

Xuelian sat up again.

"Even if I follow your advice to stop protesting, I can't go back just yet."

"Why?"

"I have to stick it to them one last time. If we head back home now, they'll know I've stopped protesting. But if we don't, they'll think we're on our way to Beijing, and that scares them. If I'm in Beijing, that's where they'll look for me. Except this year there'll be no protest. I want them to try to find me in Beijing."

"You're right," Big Head agreed, "you're absolutely right. Stick it to them one more time. They'll never find us in Beijing, and they'll be frantic."

He paused.

"But we can't stay here," he continued. "Not far enough from the county. They'll likely find us if we don't leave."

"Where should we go?" she asked, a note of concern creeping in.

"I'll take you to Mt. Tai. You've never been there, have you?"

"All I've done for the past twenty years is protest, and Beijing is the only place I've been to."

"Mt. Tai is a beautiful spot. We'll watch the sunrise together. It's a sight that'll open up your heart."

They had begun seeing things the same way. Zhao rolled over, laid Xuelian across the bed, and mounted her. She tried to push him away.

"Again? she said. "Are we ready?"

He took her hand and moved it down below. "You tell me."

He returned to the harbor, and as he moved he said:

"Here with you, I'm like a youngster again."

The following morning, they left their bicycle at the inn and took a bus to Mt. Tai. The highway was under construction, though still open to traffic, and was stop-and-go all the way to the town of Tai'an, which they didn't reach until 5:30 in the afternoon, too late for mountain climbing that day. So they found an out-of-the-way inn down a small lane and checked in for the night. Big Head was in no mood to rest that night either. In the morning, after a quick breakfast by the gate, they went climbing. To save money, they climbed a serpentine path up the mountain instead of riding to the top in a cable car. They were surrounded by a cacophony of accents. Xuelian was in such high spirits on this, her very first sightseeing trip, that she struck up a conversation with just about every woman she met on the way. For Big Head, on the other hand, two nights of heavy activity had taken its toll, and he had to stop at every stage to catch his breath; he lacked the energy to talk to anyone, including Xuelian, who giggled when she saw him gasping for breath, and tapped him on the forehead.

"A bad boy at night. Let's see how bad you can be now."

He stiffened his neck defiantly.

"It's not what we did at night, it's my arthritic knees."

Most people can reach the peak of Mt. Tai before noon. But, slowed down by Big Head's snail's pace, at noon they had only made it halfway, to Mid Sky Gate, where the western and eastern paths converged. He sat down in front of a little temple around the bend and mopped his brow.

"Why don't you go on alone?" he said. "I'll wait for you here."

"How much fun can it be for one person to go alone on an outing for two?" she said, her disappointment showing.

But it was clear he could not keep climbing, so there was no use pushing the issue.

"Then we'll just rest here," she said, "and head back down in a while."

"I said we were going to the top today," he said, feeling pangs of regret. "If we don't we'll miss the chance to see the sunrise in the morning."

"At home," Xuelian said to make him feel better, "I'm out in the field before dawn every day, so I never miss a sunrise."

"It's different on Mt. Tai."

"Isn't it the same sun?"

They ate their lunch of bread and tea-steeped eggs, and washed it down with bottled water they'd brought along, then started back down the mountain. The easy trip down breathed life into Big Head.

"We'll come back next year," he said. "This shortened climb doesn't count."

"I've seen the mountain," Xuelian said, "so why spend the money to return? We'll go somewhere else."

At the foot of the mountain they had a lunch of flatbreads and noodles with marinated mutton at a roadside stand, and then returned to the inn to rest. Zhao was on his best behavior at night, lying beside

Xuelian as they talked about their schooldays thirty years before. She asked him when he first became interested in her.

"You have to ask? It was the first time I laid eyes on you."

Xuelian puffed in disbelief.

"We were in middle school. I was thirteen."

Then:

"You ignored me all through middle school."

Zhao had to admit that he didn't have real feelings for her until high school.

"You were just a kid in middle school. You blossomed in high school."

She next asked him where he'd gotten the money to buy the "Big White Rabbit" candy he'd given her.

"Filched it from my father," he said. "That candy cost me plenty of whippings."

Xuelian laughed. Wrapping her arms around him, she planted a kiss on the top of his head. She then brought up the incident in high school where he'd called her out to the threshing ground and wondered why he'd run off when she pushed him away.

He slapped the side of the bed.

"I was a coward back then," he said, displaying feelings of regret. "If I'd had any guts, I could have changed the course of a couple of lives."

He shook his head.

"It's taken me thirty years to find some courage."

"So now you've got courage?" Xuelian puffed a second time. "More like no shame!"

They laughed. Their talk then turned to their classmates and teachers. By now most of their teachers had passed on, and they had trouble recalling some of their middle school classmates. Five of their high school classmates had died, the rest had dispersed to all corners, and most were likely grandparents, after thirty years. Few had done especially well in life; the majority had been dragged into a life of exhaustion from raising children. With the mention of children, Xuelian told him that she'd raised her daughter as a single mom, only to be betrayed by someone with whom she could never see eye to eye. The girl wasn't disobedient though; it was all because of Xuelian's protests. Other people, ignorant of the details behind what she was doing, could be excused for pointing at her behind her back, but her own daughter, who had spent all those years by her side and knew the whole story, not only lacked understanding, but complained of being embarrassed by the way her mother had lodged public protests all those years. That incensed Xuelian. Her daughter, who had married at nineteen to get away, seldom came to see her. Her son, on the other hand, who had grown up in Qin Yuhe's home, was affectionate toward his mother, who had given him the name Youcai, in hopes of investing him with "talent." The previous autumn, they had passed one another on the street. He was in his thirties with a son at home, and Xuelian hadn't recognized him at first, not having seen him in years. But he had stopped abruptly, turned and caught up with her. "Ma," he'd called out.

"You've gotten old, Ma," he'd said as Mother and son stood there looking at one another for a moment. "I know you've suffered tremendous injustice, but you have to take care of yourself."

When they said good-bye, Youcai had slipped her two hundred yuan. At this point in her account she teared up.

"Youcai was right," Big Head said as he dried her tears.

He sighed, as thoughts of his own son surfaced. Since the boy wasn't much of a student, Big Head had taken him into the kitchen to learn the trade. But that hadn't lasted long, since the youngster could not stay put. Now, some thirty years later, the best he could manage was a part-time job in the county Bureau of Animal Husbandry and spent the rest of his time with his no-account friends. Since he never earned enough to support his wife and child, he regularly borrowed money from Big Head, who did not earn enough at the restaurant to help out his son as well, and was fortunate to have a pension that helped him make ends meet.

"Our children have turned out to be the bane of our existence," he said emotionally. "I must have owed him something in a previous life."

And so they slept. The next morning they took a walking tour of Tai'an city, not stopping to buy anything, since the nice things were too expensive and the affordable things served no purpose. They returned to the inn at noon, where Big Head suggested they travel to Qufu, the birthplace of Confucius, little more than a hundred li away. No mountains to climb there. They'd studied the wise sayings of Confucius in middle school, but had never encountered the man himself.

"Why not?" Xuelian said, feeling they ought to go some place, since they needed to stay away from home. "But for the city's famous sesame candy, not for Confucius. I'd like to try some of that."

"Good point. Let's see which is better, the sesame candy Confucius ate or the Big White Rabbit candy I gave you when we were kids."

They decided to travel to Qufu that afternoon to enjoy some of its sesame candy. Big Head went to buy bus tickets, leaving Xuelian at the inn to pack their things. That done, she went out to buy Big Head a sweater. Though spring was in the air, there was a chill in the morning and evening. She'd brought a sweater along when she left the house, but Big Head had been so busy tricking the police into getting drunk he'd left wearing only a thin jacket. Xuelian noticed that he'd left the hotel that morning shivering from the cold and sneezing. She'd wanted to buy him a sweater on their tour of the city, had even spotted one at a mall for ninety-six yuan. But he wouldn't let her spend that much on him. Now, as they were getting ready to travel, she was worried he might fall ill in the cold air, and the medicine to fight a cold would cost more than a sweater. So she walked the two li to the mall they'd passed that morning and managed to knock the price down to eighty-five. On her way back she bought some rolls and pickled mustard root to eat on the road. She heard Big Head's voice outside the room, which meant he'd already bought the tickets. But who was he talking to? She listened a bit more and could tell that he was on his cell phone, but before she opened the door and walked in, she heard that he was arguing with whoever was on the other end. She waited in the doorway.

"I haven't been calling you. I've taken care of my end. Have you done what I asked you to do?"

She couldn't hear what the other party said.

"All you care about is reporting to the county government how I've taken care of Li Xuelian. How about my son's job?"

Again, what the other party said was lost.

"I trust the government, but I want to see for myself."

Another inaudible pause.

"What the hell does that mean? There's no comparing the two things. How am I supposed to let you see for yourself? Forget about

Shandong, even back in the county, you can't stand by the bed when I'm doing it with her."

Silence, then:

"Of course it's all wrapped up. We're going to be married when we get back, and lodging a protest will be the furthest thing from her mind."

Li Xuelian felt like a bomb had gone off in her head.

9

Jia Congming was a standing member of the County Judicial Committee, a position held twenty years earlier by a man named Dong Xianfa. Li Xuelian had gone to Dong twenty years earlier to lodge a protest, which he said was out of his jurisdiction. An argument had ensued, at the end of which he'd called her a troublemaker and told her to get lost. Eventually, she'd crashed the NPC in Beijing and he, along with the chief justice, county chief, and the city's mayor, had all been sacked. Dong had retired to the marketplace, where he'd sold livestock until suffering a stroke and dying a few years later, thus fading into history.

Jia Congming, a man in his forties, had been in the position for three years. Six months earlier, a deputy chief justice had retired, and Jia had hopes of filling the vacancy. Promotion to deputy chief justice was not a dizzying advancement for a standing member of the Judicial Committee; on paper he outranked a judge, but no power was attached to the position, which made it a less desirable post. The legal establishment included Criminal Court #1, Criminal Court #2, Civil Court #1, Civil Court #2, Commerce Court, Juvenile Court, Executive Court, altogether a dozen or so branches, each of which had a section chief. Beyond that were the townships, each of which had its own court of law. Added together, there were more than thirty section chiefs in the legal establishment, all of whom had the same idea Jia Congming had, which was to become a deputy chief justice. Few of his competitors considered the powerless standing committee member a viable rival. They vied over the prized bone for a full six months, which evaded them all, upsetting them but not Chief

Justice Wang Gongdao. It was like three dozen monkeys fighting over a single grape; since only one would end up with it, they'd surround you so long as you held the grape in your hand. Once you let it drop into the mouth of one monkey, the others would quickly disperse. Even the one with the grape would turn its back on you as soon it ate it. People these days don't take the long view, and they play politics like doing business, parting ways when the deal's done. But if you hold on to the grape, the monkeys will not only surround you but you will reap a bigger harvest, in that they will offer you peaches every once in a while. That was how Wang Gongdao climbed the ladder to the position of chief justice; now he played the same game on these people. The deputy chief justices at the courthouse were quite happy with his strategy, since they also enjoyed some trickle-down benefits, like getting a few dates when Wang was given a peach. Dates were better than nothing. So the longer it dragged on, the more everyone benefitted from the vacancy, and not just Wang, but the county chiefs and their deputies as well. Some of the judges even tried working on the mayor.

These campaigns tended to be expensive, a fact that lessened Jia's chances, since gifts from plaintiffs seldom find their way into the hands of people with no power, people like him. Judges, on the other hand, wielded considerable power, which not only brought in revenue above their salaries, but allowed them reimbursement for their expenses. Discouraged by not being able to feed at the public trough, Jia could only turn to personal means. His salary was a bit over two thousand a month; his wife earned a little more than a thousand as a hospital nurse; and his father sold ginger on the street for a pittance, not the sort of thing you gave as a gift for your superiors. How would it look if you gave one of them a pot of peanut oil or a couple of live hens or a basket of ginger? These days, even expensive objects were out of fashion; money had become the gift of choice. The thirty judges, with their access to government funds, were able to help their candidacy along with gifts of money, leaving Jia Congming in their dust after half a year. Worse yet, he was squeezed dry, with no more money to give. But since he'd already spent money on the position, it would be a waste if the job went to someone else. In name, a judicial committee member was above a chief justice, but missing out on the promotion would also cause a huge loss of face if the new chief justice became his superior. Which was why Jia could not simply throw in the towel. But money was hard currency and he could not count on any of his poor relatives, who actually came to him for help. And with no real power, he had no rich friends. No matter how hard he thought, he failed to come up with a solution, and he could only sigh and complain after he came home, since he did not want to unburden himself at work.

On this particular evening, Jia's father returned home from a day of selling ginger and saw that his son was unhappy. He asked what was wrong.

"It's all your fault," Jia said gruffly.

"What did I do?" his puzzled father asked.

Jia told his father how he'd wanted to send a gift in hopes of getting a promotion to deputy chief justice, but could not come up with the money. So he took that out on his father.

"If you wanted to be involved in business, why ginger? Why not go into real estate. I wouldn't be unhappy if I had a wealthy father at home."

"Is sending a gift of money the only thing you can think of?" his father asked, also disheartened.

"No. Instead of selling ginger, you could have become the provincial governor. Then I wouldn't have to worry about sending gifts, since people would beg me to take the job of deputy chief justice."

"Before I started selling ginger," his increasingly downcast father said, "I sold fake liquor for a fellow named Hua. And I had to go around begging people. That experience taught me that if you want someone to do something for you, do something for them first, like help them out of a jam. Do that, and they'll return the favor. That's much better than handing them money."

Something suddenly became clear to Jia Congming.

"All those lawsuits you got me involved in that year," he said angrily, "had to do with helping out purveyors of fake liquor."

He sighed.

"But this isn't about fake liquor. We're talking about high officials, not piddling tradesmen or peddlers who come to us for help. What problem could a leading official have that I could help with?"

He walked off. But as they say, the heavens always leave a way out. An official's dilemma urgently needing resolution fell into Jia's lap. His father was a good friend of Big Head Zhao, a chef at the Hongyun lou Restaurant in town. Their friendship was born not because Zhao was one of Elder Jia's customers, but because they were both incurable gossips. For Jia, that had been a lifetime pursuit, but Big Head had been taciturn until the age of forty-five, when he abruptly took to gossiping. For the lifetime gossip, idle chatter became habit, and it was an easy addiction for people had been uncommunicative most of their lives. For them, going without food for a day could lay no claim to starvation, but twenty-four hours with no gossip was a day of deadly tedium. To satisfy his craving for chitchat, Big Head paid frequent calls on his neighbors, and those visits increased after his wife died, leaving him with too much time on his hands. Once he and Jia became friends, after getting off work at the restaurant, instead of going straight home, he headed to Jia's to exchange the latest gossip.

The annual National People's Congress was about to convene during one of their conversations, and by then talk of Li Xuelian's protest had spread like wildfire from the county to the city. The two men's talk naturally turned to her, and Big Head, who could not keep a secret, revealed their relationship to elder Jia. He began with their middle-school days, and the Big White Rabbit candies he'd given her; he told how he'd tried to kiss her on the threshing ground, how they'd met in Beijing on one of her protests, and how he'd let her spend the night in his bed when they'd come that close to having sex, and so on. He talked up a storm. Jia Congming happened to be home during this particular conversation, and at first paid no attention to what was being said around him. Until, that is, something clicked. He knew that Chief Justice Wang Gongdao, County Chief Zheng Zhong, and Mayor Ma Wenbin were agonizing over Li Xuelian's trips to Beijing to lodge her protest. They had reached the end of their tether over this affair, and Jia realized that if he could come to their aid on this, he'd be doing exactly what his father had suggested. That could make his promotion a foregone conclusion. It sure had it all over monetary bribes. Ensuring that she took a new husband was a better means of getting Li Xuelian to give up her protests than mediation or surveillance. Since her issue was whether the divorce was real or a sham, if she married another man, her legal case would become moot. There was also her former husband's slander in calling her Pan Jinlian to deal with; Pan Jinlian finding a husband was pretty much the same as a prostitute getting married. Jia was ecstatic, though he took pains not to show it.

"Uncle," he said to Zhao, "since you and Li Xuelian have an intimate history, and your wife is dead, isn't this a golden opportunity for you?"

"How's that?"

"Keep chipping away her resistance until she's yours. Didn't I hear that she was quite a beauty in her youth?"

"She sure was," Zhao agreed. "I wouldn't have kept up the relationship all those years if she hadn't been." He sighed. "I just messed up at the critical moment."

"It's not too late to start over."

Zhao shook his head. "It's not the same now; everything has changed. And even if I wanted to, she's tied up with her protest."

"That's exactly why I think you should get her to marry you," Jia said.

"What do you mean by that?"

Jia told him about the officials' dilemma, though he knew that as well as everyone else in the county and city, where word of her protest had reached the ears even of women and children. Still, Jia thought it worth repeating.

"If you can make this public headache go away by marrying her, not only will you have gained a wife, but the officials will be in your debt."

"Those are two different things, getting married and coming to the aid of government officials."

He paused.

"And if I did help them, what would be in it for me?"

"You help them, they help you."

"How can they help me?"

"You can't tell me that everything is perfect in your life. Isn't there anything you'd like to be better?"

Zhao thought for a moment.

"Everybody has something they'd like improved. For me, it's my no-account son. He has a part-time job in the Bureau of Animal Husbandry. He'd like to become a permanent employee, but nothing has panned out so far. He comes home every evening just itching for a fight."

"There you go," Jia said with a clap of his hands. "If you can resolve the Li Xuelian issue, get her to stop her protests, while the chief justice has no leverage in the Bureau of Animal Husbandry, the county chief and mayor do. Improving his job situation would be easier than shit, and I wouldn't be surprised if they made him a division head."

Big Head Zhao got lost in thoughts.

"What's there to think about?" Jia asked him. "We're talking two birds with one stone here."

"But what if I handle my end, and they don't do what they promised?"

"You still wind up with a wife. But if they do as they promise, you get both."

Zhao shook his head. "What worries me isn't that I don't have a wife, and that my son picks a fight with me every day."

"That's why you have to give it a try, for your son. I can't think of any other way for you to come to the attention of the county chief or the mayor."

Zhao began to waver. "I could try," he said, "but how do I know they'd keep their word?"

"Don't you trust the government? In the name of the courts and the legal system," he said solemnly, "I promise you that if you help them, nothing will keep them from looking after your son."

Zhao still had doubts.

"The way you're so eagerly making this your business, I wonder what's in it for you."

Jia laid it all out, revealing his desire to become deputy chief justice.

"My good uncle," he said with a clap of his hands, "you and I are grasshoppers tied to the same string. We live or die together. If you perform a service for the leadership, I'll benefit along with you. The day I become deputy chief justice, you and I will run that court-house, won't we?"

"You make it sound so simple," Zhao said, "but I need to think about it." He returned home.

Jia Congming had had his say. He lost nothing if Zhao failed to do what they'd talked about, and stood to score big if he did. No need to be concerned, either way. And so he was surprised when Big Head came to see him the next day, prepared to give it a try, not because he was particularly keen on it, but because he'd talked it over with his son. What started out as a casual conversation, a bit show-offy, perhaps, had his son, who'd been in a funk over his job situation, raring to go. He forced Big Head into it. Sons everywhere will fight to keep their fathers from remarrying, while Big Head Zhao's son actually nagged his to find him a stepmother. For Big Head, it was a matter of negotiating a way out of a predicament. Jia was thrilled with the news.

"Do it, then. If it turns out well, for you and me, the sky's the limit. If it doesn't, it's no skin off our noses."

"That's how I see it, too," Zhao said.

They said good-bye, and Big Head went off to deal with Li Xuelian. Jia wasn't especially confident that Zhao could manage, but as he said, either the sky was the limit, or it was no skin off his nose. With that he put the matter out of his mind. He was surprised when Big Head called him almost immediately to report on his progress with Li Xuelian; he was not surprised to hear that things were not going well. Big Head and Xuelian were seeing things differently, and Jia knew that it was too early to report to his superiors. If he jumped the gun, and Big Head made things go from bad to worse, that would sour his superiors' impression of him, Jia Congming. You don't lift the lid off the pot till the rice is cooked. If people familiar with Big Head got a whiff of the rice, they'd steal the glory from him. Jia was attempting an experiment, pausing after each step to see how things were going, or, as they say, crossing the river by feeling the stones. To his astonishment, Big Head actually felt his way to the opposite bank of the river, accomplishing his goal. Not in his home county, but a neighboring one; and not in his home province, but in Shandong. Big Head sent Jia a short message, saying he'd done it, but Jia remained doubtful. So he sent a short message of his own:

"For real?"

Big Head replied solemnly:

"We've slept together. Isn't that enough for you?"

Now Jia believed him, and the blood surged through his veins. He couldn't wait to report to his superiors. The authorities had chased Li Xuelian for three days after she'd escaped from her home, and, infuriatingly, had come up empty. Now was the moment to make his report. But report to whom? He wasn't sure. As a member of the judicial committee, by rights he should report to his immediate superior, Chief Justice Wang Gongdao. But he had second thoughts. He did not like Justice Wang, with whom he'd argued back when Wang was a

courtroom judge. Wang held grudges, and constituted the main obsta-
cle to Jia's promotion to deputy chief. He'd showered the man with
gifts, none of which had wiped the slate clean. How, he wondered,
could a squat, overweight man with no eyebrows be so narrow-minded?
Next in line would be County Chief Zheng Zhong, Wang's boss. He
would be a better person to receive Jia's report, since it would be more
beneficial to report directly to the County Chief; if Jia went first to
Wang, Wang would get the credit when he passed the report on to the
county chief. Taking that route would be the height of stupidity. Addi-
tionally, going over Wang's head would make Wang look bad, as a man
who could not manage what his underling—Jia Congming—did. That
could well lay even better groundwork for Jia's promotion. Filled with
excitement, he went to the county office building to see Zheng Zhong.

In the three days Li Xuelian had evaded the forces looking for
her, Zheng Zhong had completely lost his appetite. He'd skipped
meals, but wasn't the least bit hungry, and his lips had begun to blister, manifestations of his worried state, but that had not helped him
find his quarry. Under normal circumstances, a judicial committee
member could not easily obtain an audience with the county chief.
But these were special times, and all Jia had to say was that he had
news of Li Xuelian to be treated differently. Zheng summoned Jia to
his office, where he was given details on the situation involving Big
Head Zhao and Li Xuelian. It came as a stunning and unexpected
development. One he did not entirely believe at first.

"For real?"

The same thing Jia had asked Big Head Zhao. He whipped
out his cell phone and showed Zheng the short message from Zhao.
Beyond the news that Zhao had slept with her, he showed Zheng a
message Zhao had sent only an hour earlier:

We're at Mt. Tai. We're getting married when we get home.

"It's all right there, Chief Zheng. It has to be real. And if Li
Xuelian gets married, what would she gain by continuing to protest?
The fact that she went with him to Shandong, not to Beijing, is even
more proof."

Zheng was still not totally convinced.

"This is a serious affair. I'll not tolerate the slightest screw-up."

"In the spirit of the Party, Chief Zheng, I guarantee you that
nothing will go wrong. I've spent the last two years working on this.
As the saying goes, I waited till the rice was cooked to lift the lid."

That sealed the deal. Convinced at last, Zheng felt as if a heavy weight had been lifted from his shoulders. He was enormously relieved. Three chaotic days, mobilizing more than four hundred policemen, all wasted. She'd gone to Shandong. Jia Congming had accomplished what had confounded all those policemen. Zheng knew what had driven Jia to devote time and energy to this: there was a vacancy at the deputy chief justice level.

"You've performed quite a service to the government. I hear there's a deputy chief justice vacancy. When this is all wrapped up, the organization department will take this into consideration."

Zheng's comment regarding the deputy chief position over-whelmed Jia's initial plan to mention Big Head Zhao's request about his son's job. The county chief had only hinted at his promotion, and he could not possibly bring up an additional request, giving the impression that he was bargaining with the Organization Depart-ment. So he kept his mouth shut; he could always broach the subject of Big Head's son once his promotion was a fait accompli.

"Don't mention this to anyone," Zheng said.

"Not a word, Chief Zheng."

Jia left the office in high spirits, and was no sooner out the door than Zheng Zhong felt ravenously hungry. Reminded that he hadn't had a proper meal in three days, he got on the phone and told his sec-retary to order a bowl of noodles. He then phoned Mayor Ma Wenbin. Back when Li Xuelian had fled her home, he'd wanted to confine the incident to the county and keep the mayor in the dark. But Ma had found out and put Zheng on the defensive with his first angry phone call, expressing his disappointment in Zheng for forgetting the three wise sayings. Zheng had reacted by soaking his underwear in sweat. Over the three days of failed pursuit that followed, Zheng had sunk into lip-blistering despair. The next time Ma blew up, he figured, the Organization Department would get involved. But then, unexpect-edly, everything turned around, proving the adage that "the heavens always leave a way out." The problem was solved, finally, and all he could think of was to inform Mayor Ma in order to overcome the negative impact left by Li Xuelian's escape. Ma was in Beijing on opening day of the NPC. At lunch when Zheng's phone call went through, Ma was surprised by the news and by how the results had been accomplished.

"Who thought up this strategy?" he asked.

Zheng's first instinct was to take the credit himself, but if the truth came out later and Ma learned of it, Zheng would have out-smarted himself again, as he had done before, by hiding the news of Li Xuelian's escape.

"Just someone who works in the judicial system, a relative of the man who got it done, and someone who knows Li Xuelian."

"Not just someone," Ma said, "but someone with political savvy."

Zheng couldn't believe his ears, and since he could not predict what Ma might say next, he didn't dare open his mouth.

"He approached the Li Xuelian affair with a clear mind. While we were all caught up in her divorce, he focused on getting her married."

Zheng was happy to hear Ma Wenbin's praise, even if it wasn't for him.

"I agree. Like sealing off the enemy's path of retreat in war," he said obsequiously.

"That's not what I was referring to," Ma corrected him. "What I meant was, in cases like this, for the past twenty years, if it was a headache, we treated the head, if it was sore feet, we treated the feet. Year after year, the same thing, taking one year at a time. It's what we call 'step on a watermelon rind and you go where your feet take you.' But this fellow went to the cause, not the symptom, and figured out how to get Li Xuelian married. Our problem was solved."

"I agree," Zheng replied. "Once she's married, she's out of our hair for good."

"What's the fellow's name?"

Zheng knew this was no casual question; the star of this individual's political future was getting brighter. Ma had asked a similar question about Zheng himself when he'd successfully dealt with the crowd that had besieged the office in the county where he served as deputy county chief. Now he wanted to know the name of the man who had earned his gratitude by arranging for Li Xuelian to get married. Zheng would have preferred not to give it, but he knew that Ma had other means of finding out; where cadre affairs were involved, Ma's word was law, one no one dared to violate.

"The man's name is Jia Congming."

"A clever man indeed," Ma said with a sigh of appreciation. "Not phony smart, as indicated by his name."

"We're gearing up to promote him to the position of deputy chief justice."

With that, Ma hung up.

The entire incident ended happily for all concerned.

But while things had worked out on his end, Jia Congming had not counted on receiving a message from Big Head Zhao, saying that his son was still waiting to hear about the job at the Bureau of Animal Husbandry. Concerned only about his promotion to deputy chief justice, Jia had not mentioned Big Head's son in his report to County Chief Zheng, figuring he'd wait till the job was his before taking action. Feeling sheepish when he received the latest text message, he first responded with a pompous "soon." When Big Head had asked him just how "soon"—three days? Five? Jia had stalled Big Head, who angrily phoned Jia, a call that led to the argument that messed up everything for them when Li Xuelian overheard Zhao's end of the conversation.

"Who were you talking to just now, Big Head?" she demanded when he shut his cell phone.

Seeing the anger in her eyes, Big Head feared that the game was up. He tried his best to paint over the truth.

"It was Old Chu, a donkey butcher in the county. We had words over the two thousand yuan he owes me."

Li Xuelian slapped him across both cheeks.

"You damned liar. I heard every word you said. I thought you were serious about marrying me, Big Head. Now I know it was all a pack of lies. And if that weren't bad enough, you decided to enlist a bunch of corrupt officials to scheme against me behind my back."

She was so worked up she took off one of her shoes and hit Zhao with it—face, head, body—until he wrapped his arms around his head and scooted under the bed.

"I wasn't lying, and I wasn't scheming," he defended himself from his hiding place. "I meant it when I said we should get married. I'm telling you, these are two different matters."

Xuelian was having none of it. She began slapping her own face.

"I'm a dumb cunt," she said through her tears. "I'm getting exactly what I deserve. Twenty years of protests only to wind up lied to and taken to bed! There was nothing shameful about those twenty years, but how am I going to live now that the whole world knows I was cheated and tricked into a man's bed?" Her tears turned to wails of sadness.

Big Head crawled out from under the bed, but didn't know what to do. If he tried to explain things, even lie, she wouldn't believe a word. It was time for self-criticism:

"I was forced to do it. My son was hoping to get a full-time job at the Bureau of Animal Husbandry. It was Judicial Committee Member Jia Congming's idea, not mine. Don't be so unhappy," he said impulsively. "To hell with my son, you and I will get married."

Xuelian's tears stopped as abruptly as they'd started. Ignoring him, she began packing her things, stuffing her clothes and water bottle into her satchel; then she kicked the door open and stormed out. Knowing how badly he'd screwed up, Big Head ran after her.

"Don't leave," he said, "let's talk about this."

As if he weren't there, she strode out of the inn, Big Head hard on her heels.

"I was wrong," he pleaded, "wrong to work with them to cheat you. If it'll make you feel better, together you and I can turn the tables on them, what do you say?"

That had no effect on Xuelian, who walked to the end of the lane and turned into a market that was swarming with peddlers and customers for the fresh produce. She walked from one end of the market to the other, where Big Head caught up and grabbed her by the arm.

"If you're still angry, hit me as much as you want."

Xuelian walked up to a butcher's stand, where she picked up a knife.

"I think I could kill you, you know that?"

She thrust the knife at Zhao's chest; he broke out in a cold sweat and backed up in fright. The butcher and everyone in sight was as frightened as Zhao. But, thinking it was a domestic fight, they tried their best to make peace.

"Go ahead, leave if you want," Zhao shouted in the midst of the crowd. "But tell me, where do you plan to go, not knowing anyone in a strange place?"

Xuelian responded the same way.

"If all this hadn't happened, Big Head Zhao," she said, "there'd be no need for me to protest. But it did, so I will. If you'd forced me not to go to my face, I wouldn't have gone ahead, but you went behind my back, so I'll expose every one of you. Go make your phone calls and tell on me. This time either the fish dies or the net breaks, or my name isn't Li Xuelian!"

10

Chaos reigned back home while Li Xuelian was fleeing from Shandong's Tai'an city. The county had been able to mobilize a large contingent of police to chase her down once. Doing the same this time would have created too great a drain on time and resources to pursue her in Shandong, something they would have failed at anyway. Besides, she had no interest in staying there for long, and would surely be on her way to protest in Beijing, where everything had changed over the past few days: the curtain had been raised on the National People's Congress, and if she managed to break into the Congress this time, the impact would be far greater than it had been twenty years before. Then she had been labeled a modern-day Little Cabbage. This time, if the same woman managed to storm the Congress, she would gain notoriety on a scale of international terrorist Bin Laden, and many county and city officials would suffer the same fate as their predecessors.

Chaos reigned in County Chief Zheng's mind as well. Without a thought for Li Xuelian, he summoned Chief Justice Wang Gongdao and Judicial Committee Member Jia Congming to his office, where he demanded angrily:

"How the hell did this happen?"

This was the last thing Jia had expected, and he shook in his boots. Wang reacted differently: he was incensed, not because of Li Xuelian's second escape, but because his subordinate, Jia Congming, had stuck his hand into this pile of dog shit on his own. The police had been responsible for Li Xuelian's earlier escape; the responsibility for her escape from Shandong, on the other hand, would be laid at his doorstep. His anger mushroomed over the knowledge that Jia had done this in order to be promoted to deputy chief justice. Selfish motives could be forgiven; what sparked Wang's anger was how Jia had gone over his head to report a successful resolution, an attempt to take the credit as well as implied criticism of Wang as incompetent. To his surprise, the pot broke after the rice was ready, and a cooked duck flew into the air. Wang could be forgiven for gloating over Jia's distress. But that was no concern of Chief Zheng's, since he had been drawn into the mess when Jia reported to him instead of to his immediate superior. Zheng was ready to explode, so Wang knew this was no time to argue about any fine distinctions in defending himself. So he held his tongue for the time being. As for Jia, he knew how badly he had screwed up, and that Chief Justice Wang was choking with resentment. His options were limited to one: sputter the truth, from start to finish, ending with Li Xuelian overhearing the argument between him and Big Head Zhao over finding a job for Big Head's son in payment for tricking Li Xuelian into marrying Big Head. She had run off for the second time. County Chief Zheng listened to how the debacle had unfolded.

"Why the hell didn't you report this earlier!" Zheng roared. "This is what's known as a cover-up, a case of saving a little only to lose a lot."

The same idiom Mayor Ma Wenbin had used on previous occasions. Seeing an opportunity to make Jia look bad, Wang added fuel to the flames:

"By engaging in a cover-up, he wasn't saving a little to lose a lot, he was selfishly scheming for a promotion to deputy chief justice. His selfish desire created chaos at all levels of government over what should have been a positive result."

Wang indeed stoked the fire in County Chief Zheng's anger.

"Where has Li Xuelian run to this time?" he asked Wang.

"I don't know," Wang said, seeing the anger in Zheng's eyes, "but I'll bet she's off to Beijing again to protest."

"So you do know. Then why are you hanging around here? Get your ass to Beijing and arrest her for me!"

"A . . . arrest her?" Wang stammered. "Isn't that a job for the police, County Chief? That isn't the court's business."

"Not your business? It's you people who handed down the court decision that started this twenty years ago. Besides, you and she are related, aren't you?"

"Related? We're not even shirttail cousins."

"You listen close," Zheng said pointedly, "this case isn't going away. If anything more happens, they'll be looking for a new county chief *and* a new chief justice." He glared at Wang. "Don't try to lie to me. I know the court has sent people to Beijing to find Li Xuelian in the past."

By now Wang was sweating profusely.

"You don't have to say any more, Chief Zheng, I'll take some people to Beijing right away."

"Just going there isn't enough. I want you to comb the streets of the city until you have Li Xuelian in custody."

So a fearful Wang Gongdao, with Jia Congming in tow, left for Beijing. Once they were gone, Zheng decided to phone Mayor Ma, who was in Beijing for the Congress. During his previous call he had informed Ma that everything had been taken care of, that Li Xuelian was getting married. He had only two days to bathe in the praise he'd received when the hen flew the nest and the egg broke. Faced with the question of whether or not he should make a second call now that it had all fallen apart, he didn't dare hold back, as he had the first time Xuelian had vanished. When Ma found out on his own, Zheng had been thrown on the defensive, forced to listen to Ma saying he was "a little disappointed" in him. Xuelian's latest escape was more serious, far more serious. That other time, she'd only run to Beijing to petition the government over an injustice. But all the unpleasantness with Big Head Zhao had filled her with anger. The NPC hadn't begun the first time she staged her protest; now it was in full swing. If he held back from reporting, and Ma found out about it, "a little disappointed" would become "deeply disappointed," and there would be no salvation—not for Li Xuelian's protest, but for Zheng Zhong's political career. Still, his heart was racing as he picked up the telephone. In two days, a triumph had suffered a complete reversal, and calling now to make a report would do nothing to lessen Ma Wenbin's anger when he received the news, anger that replicated his own, directed at Wang Gongdao and Jia Congming. He put the handset back, but then picked it up and laid it back down three times. Finally, he decided to phone the secretary-general of the municipal government instead of Ma Wenbin, for now. Both Ma and the secretary-general were in Beijing, so he'd sound out the latter before considering whether or not to inform the mayor. Zheng heaved an emotional sigh. A once fearless official who had deftly defused a dangerous situation soon after his transfer to a new county, he had encountered Li Xuelian and turned into a man who feared the wolf in front and the tiger behind. What puzzled him was why people at all levels of government had gotten involved in a citizen's domestic affair, deeper and deeper each year, for twenty years. How had Li Xuelian, an ordinary village woman, succeeded in leading all those people by the nose? How had it all come about? What were they all afraid of? Zheng hadn't the foggiest idea. But emotional sighs accomplished nothing; needed now was an urgent resolution of this twisted state of affairs. When his call went through, he described the latest developments of the Li Xuelian affair to the secretary-general, who received the news with alarm.

"Wasn't she getting married?" he asked Zheng. "Then why is she coming back to protest?"

He was unwilling to lay the blame on Jia Congming's selfishly motivated scheme, which had backfired, since reporting subordinate incompetence always reflected badly upon the person reporting, a complication he did not need.

"That was the plan," he said, "but they quarreled when they were out of town, and the woman ran off."

He placed the blame squarely on Big Head Zhao and Li Xuelian.

"This is a problem," the man said.

"You're absolutely right," Zheng hastened to agree. "But there was no way we could anticipate what the two of them would do."

"When I said this is not good news, that's not what I meant. Last night Mayor Ma had dinner with the governor, who asked him about the 'Little Cabbage' affair. The mayor treated her marriage as a joke. Well, the governor laughed, and so did the other bigwigs. But now a day later, the joke is on him. How is he going to explain this to the governor?"

Zheng Zhong broke out in a cold sweat, for he knew that this was worse than he'd feared, now that the governor was involved. Not wanting to explain things to the mayor was one thing, making it necessary for the mayor to explain things to the governor was something else again. It would be hard for the mayor, who would be "a little disappointed" in him, but making it necessary for the mayor to then explain things to the governor would result in more than "a little" or even "deeply disappointed." Handing everything over to the Organization Department would very likely be his immediate action.

Ma Wenbin was always speedy and resolute in his dealings with subordinates, and even though he had been responsible for Zheng's promotion, that was then, this was now; there was success, and there was failure. By now Zheng's clothing was damp.

"Secretary-general, I fell down on the job and have caused much trouble for you. But now that events have reached this point, what should I do? As my long-time superior, you can't abandon someone who has served you faithfully."

The secretary-general, a man with a heart, thought for a moment, wanting to help Zheng Zhong.

"Given the state of affairs, we'll have to do it the cumbersome way."

"The cumbersome way? What's that?"

"Send a team of plainclothes policemen from your county to Beijing ahead of Li Xuelian, where they will throw up a dragnet around the People's Hall. Now we know that Beijing police are already ringing the hall, so you set yours up outside theirs. That way, if she's planning to break into the hall again, you'll nab her before the Beijing police can. If she causes an incident somewhere other than the People's Hall, it's no big deal. Treat this as protecting the Hall."

Zheng saw something bright ahead when the secretary-general finished with what Zheng considered a brilliant plan.

"On behalf of the million-plus residents of the county," he said excitedly, "I thank the secretary-general for his kindness, his big heart. I'll get to work immediately. One more favor. Would it be possible not to say anything to the mayor yet? We can handle this internally. You know how he gets." He quickly added, "Obviously, you will be shouldering much of the responsibility."

"I'll do my best," the secretary-general said. "But you are the key here. You need to throw up a steel curtain, something no one can get through."

"Don't you worry," Zheng said confidently. "We've screwed up too often already. There won't be any slipups this time. We'll make the net so tight not even a moth could get through."

As soon as he hung up, the county chief summoned his police chief and told him to send several dozen of his men, all in civilian clothes, to Beijing, where they were to throw up a dragnet outside the Beijing police perimeter and catch Li Xuelian when she tried to get to the Great Hall of the People.

"You lost her the first time," he said. "This is your last chance. If you slip up, losing your job will be the least of your worries. You'll be the Li Xuelian who gets arrested!"

Li Xuelian's earlier flight from home had made the police chief as fearful as a bird from the bow. He had breathed a sigh of relief upon hearing that she was going to be married and abandon her protest. That lasted only until he learned that she'd run off a second time. And even though the police were not responsible in this new complication, if she hadn't gotten free the first time, there would have been no second time. Seeing the stern look on Zheng Zhong's face, he said:

"Leave it to me, County Chief, I'll mobilize the men immediately and put them on a train to Beijing."

That really set Zheng off.

"With a fire on your ass, who takes a fucking train! What about airplanes? Time is more than money, it's your life!"

"We'll take planes," the police chief sputtered, "we'll take planes. But what about the cost? We haven't budgeted for something like this."

Zheng Zhong had a thought. He had no plan to tell Chief Justice Wang Gongdao about the dragnet in Beijing. Instead, he'd leave it up to Wang to take court personnel to Beijing to scour the city's streets and byways for Li Xuelian. A two-pronged strategy was just cumbersome enough.

"Keep this plan secret," he cautioned the police chief. "Don't tell a soul, including anyone at court."

"At court?" the police chief said. "I won't even tell my own father."

He left, scared shitless.

11

Wang Gongdao and fourteen of his men had been in Beijing three days without spotting Li Xuelian. Unaware that dozens of county police had thrown up a net around the Great Hall of the People, Wang assumed that he had sole responsibility for finding her. He divided his cadre of personnel, including himself, into five teams of three to conduct a carpet search through the city. Two of his people had been in Beijing to look for Li before, so they led teams to the inns and hostels she'd stayed in. Located mainly in remote lanes, they were dirty, smelly places often in the basements of tall buildings. They also looked up all the people she'd known back home who now lived and worked in Beijing—diner owners, construction workers, food peddlers, even trash pickers. They failed to find a trace of her. The other three teams concentrated on Beijing's train and long-distance bus stations, in hopes either that Li would arrive in the city after them and they'd be there waiting for her or that she would not have money to rent a room and would spend her nights in one of those stations. But not one of the hundreds of thousands of people who came and went in any of those spots was Li Xuelian.

Wang Gongdao took his frustration out on Jia Congming, who hadn't planned on coming to Beijing, but had been forced into it the same way Wang had been forced by the county chief.

"What makes you think you could get out of this mess? It was all your doing. If not for you, we wouldn't be here searching for her. You're not the only victim of your selfish desires. We all are, and you're not getting out of the search.

"The question isn't whether or not you'll join in the search, but whether or not you find Li Xuelian. If you don't, before I get sacked, I won't just remove you from the judicial committee, I'll see that you're barred from public office."

Knowing how badly he'd screwed up, Jia came along, a doleful look on his face, hoping to atone for his misdeeds by working hard to find the woman. But finding someone is not the same as working hard to find the person. There was no assurance that Li had come to Beijing in the first place, and if she had, she could be staying anywhere. An unsystematic search was a waste of time. He didn't realize how big a city Beijing was or how many people lived there until he started searching. Finding her would be a stroke of luck; not finding her was inevitable. But search he must, with no earthly idea when or even if that search might succeed.

He contacted the Beijing police, checking in at precinct stations near every hotel, every construction site, every marketplace, and every trash picker hangout he searched. He visited every train and bus station, showing Li Xuelian's photo around. Partly because they were especially busy during that time, owing to the ongoing National People's Congress, and partly because people from all over the country were in Beijing searching for missing people, the police had no time to help. They were ignoring all requests from outsiders. You could take out letters of introduction from the county or the city, even the province, and nothing helped; no wonder Wang Gongdao and the others were discouraged. At a few of the stations, the police were puzzled by the letters they were shown.

"Missing persons are police matters. Why are the courts involved?"

Seized with anger, Wang pointed to Jia Congming.

"Ask him!"

The comment surprised the local police. Jia Congming, shamed by his own misdeed, felt like crawling into a hole. Wang wasn't the only one whose blood was boiling over what Jia had done; his thirteen fellow searchers were angry at him for making such a mess of things and creating problems for them just so he could wrangle a promotion. Beijing wasn't a tourist spot if you were there to search for a person. Tourists toured the city with a carefree mind; searchers' heads were filled with legal matters. Tourists turned in nice and early; the people searching for Li Xuelian were out till two in the morning, the best time to look for people in the hotels and train and bus stations, no matter how exhausted the searchers were. On this night, after searching for her till two in the morning, they returned to the hostel tired and hungry, grousing at Jia Congming, who tried to placate them by offering to treat them to a midnight snack. Like what? they asked. If it's a bowl of wontons, skip it. We'll be better off getting some sleep. When Jia said he'd treat them to a full meal and a couple of bottles of liquor, the carping stopped, so he went to get Wang Gongdao to join them.

"How can you can think about food before we've found her?" Wang demanded icily.

Jia could see that Wang's unwillingness to join them for food was not just about the search that had so far failed, but that he did not want to help Jia look good. And yet the gesture would be meaningless if Wang did not join them, So Jia put aside his pride and implored:

"I know you're angry, Chief Wang, but a great man does not hold petty grudges."

He slapped himself across the face for added effect.

"It's all my father's fault," he said. "He talked me into trying to help my leaders out of a jam."

So Wang thought it over and wound up joining the others in their late-night meal. He took some pleasure in knowing that while they hadn't found Li Xuelian in the three days they'd been in Beijing, she hadn't caused a scene during that time. If they spent another ten days in blind pursuit of her, till the curtain came down on the NPC, and she did not make an appearance, they could return home without her and still say they'd done their job. County Chief Zheng phoned every day to ask if they'd apprehended her. Admitting that the search had been futile so far, Wang explained that as long as nothing happened in the ten days the NPC was still in session, they could still say they'd accomplished their mission. Imagine his surprise when Zheng Zhong exploded:

"Crazy talk! If that's what you're thinking, then a slipup is guaranteed. Li Xuelian has a pair of feet attached to two good legs, so how can you be sure she won't show up during those ten days? The NPC is only one third finished. The longer it goes on, the greater the chance of something happening. This is no time to drop our guard. Remember what I said: If you don't catch her, bring a letter of resignation the next time you come to see me."

"Yes, yes," Wang sputtered. But catching someone on the run was tough. Of course they would continue to look for her but was is it wrong to hope that she wouldn't stir up any trouble?

They were out in the cold each day till two a.m. looking for Li Xuelian. On the fourth day, two of the searchers fell ill, coughing during the day and spiking a fever at night, one as high as 102. Wang Gongdao sent them to a local hospital for IVs, but by the next morning, the fevers had not broken and one of the men had traces of blood in his sputum from coughing so badly. So when the teams went out to continue the search that day, they were short the two sick men and a third who stayed with them at the hospital. Wang had no choice but to reorganize the five teams into four for the time being. Then a man named Hou complained that he had to return home to prepare for the third anniversary of his mother's death. His father had died years before, and she had raised him all by herself. He was in charge of the preparations, and had been under the impression that they'd only search for a few days; he could not take part in a drawn-out campaign. When the others heard his complaint, they too were getting antsy. Wang criticized Hou by asking what was more important, personal interests or the job. Under normal circumstances, Wang would have done more than simply give Hou time off to make preparations; he'd have personally showed up on the day of the anniversary. The problem was, Li Xuelian could be on her way to protest while the NPC was in session. Now, which was more important, he asked, the People's Congress or the third anniversary of your mother's death? How could a Party cadre not weigh the importance of contrasting affairs? That would be like an itinerant barber not knowing which end of his carrying pole was light and which was heavy, which was cold and which was hot. Why is the Congress tied to your mother's rite? Because Li Xuelian is on her way to protest. If you want to vent your unhappiness, vent it on her. He concluded with a promise that if Hou focused on the big picture and decided not to return home for the anniversary, once she had been apprehended and they were back home, he would ask the Party organization committee to consider Hou for a promotion from assistant to regular justice. By cajoling, employing both the carrot and the stick, he managed to convince Hou to stay put and, in the process, calm the others, thereby stabilizing morale.

Another three days passed, and Li Xuelian remained at large. She had not been heard from. Wang was experiencing contradictory feelings: anxiety over three more days of fruitless searching, but relief that nothing amiss had occurred during that time. Another week was all he needed, up to the day the Congress closed, for everyone to breathe a sigh of relief. That said, he was worried that Li might be playing a game of cat-and-mouse, that she had gone somewhere other than Beijing and had once again changed her mind about making her protest. And yet, she'd been doing it for twenty years, and habits are hard to break. When her fight with Big Head Zhao was added to the mixture, maybe she was just waiting for the right time to vent her anger in a new protest and was hiding out in Beijing, waiting for the Congress to move to the election phase to cause a disruption. That last thought had him in a cold sweat; County Chief Zheng's outburst was starting to make sense.

As he was walking out the door that morning, a man from home who had opened a restaurant in Beijing, a fellow named Bai, came to see Wang, who had visited him a few days earlier as part of the search. "Restaurant" was a stretch for a little eatery with no more than five tables where wontons, dumplings, and pig intestine soups were sold. Assuming that Bai had a lead on the search, Wang's spirits soared. No such luck.

"Chief Wang," he said, introducing him to a man he'd come with, "this is Manager Mao, who's from our township. He'd like to buy you dinner."

"Afraid not," Wang replied, abruptly deflated, "I've got a job to do."

Aware that Wang was trying to locate Li Xuelian before she caused an incident, Bai said:

"This is dinner we're talking about. The Congress isn't in session at night, so Li would be wasting her time crashing the party then. There's nothing to worry about. You've been at this for more than a week and deserve a break, with some good food and drink."

Bai led Wang off to the side and, sort of on the sly, pointed to Wang's men.

"They can conduct the search without you for one night. You're their leader."

However bad that sounded, the logic was irrefutable. Wang had to laugh.

"Exactly who is he?" Wang asked, pointing to the man who'd come with Bai.

"I won't lie to you. He calls himself a manager and says he's involved in commerce, while the truth is, he sells pigs' guts."

That stopped Wang. Sitting at the same table as a seller of pigs' guts might not look so good for a chief justice.

"But not your ordinary pigs' guts seller," Bai said, noticing Wang's discomfort. "He's the wholesaler for all the guts sold in Beijing. It's made him a rich man."

Wang nodded. He had to reproach himself for wanting not to be seen with a man just because of his trade. You can't tell a person by his looks or measure the ocean by the water you see. But doubts crept back in.

"Why does a pigs' guts seller want to buy me dinner?"

"No reason. We're all from the same county and just happened to meet in Beijing. He'd like to get to know you."

"Hardly! It's the people who say 'no reason' who have all the reasons."

"Well," Bai said, deciding to come clean, "he has a case he'd like help on."

"Not a divorce case, is it?" Wang said fearfully.

Aware of how Li Xuelian's divorce case had put the fear of domestic quarrels in Wang, Bai was quick to respond:

"No, not a divorce. A minor financial dispute."

Wang Gongdao was fearless where financial disputes were concerned. But before agreeing to anything, he needed more information. "We'll see," he said and took his men out to keep searching for Li Xuelian.

By the end of the day Wang had forgotten about the invitation, and was surprised to receive a phone call from Bai at five that evening. Bai asked Wang where he was, saying that Mao wanted to treat him to dinner that night.

"I'm at the Yongding Gate train station," he said, reminded of their conversation that morning. "I think I'll skip it."

If he thought that was the end of it, he was wrong, because half an hour later, Mao the pigs' guts man drove up to the Yongding Gate station in a Mercedes Benz, with Bai in tow, to pick up Wang. One look at the car was all Wang needed to see that he should not have underestimated the man. Taking note of Mao's apparent good faith and the fact that he hadn't had a proper meal for seven or eight hard days, Wang looked forward to a nice, clean spot to enjoy some good food and drink. And so, with a show of reluctance, he climbed into Mr. Mao's Mercedes after instructing his team to continue the search.

Mao was savvy enough not to take Wang to Bai's eatery; instead, he drove straight to the upscale Mansion 888 on West Fourth Ring Road, where they were greeted by two rows of beautiful hostesses. With a sigh, Wang reveled in a feeling that he had returned to the realm of humanity. First to the sauna, where he bathed, took a steam bath, and gave himself a good rub; then, refreshed and clean from head to toe, he was taken to a brightly lit private room of more than a hundred square meters, with a bridge over a flowing stream through the center, through which the kitchen sent in an array of exotic dishes: shark's fin and bird's nest soups, geoduck clams, sea cucumbers stewed in millet . . . it was the sort of banquet Wang was used to at Peach Blossom Heaven back home, a remote, inland county restaurant that did not lack world-class seafood. After spending a hard week in Beijing without a decent meal, this banquet felt just right. As he took in the fairyland-like décor, he had to admit that Beijing and home were quite different places. The food was the same, the surroundings weren't; or the food was the same, he was not. The him at home and the him in Beijing were two different people. Really a case of: that was then and this is now.

Wang was a little drunk after seven or eight cups of strong liquor, but even if he hadn't been, he'd have acted as if he were; that was something he'd learned from nearly a decade of being chief justice. The richer the spread, the greater the implications behind it, and the harder the fine food was to digest. But the word "drunk" could ward off a mighty force. After ten rounds, Bai gave Mao a sign that it was time to broach the subject. Wang pretended he didn't notice.

Mao said he had a cousin who'd gone into the business of selling hog bristles to the foreign trade bureau back home. Everything had run smoothly until the beginning of last year, when the trade bureau had stopped paying its bills. All attempts at mediation had failed, and a lawsuit was filed. Mao asked Wang for his advice.

"How much are we talking about?"

"Twenty million yuan."

Wang was bowled over. That much money for hog bristles! This was a recipe for a very difficult case.

"I think I'm a little drunk," Wang said, slurring his words.

Again showing how savvy he was, Mao said:

"Chief Justice Wang, we can talk about this some other day. I'm a fan of the saying, 'Don't talk business when drinking, and don't drink when you're talking business.'"

Wang was impressed by Mao's thoughtfulness, and by the time another ten rounds had occupied them, he was about as drunk as a man could get. So drunk that his mind betrayed him: he asked Mao for details about the case. Mao was happy to oblige. But Wang felt as if a battle for the ages was being fought in his head, since not a word of Mao's explanation got through

"Justice Wang," Bai interjected, "this case is a snap compared to Li Xuelian."

The mere mention of the name had a sobering effect on Wang, sending the army of neurons in his head in her direction, and with that he interrupted Mao's explanation to begin talking about the Li Xuelian case. Though he hadn't grasped a word Mao had said, he was clear as a bell in talking about the Li case. Why? Because twenty years earlier it was he who had handed down the fateful decision; since then he had suffered every hardship, tasted every bitterness involved with the case, and there was no telling when, or if, it would ever end. On and on he talked, until he was weeping and pounding the table with his fists.

"Li Xuelian, you old whore, you've made my life a living hell!"

Bai and Mao exchanged puzzled glances as Wang stammered a few more words before his head drooped onto the table and he was out. They had no choice but to carry him out of the place, fold him into the car, and deliver him to his guesthouse.

Wang had no memory of what had transpired the night before when he woke up in the morning. He was hung over and had a splitting headache. The Maotai they'd drunk was probably fake. With his head in his hands, he wished he hadn't gone; sitting next to a pigs' guts seller for the sake of a meal was not worth it and worse yet, he was unable to recall what he might have said to the man. But regret belonged to yesterday and had no place in today's continuing search for Li Xuelian, so headache or no, Wang led his team out for the day's search. His hangover hung on all morning. At noon, his team of three broke for lunch at a noodle shop. While the other two slurped their noodles, Wang sat there drinking water, the noodles and stewed eggs seeming to shimmer in the bowls in front of him. His cell phone rang. He opened it and looked at the screen. It was Hou, who was leading one of the other teams. Assuming he was going to make another attempt to take off to prepare for his mother's funeral, he said listlessly:

"Is this about going home again? I already said no."

"Chief Wang," Hou said, "I've found Li Xuelian."

All the alcohol remaining in Wang's body emerged from pores as cold sweat. His mind was suddenly clear, and his tone changed.

"Where are you?" he demanded.

"At the Songjiazhuang subway entrance."

"What the fuck are you waiting for? Arrest her."

"I'm all by myself here," Hou complained, "and the station is packed with people. If she starts a fight, I won't be able to stop her."

"Where are the other two?"

"At lunch. I've got kind of a bad stomach, so I came out looking for a toilet when I spotted her."

Wang was in no mood to continue the conversation.

"Don't do anything to scare her off," he said. "And don't let her out of your sight. I'll send help."

His headache gone, he told his men to put down their bowls and follow him outside, where he had them phone the other two teams and tell them to get to Songjiazhuang as fast as possible; then they were to take a taxi to the subway station.

Half an hour later Wang and his men arrived at the station, just as one of the other teams came up in a taxi. Hou's teammates were back on duty with him. He told Wang he'd lost her.

"Didn't I tell you not to let her out of your sight?" Wang sputtered.

Hou pointed to the people streaming in and out of the entrance.

"That's easy for you to say. How was I supposed to do that with all those people? One second she was there, the next she wasn't."

"Split up, and hurry," Wang said to his men, not wanting to waste time fixing blame. "Turn this station inside out until you find her."

The men spread out, some inside, others outside, joined by the fourth team, which had just arrived. But from noon till late in the afternoon, the twelve men combed the station and its surroundings seven or eight times and found no trace of Li Xuelian. She could have taken the subway anywhere; after all, that's what people do in

subway stations. So the searchers boarded subway cars to search for
her at other stations. But with a dozen subway lines and more than
two hundred stations, it was hopeless. You could search subway cars
and stations on the same line and be heading one way while she was
heading the other. Line after line, station after station, they rode the
subway till midnight, skipping dinner, and not a trace of Li Xuelian.
At one in the morning the subway stopped running and the stations
closed. The four teams met up outside the Songjiazhuang subway
entrance. They would not have been so disheartened if it had been a
case of not finding her. But finding and then losing her, not knowing
what she had in mind, was a different matter. They'd been hoping
that the Congress would close in a few days without incident. But
now they knew she was in Beijing, and that spelled trouble. It could
happen tomorrow, it could happen the day after. The events of that
day so distressed Wang Gongdao that his lips began to blister. But
that didn't stop him from raking Hou over the coals:

"The minute you spotted her you should have rushed her. A fat
guy like you could easily overwhelm a woman, couldn't you?"

"I thought you told me not to scare her off," Hou defended
himself. "I wasn't in uniform, and I was afraid that if I rushed her and
she screamed, I might get the shit kicked out of me."

The others laughed, but not Wang.

"Are you sure it was her?" Wang asked.

He wasn't. "I just saw her back. She didn't turn around, so I
never got a good look at her face."

"Then how can you be so sure it was her?"

He'd been sure then, not so sure anymore.

"It looked like her."

"You're seeing things," one of the others complained. "And for
that we searched from noon till the middle of the night, not even
breaking for dinner."

That mirrored Wang Gongdao's sentiments. Hou had seen
someone who "looked like her," but could not be sure. Which meant
one of two things: it probably was Li Xuelian, or it probably wasn't.
If it wasn't, it was a false alarm. But if it was? That meant big trouble. Wang did not dare relax. The next day he had three of his teams
concentrate on the subway system, while the fourth focused on the
streets, and train and bus stations. That went on for two more days,
with no success. But Li still had not made an appearance, and Wang

was leaning toward the opinion that the woman Hou had spotted at Songjiazhuang was not Li Xuelian. It was a comforting thought. The Congress would ring down the curtain in five days, and if Li remained out of sight all that time, Wang could raise a prayer to Buddha, whether she was caught or not.

His men returned to the guesthouse to sleep after another fruitless day of searching; fruitless for them, but not for the Beijing police, who had in fact apprehended her. Wang had barely dressed for bed when his cell phone rang. The call was from a precinct station in Beijing's Xicheng District. Ten days earlier, soon after arriving in Beijing, Wang's team had searched a basement hostel in Xicheng, where Li Xuelian had stayed on earlier trips to the city. Finding no trace of her, Wang had left his card and phone number with the precinct station. The voice on the phone told him that during their patrol around the Zhongnanhai Central Government compound that evening, they'd come across a countrywoman who looked to them to be a petitioner. Back at the stationhouse, she refused to answer their questions, but didn't appear to be a mute, since most mutes are also deaf, and she obviously heard what they were saying. On further examination, she resembled the description Wang had given them of the woman they were looking for. Wang could barely contain his excitement.

"How old is she?"

"Appears to be in her fifties," the policeman replied.

"What does she look like?"

"Medium height, short hair."

"Heavy or thin?"

"Neither, I'd say."

"It has to be her!" Wang exclaimed. "We'll be right there."

Wang hurriedly woke up his men. They rushed out of the guesthouse, hailed three taxis, and headed at full speed to the precinct station. A weight had been lifted off of Wang's shoulders. Li Xuelian had come to Beijing, after all. Whether or not she'd done what she'd come to do at the Congress, having her in custody was a lot better than going home to face his superiors empty handed. He had shed a heavy responsibility, and the three men who shared his cab could barely contain their excitement.

"We're no match for the Beijing police," one of them said. "We looked for more than ten days and found neither hide nor hair of her. They caught her in one night."

"Who cares who caught her," another commented. "As long as we take her back home, we'll get the credit."

Even Jia Congming, who hadn't raised his head the whole time, snatched the moment to sidle up to Wang.

"Now that we've got her," he said, "I guess you'll be hosting a celebratory dinner, Chief."

Unable to contain his excitement, Wang decided to let Jia off this time. He slapped his thigh.

"Host a dinner? You bet I will. We've all put in many hard days, so we'll enjoy some Peking duck tomorrow for lunch."

With that they arrived at the station entrance, where they climbed out of their taxis and went inside. After greeting them, the duty officer went out back and returned in two minutes with a countrywoman. One look—they were dumbfounded. It wasn't Li Xuelian. She was the right age and appearance, but she didn't have Li Xuelian's face.

"We spotted her right off as a sly old petitioner," the policeman said.

Wang Gongdao was appalled. He just shook his head, looking like a common fool.

Early the next morning they were back out on the streets of Beijing searching for Li Xuelian.

12

The National People's Congress had been in session for twelve days, and Li Xuelian still had not made an appearance in Beijing. While Chief Justice Wang Gongdao and his team of men were searching for her, dozens of county police had formed a dragnet around the Great Hall of the People beyond the web formed by Beijing police, all in vain. She hadn't changed her mind about coming to Beijing to protest; she had fallen ill. Knowing that county officials would send people to stop her from entering the city, she'd avoided Beijing bound trains and long-distance buses and instead traveled from one town to the next, where she'd switch to another local bus for another town, zigzagging her way into the Capital. Twenty-years of traveling to Beijing had taught her that was the best way to elude the police. Constantly stopping to change buses was exhausting and expensive, but she preferred forgoing an ease of journey over getting nabbed by the police. While her travel style had consumed great chunks of time, she knew that she'd manage to carry out her protest so long as she made it to Beijing during the two weeks the Congress was in session.

In the twenty times she'd set out in the past, she'd actually made it to Beijing on five occasions, each time with police hot on her heels. From her cat-and-mouse experiences with them, she'd learned that they were on highest alert during the early days of the Congress, when the chances of getting caught were greatest. By entering the city later, when police vigilance had flagged, it was far easier to find a way past them.

She set out from Tai'an and traveled five days, stopping when necessary; the trip was tiring, but she made it to Gu'an in Hebei province without incident. Two bus trips from Gu'an would put her in Beijing, a stimulating prospect. Arriving at night, she found an inn down a small lane and went straight to bed to get a good night's sleep in preparation for the final leg of her journey—to Beijing. The night passed quickly, but when she awoke in the morning she did not feel well. She touched her forehead; it was burning up. Oh, no! she said to herself, traveling is no time to get sick. Her body had to hold up; if it didn't, besides the obvious dangers to her health, it could spell disaster for her protest. But she'd made it to Gu'an, a stone's throw from Beijing, while the Congress was entering its final days and she could not allow herself to rest just because she'd taken sick. So she got out of bed, washed up, left the inn, and walked down the lane to the main road. She managed to make it to the bus station, where she bought a bowl of porridge at an outdoor stall, hoping the fever would break from a good sweat. But when she ate the first spoonful of porridge, her stomach sent it right back up. She put down the bowl, determined to leave Gu'an, and bought a bus ticket to a place called Daxing. Once aboard, she reflected on her trip from Tai'an, during which she'd taken a dozen or more exhausting bus rides and economized by subsisting on flatbreads and pickled vegetables, going three days without fresh greens or a mouthful of hot soup. Regret set in, as she recalled the saying "Scrimp at home, spend on the road." She knew she should not have treated herself so shabbily on the road, but she could not let a bad spell of health hold up her entrance into the city; that would be too great a sacrifice. As she reflected on why her travel over the past several days had been so wearying, she determined two causes: scrimping on food and rest, and, more importantly, her anger at Big Head Zhao. He'd put her up during her first visit to Beijing. Now, twenty years later, he'd initiated a romantic relationship and had helped her escape her virtual house arrest. She'd let him talk her out of continuing the protests and travel instead to Mt. Tai. It had all been a trap that he had worked out with county officials. But while Zhao and the officials could not escape her loathing, she reserved most of it for herself. For a forty-nine-year-old woman who had traipsed all over the place to stage protests for twenty years, there was little she hadn't seen. She'd forded rivers, only to have her boat capsize in a sewer and throw her into Zhao's hands. Being tricked was bad enough, but then she'd let Zhao have his way with her. Tricks were easily avenged, but how could she cleanse a sullied body? A soiled bowl can be washed, but not a besmirched body. One of her reasons for staging protests had been to disprove the label of a Pan Jinlian. Now, after twenty years, that's exactly what she was, thanks to Big Head Zhao. She entertained thoughts of killing him, but all that would solve is to end her life as well. Sparing the officials involved in the matter would be a sort of exoneration for them. No, the protest came before everything, including killing Big Head Zhao; there'd be plenty of time for that later. This year her protest was going to be different. Actually, the only difference was that instead of targeting Qin Yuhe, she'd expose the officials who had conspired with Zhao, for it was they who had driven her to this juncture. She'd boarded buses seething with flames of anger, overheating her body, and then cooling off by opening windows. Though it was early spring, the wind carried a chill, turning heat into a fever, which had then spiked. So from Gu'an to Daxing she kept the window tightly shut, but leaning against her head it only resulted in more heat. She'd gotten up in the morning with a fever, and now her whole body felt like it was burning up. All that heat clouded her mind. When the bus arrived at the Daxing county line she saw that the way ahead was blocked by police cars with flashing lights and policemen with batons signaling all vehicles to pull over for inspection. Tourist buses, trucks, minivans, and sedans were lined up waiting to be checked. Li Xuelian broke out in a cold sweat. In addition to shunning the Shanghai-Beijing rail line, she had chosen not to take a bus directly from Tai'an to Beijing and to make her way on country buses in order to avoid an inspection. That had been a waste of time and effort and had brought on a bad cold in the process. A cold sweat actually made her feel better. The line crept forward for an hour before a pair of policemen boarded her bus. One by one they checked passengers' papers, asking their reasons for coming to Beijing, and demanding to see authorization letters from home. It was a repeat of the inspection Xuelian had encountered twenty years earlier, when she'd tried to enter the city from Hebei. But this time she was prepared, experiencing no sense of dread as she watched the policeman make their way toward her. Some of the passengers passed inspection, others were taken off the bus in silent dejection. Eventually, one of them came up to Li Xuelian. He asked for her papers. She handed him a false set she'd spent two hundred yuan for three years before in a lane in Beijing's Haidian District specifically to avoid interrogations. They were so authentic looking they fooled the police, then and now. He handed them back.

"Your reason for coming to Beijing?"

"Medical." The same answer she'd given twenty years before.

"Which hospital?"

"Beijing Hospital." Again, the same answer.

"What illness?"

"Feel my forehead."

He hesitated, then reached out and felt Xuelian's forehead. Though she'd broken out in a cold sweat only moments before, her forehead felt like hot coals. The policeman jerked his hand back.

"Your county authorization letter?"

"Sick as I am, good brother, when did I have time to wait for one of those?"

"Sorry, but you'll have to get off the bus."

"I can barely think straight. Will you take the responsibility if I get off and keel over dead?"

"That's a separate matter," he said impatiently. "Have local doctors see you. You can come back to Beijing after the Congress closes."

She'd heard that before, twenty years before, to be exact.

She leaned her head against the window. "I have asthma, and I'll die if I can't breathe. I'm too far from home, and I'm not getting off."

"Now you're being unreasonable. Without authorization, you have to get off." They scuffled until an elderly man sitting next to Li Xuelian stood up. Wearing a travel worn military uniform, he appeared to be a Party cadre.

"If it's proof you want," he said, pointing at the policeman, "the state of her health ought to be all you need. I've been sitting next to her since she boarded the bus, and she's been burning up the whole time. Would you be so uncaring if she were your sister?"

Xuelian was moved by the man's remarks; they were the first kind words she'd heard in days. Someone she'd never met ignited a range of emotions, and as she thought back over the hardships she'd endured for a week or more, that reminded her of what she'd suffered for twenty years; she began to wail, and the stunned policeman could only wave his hand defensively.

"I don't want to keep her from entering the city," he said, "but the Congress is in session."

"So what?" the old man responded. "Aren't the people permitted to go in to see a doctor? Doesn't that include her?"

Xuelian's crying elicited expressions of anger from her fellow passengers. Many stood up and added their criticisms of the policeman's behavior.

"Who do you think you are?"

"What happened to your humanity?"

A young man with a crew cut shouted:

"We're not going to take it anymore. Let's torch this bus!"

In the face of all that anger, the flustered policeman could only say:

"Don't think I like doing this, but I have my orders."

He turned and got off the bus.

With him gone, the bus proceeded on to Daxing. Li Xuelian thanked the elderly man and the other passengers; she stopped crying. But all that crying had weakened an already frail body. Before her tearful outburst she had been burning up; now she was so cold her teeth chattered and she couldn't stop shivering. But she said nothing; getting into Beijing was all that mattered. Cold one minute, hot the next, but no more sweating. Cold and hot, back and forth, till she passed out and slumped against her fellow passenger.

The man called out to stop the bus. The driver came back to look at Xuelian, and the sight of her lying there unconscious, added to the comment he'd overheard about asthma, alarmed him. He was less worried about his sick passenger than about the possibility of her dying on his bus. That was the sort of involvement he did not need.

"Don't just stand there," the elderly man shouted, "get back up there and drive to the nearest hospital."

That snapped the driver out of his daze. He rushed to his seat, started the engine, and drove off down highway, then turned and roared down a paved village road as fast as the bus would go for fifteen kilometers, to a spot called Bullhead Town, where Hebei province bordered Beijing. He drove around until he spotted a hospital in the western part of town.

After lying unconscious in the Bullhead Hospital for four days, Xuelian awoke to find a needle in her arm and an IV bottle hanging from a rack by her bed. Never in all the years she had been protesting had she fallen ill, despite all the lumps she had taken, not even a bad headache. The hard slogs had actually made her stronger. Until now, when all the illnesses-in-waiting erupted full-blown. The doctor told her that her bad cold had led to malaria-like symptoms; to that was added gastritis and enteritis. Somewhere along the line she had eaten something that wasn't clean, and was told that during the time she was bedridden she had suffered from dysentery. Finally, the asthma she had spoken of on the bus appeared to have become a reality. All these maladies were a form of inflammation, which was why her fever hadn't broken over the four days. Her white blood cell count was nightmarishly high.

For four days she was hooked up to the IV drip; during that time she had pretty much exhausted the center's meager supply of anti-inflammatories. She thanked the doctor for treating her, but was already experiencing extreme anxiety, not over the state of her health, but, as she spotted the calendar at the foot of her bed, the fact that she had lost four whole days, days that carried the National People's Congress toward closing, which was now only four days away. If she didn't find a way to get to Beijing soon she would miss the opportunity to stage her protest while the Congress was in session, making it ineffective. A tiger would become a cat, a protest would be little more than a petition, and none of those people back in the county or the city would have anything to fear.

As soon as the doctor left, Xuelian tried to get out of bed for the first time in days, but the minute her feet touched the floor she realized how weak she was. The room spun, her legs felt like rubber, and walking was out of the question. How then was she going to leave the hospital and get on the road to Beijing? She crouched down, breathless. She had to get back in bed.

Two more days passed, and the curtain was coming down on the Congress. Xuelian would not allow herself to stay in bed any longer. She made up her mind to leave, even if she had to crawl all the way to Beijing. She asked one of her ward-mates to call for the doctor, a slight, middle-aged man with buckteeth; Xuelian had formed a good opinion of him during her hospitalization, but when he heard that she wanted to leave, his anxiety exceeded hers.

"Are you tired of living? You can't leave, not in your condition."

She couldn't tell him the real reason she had to leave and had to come up with something else.

"I don't have any money," she said.

The doctor froze for a moment, then spun around and walked out. He returned a moment later with the hospital's manager, a middle-aged, heavyset woman with a perm.

"How much money do you have?" she asked.

Xuelian reached behind her for her bag, opened it, and took out her purse. All the bills and change added up to five hundred sixteen yuan.

"What were you thinking?" the manager said angrily. "You've been here for six days, hooked up to a drip, and you've just about exhausted our pharmacy. Your treatment and hospital stay add up to more than five thousand."

"I guess I'll have to leave," Xuelian said.

"Certainly not, if that's all the money you have."

"If I stay here I'll just owe you more, won't I?"

"Get a relative to bring money," the woman said, seeing Xuelian's point.

"My home is three thousand li from here. My family is poor. My relatives would happily come if there was money in it for them, but not if they were asked to bring money to me."

"Then what do you suggest?"

Xuelian thought for a moment.

"Beijing is only two hundred li from here. I have a relative who sells sesame oil at a farmer's market in Donggaodi district. You can send someone with me to Beijing to get money from him."

13

The next morning Li Xuelian rode into Beijing in the back of an ambulance. Belonging to the Bullhead Township Hospital, the vehicle had seen better days, wheezing like an asthmatic old man and complaining with hacks every so often. Normally reserved for the transportation of the sick and dying, this time it was delivering its patient not to a doctor or a new hospital, but to the farmer's market in Donggaodi district for money to pay her hospital bill. If that had been the sole reason for going to the city, the ambulance would not have been required, since a trip was planned for the next day to purchase medical supplies. But Li Xuelian's outstanding hospital bill moved everything up a day, thus saving the hospital one trip. For her, this was a departure from her earlier rides into Beijing. The ambulance negotiated several kilometers of country roads before reaching a highway that took them to the Hebei-Beijing checkpoint, where police checked incoming traffic, something she had experienced twice before on buses. This time, however, instead of directing her conveyance to the side of the road for inspection, the police waved them through, despite the vehicle's unhealthy appearance. It was a trouble-free entrance.

Xuelian's planned protest at the Great Hall of the People would have to be delayed by a stop in Donggaodi district. A thirty-something young man, whom the driver called Anjing, or "silence," accompanied her on the journey. He was anything but silent, however, complaining the whole way about the hospital and Xuelian.

"I was supposed to make this trip tomorrow," he said. "I had other plans for today. I keep telling them to get payment for treatment up front. But they won't listen, and now look at the trouble that's caused. Humanitarianism is all well and good, but there are always people who will take advantage of you."

Xuelian felt like explaining that it wasn't her idea to be admitted to the hospital, that someone had brought her there unconscious. Nor had she asked to spend all the time in the hospital, where she'd been given an array of medicines and lain there for four days without regaining consciousness. She wanted him to know that she was not a deadbeat and that it had been her idea to go to the farmer's market expressly to get the money she owed. But she was too weak to get into a long discussion, and since this was likely the only time in her life she'd see him, why waste time trying to win him over? That might work on some people, but not on the likes of a person who would not be understanding, no matter what she said. She opened her mouth, but quickly shut it and stared silently out the window.

An hour after they entered the city they arrived at the Donggaodi farmer's market, where her cousin, Yue Xiaoyi, who had come to Beijing seven years earlier, sold sesame oil. He was twelve years younger than Xuelian and had stayed with her family as a three-year-old when his mother was stricken with hepatitis and his father, who had to take care of her, was afraid that the disease might spread to his son. He stayed with Xuelian's family for three years. Slow in starting to talk, he could not form a complete sentence even at the age of three, and was taken advantage of by Xuelian's eight-year-old brother, who rode him like a horse. Feeling sorry for the boy, Xuelian often carried him piggyback into the fields when she went to cut grass, and caught grasshoppers for him. He never forgot her kindness, and after he moved to Beijing, whenever he came home to visit, he made a point of stopping to see her. On several of her protest trips to Beijing, she'd stayed in his shop, with never a word of complaint from him over the expense. Beyond that, when she explained one night why she'd come to Beijing, even though he had no idea how it had grown into such a major event, he was solidly on her side. He was a good man, this cousin, and now that she was in a jam, he was the one she came to. She recalled that he was on the northeast corner of the market, between a shop that sold donkey intestines and one that slaughtered and sold chickens. Now that she was back, she walked haltingly with the hospital traveling companion to the northeast corner. The intestines and chicken shops were still there, but Xiaoyi's sesame oil space was now occupied by a man who sold roasted seeds and nuts.

"What happened to Yue Xiaoyi, the sesame oil seller?" she asked.

"Don't know who that is," the fellow said. "This spot was unoccupied when I set up shop."

"Good brother," Xuelian said to the proprietor of the intestines shop, "what happened to Yue Xiaoyi, who used to sell sesame oil here?"

"He left three months ago."

"Do you know where he went?"

"No."

She next asked the owner of the chicken shop, who was slaughtering a chicken as she walked up, if he knew. He shook his head impatiently, without so much as a glance at her. Xuelian panicked. So did Anjing, her traveling companion. But there was a difference. She panicked over not finding her cousin. He panicked over being taken for a ride. He grabbed her.

"What kind of scam are you pulling? I'm not going to waste my time following you from one end to the other. I've got better things to do."

Xuelian's hands shook.

"He was here the last time I came. How was I to know he moved?"

"Stop wasting your breath and give me the money. If you don't I'm taking you back to Bullhead."

Xuelian began to cry, not because Yue Xiaoyi wasn't where she thought he'd be or that she couldn't pay what she owed. She was crying over the possibility that she'd be taken the two hundred li back to Bullhead if she couldn't pay, which would spell the end of her chance to protest at the Great Hall of the People. The Congress was due to close in a day and a half. The market was packed with people, some of whom gravitated toward them to see what was going on with the young man holding an older woman's arm and screaming at her. Their first impulse was to talk peace, but when they heard that the argument was over money, no one stepped forward. They just stood and watched. Until, that is, a fat man in a rubber apron with half a butchered pig over his shoulder and a butcher knife in one hand walked up, saw a crowd of gawkers, and laid down his load to see what it was. When he learned that the woman had asked after the fellow who had once sold sesame oil here, he took Xuelian by the arm and led her over to the intestines shop.

"Say there, Ji, where'd the fellow who sold sesame oil move to?"

"Don't know," the man said.

"Your stall was right next to his. Do you mean to tell me he didn't say anything when he left?"

He pointed to Xuelian.

"See the way she's crying. She owes some money and is in a real jam."

"I said I don't know."

"How about for my sake then?" the pork seller said, pointing his cleaver at the peddler. "If I hear you say that again, I'll kick your stall over. You'd be smart to believe me."

As he cocked his leg to do as he threatened, the man ran out from behind his counter and wrapped his arms around the pork seller.

"Take it easy, Brother Zhang. Three months ago he got into a fight with the chicken seller, and word has it he moved to Yuegezhuang. But that's all I heard." He glared at Li Xuelian. "Now, since I answered your question, how about buying some of my intestines?"

Yuegezhuang, located in the northern suburbs, also boasted a farmer's market. Hearing that Yue Xiaoyi hadn't left Beijing calmed Xuelian considerably. She also realized that she should have made it worth the peddler's while to give her the information she wanted. She rewarded the pork seller with profuse thanks, but he waved her off.

"I hate seeing people pick on the poor."

He shouldered his load and walked off.

The ambulance drove off on its hour-long drive to Yuegezhuang, where Xuelian and Anjing went into the market to look for Xiaoyi. Since the Donggaodi peddler hadn't said where in the market Yue had set up shop, they had to check every stall from east to west and north to south. No Yue Xiaoyi, in fact, not a single seller of sesame oil. Worried that they hadn't conducted a thorough search the first time, she and Anjing canvassed the place again. Xuelian experienced another panic attack, afraid that her cousin had moved a second time or that the intestines seller had lied to her. But none of that really mattered; Yue was not at the farmer's market. Now she didn't know what to do. Anjing's sense of restlessness matched hers.

"Is this going to get done or isn't it? I don't have time to keep searching for people!"

He looked at his watch.

"It's already noon, and all we've done is talk. I still have to buy medical supplies. No more looking. I'm taking you back to Bullhead and turning you over to the hospital manager. You can work things out with her."

This increased Xuelian's anxieties, which stemmed both from her inability to find Yue Xiyi and the further delay in her attempt to stage her protest. Noon already. Little more than a day remained before the Congress would end. Time, as the saying goes, waits for no one. At that moment she made up her mind: whether or not she found her cousin and whether or not she was able to pay the money she owed, she was not going back to the Bullhead Hospital with Anjing. But how was a woman in her fifties, so ill she could not walk without breaking out in a sweat, going to free herself from a healthy young man standing right next to her? At that moment she heard a shout behind her:

"Ribbon fish from Zhoushan, special close-out sale, fifteen yuan a catty."

That voice, it sounded familiar. She spun around to see who it was. There at a peddler's stall a man in rubber boots, with sleeve protectors on both arms and rubber gloves, was separating frozen ribbon fish with a screwdriver. It was her cousin, Yue Xiaoyi. She'd found him; her legs turned weak. He'd moved to Yuegezhuang after all, and was now selling fish instead of sesame oil. Once her legs were firmly under her again, she shouted:

"Xiaoyi."

He looked up to see who was calling him. It took a moment, but he recognized Xuelian. That was a shocker. Not that she'd trailed him from one place to another, but:

"How did you get so skinny, Sis? I barely recognized you."

As tears rained from her eyes, she said:

"I've been sick. But you, why are you selling fish now?"

"The price of sesame seeds spiked this year, so I couldn't make a living selling the oil."

He led his cousin over to a nearby wall.

"Are you here to protest again?"

She nodded.

"No wonder. People from the county have been around here many times. Every three days or so lately. Yesterday they came by twice."

The news unsettled Xuelian, who knew she had to move on before they found her.

"I have to leave."

She turned to walk away just as Anjing ran up and took her by the arm.

"You can't leave. Where's our money?"

She'd momentarily forgotten that she'd come looking for Xiaoyi because she needed money. So she told her cousin, in detail, what had happened to her in Bullhead Township, how she owed the hospital there five thousand yuan, and that she'd only paid them two hundred. Xiaoyi turned to Anjing.

"I'll pay you what my cousin owes you," he said without a moment's hesitation. "But I don't have that much on me."

"Then don't even think of leaving," he said to Xuelian.

"Wait here, both of you," Xiaoyi said. "I'll go to the bank."

He asked a pig-intestines peddler in the next stall to look after his fish stand while he was gone, took off his rubber gloves and sleeve protectors, and rushed out of the farmer's market, leaving Xuelian to wait there with Anjing. Not five minutes later, Wang Gongdao led his men into the area. When they spotted Xuelian, their gleeful surprise was as great as a hungry fly seeing blood. They quickly surrounded her. Since she had committed no crime, they could not cuff her. A breathless Wang Gongdao was smiling.

"Cousin," he said, "you've led us on a merry chase."

Ignoring him, she turned to Anjing.

"It's all your fault," she complained. "You've ruined my chances."

Anjing stood there wondering what was going on. Did she owe these people money too?

"Get in line," he said to Wang, ignoring Xuelian. "You can deal with her after she's paid what she owes us."

He had no idea who these people were, and before Wang had time to respond, the heavyset Hou stepped up and shoved Anjing.

"Step aside," he said. "If she owes you money, take her to court. We're on official business. Understand?"

Thinking he was confronted by the police, Anjing stood there blinking, not daring to say another word. Normally a chatterbox, now that he was up against someone harder than him, he kept his mouth shut.

"Cousin," Wang said to Xuelian with a smile, "come back with me instead of protesting, what do you say? We knew you'd come to see Xiaoyi sooner or later, since he's family."

Xuelian stiffened her neck.

"You wouldn't believe me when I said I wasn't going to protest. In the process you've driven me to this. If you won't let me do it, I'll kill myself right in front of you."

As Wang turned and signaled someone in the distance, she saw some men emerge from a marked car and run toward her. She assumed they were police, but when they were close enough to make out, she saw that one of them was her son, Youcai. She was stunned at the sight of the son who had grown up with his father, but had developed a fondness for his mother as a young adult. The year before, when they'd met on the street, he'd handed her two hundred yuan. Her first thought was that he was being held hostage by the court as a way to force her to go back with them. But that did not seem likely. Though she favored her son over her daughter, her daughter at least had grown up with her. They shouldn't have tried to keep her from what she wanted to do by turning her son into a pawn. But in all her dealings with these people, they had never shied from pulling tricks out of their bag.

"How did you get so skinny, Ma?" he said with a look of surprise.

"Have they brought you here in custody, Youcai?" she asked, ignoring the question about her appearance.

"No," he said. "I just came to tell you, Ma, not to protest."

"If that's what you came to do, then you might as well go back home right now. I might have listened to you if you'd done this in the past, but everything's different this year, and I'll die before I give up."

"I'm not saying you shouldn't protest, I'm saying you can't do it this year."

"Why?" she asked.

Without warning, Youcai burst into tears as he crouched down and wrapped his arms around his head.

"My dad's dead."

Xuelian did not understand him at first. But then the words "my dad" got through. He meant Qin Yuhe, and the news that he had died nearly made her head explode. She wasted no concern over Qin himself, but over the fact that with him dead she lost her reason to protest. The sham divorce had somehow become real and was the core of her action. That had spawned talk that she was Pan Jinlian and subsequent encounters with a range of officials. His death broke all those links in the chain. Where does the hair go when the skin no longer exists? In past years, he had been the target of her protest; this year was to be different—the targets were to be those officials, and Qin had faded into the background. But his death ruined everything, and the officials would be off the hook. Big Head Zhao had teamed up with them to trick her into his bed with his lies, thus actually turning her into a Pan Jinlian. She'd nearly died on the road to Beijing, but had made it somehow, only to see everything fall apart. Two wasted weeks. The officials were no longer in danger, and she had become a Pan Jinlian for nothing. All this was too much for her.

"How did he die?" was all she could ask. "I didn't know he was sick."

Youcai stood up.

"A traffic accident. Five days ago. He and my stepmother had argued that night, so he stormed off to deliver a load of fertilizer. On the Yangtze River Bridge, he tried to avoid a passing car and slammed into a bridge pier. The truck flipped over into the river, him in it." He began crying again. "At his age, with failing vision, he shouldn't have been driving when he was angry."

The fullness of the news sunk in. Qin Yuhe died while she was lying unconscious in a hospital bed.

"Qin Yuhe, you son of a bitch!" she cursed. "After ruining my life, you won't even let go in death. Just like that, you're gone, but what about me? You never told the truth about you and me. Not only that, you son of a bitch," she ranted on, "nothing else will ever be resolved."

She began to howl, tears and mucus rolling down her face. She didn't even try to wipe it away. She was crying harder over Qin Yuhe, her most bitter enemy, than she ever would over a loved one.

An eighty-six-story commercial high rise rose up across the street from the Yuegezhuang farmer's market. A gigantic video screen affixed to its wall was at that moment showing scenes of the ceremonial closing of the National People's Congress. That morning, all the resolutions had been approved by unanimous consent, greeted by a round of thunderous applause.

14

Qin Yuhe's death went unremarked the first two days, but on the third it came to the attention of County Chief Zheng Zhong, who learned of its connection to Li Xuelian's failure to protest. On his return from a meeting in the city he passed by the county fertilizer plant and spotted a clutch of people at the entrance in front of a stand with a large funeral wreath. A middle-aged woman and a child in funeral sackcloth were kneeling in front of the wreath; she was holding a cardboard sign on which was written: QIN YUHE, YOU DIED FOR NOTHING

At first the name meant nothing to Zheng, who wondered what the apparent dispute was all about.

"Stop the car," he said to his driver.

The driver pulled to the side of the road, where Zheng said to his secretary, who was sitting in the front passenger seat:

"Go find out what this is all about. We can't have something like that at the western entrance to the county seat, where cars and pedestrians stream past."

His secretary returned five minutes later to report that the family of the deceased was arguing with the plant foreman over compensation offered for the traffic death of one of its drivers. That's an internal affair at the plant, Zheng said to himself. The chief of a county has no business getting involved. All that would accomplish is to stir things up even more. Better to let them hash it out over a couple of weeks, with a little give and take by both sides, until the matter is resolved. This sort of dispute requires a cooling off period.

With that, Zheng told his driver to drive on. But when the car drove into the county government compound, a vague memory surfaced in Zheng's mind.

"Qin Yuhe, why does that name sound so familiar?"

His secretary, who hadn't made the connection either, took out his phone and punched in the number of the fertilizer plant's manager. He followed his boss into the building, and when they were in the Chief's office, he said:

"I've got your answer. The dead man, Qin Yuhe, was the ex of our 'Little Cabbage.'"

The news that Qin was Li Xuelian's ex-husband meant little to Zheng until he was sitting at his desk, when he finally made the connection between Qin Yuhe's death and Li Xuelian's protests. He banged his hand down on the desk excitedly.

"This is no run-of-the-mill incident," he said.

"What do you mean?" his secretary asked. "It's just a traffic accident."

"If it was anyone else, it would be an ordinary traffic accident. But not with Li Xuelian's ex-husband. Their marriage is what her protest is all about. Now that he's dead, the marriage issue is settled, so what reason does she have? None."

His secretary got the picture. "The accident was a godsend," he said.

Having no interest in discussing the virtues of the accident, Zheng snatched up his phone and placed a call to Chief Justice Wang Gongdao in Beijing, where he was conducting the search for Li. He told him about Qin Yuhe's death. Wang was shocked. But the significance of the news quickly became clear.

"That's wonderful news. With him dead, Li has no reason to protest. It's over." After a moment, he continued: "We can head home."

But Zheng surprised him:

"You missed my meaning. This turn of events makes taking Li into custody more urgent than ever."

"Why? If she doesn't have a case, won't we be wasting our time?"

"Li might not know that Qin is dead, and still plans to disrupt the Congress."

"There's no reason for her to do that now," Wang replied. "If she does, she'll be guilty of deliberate provocation. We've got nothing to be afraid of."

"You just don't get it, do you? It's critical to stop her now. If she crashes the Congress, when the high-ranking people investigate, they won't concern themselves with why she protested, but with the political fallout from having someone crash the Congress. If her protest succeeds, we deserve to be censured. But if it doesn't and we still suffer the consequences, wouldn't we be the losers?"

Zheng's explanation made things clear to Wang. But he and his team of a dozen or more men had searched the streets and byways of Beijing, above and underground, for over a week without finding a trace of Li Xuelian. Zheng was unsympathetic to the claim that finding someone in a city as big as Beijing was next to impossible.

"Go find her," he insisted, "and tell her that her ex is dead. Then and only then will this be over."

"Even if we find her," Wang protested, "how do you know she'll believe us when we say Qin Yuhe is dead? She could consider it a ruse."

The logic was convincing, and that is when Zheng came up with the plan to send her son to Beijing. She'd surely believe him. After ending the call with Wang, Zheng placed a call to the county police chief, who was in Beijing, informing them of Qin's death and stressing the importance of tightening the cordon around the Great Hall of the People during the final days of the Congress to keep Li Xuelian from crashing the show. He reminded him that people tend to slack off as time passes, and that is when incidents normally occur. Two months earlier, Li had escaped because of a lull by those assigned to watch her. That was back in the village. Beijing was a whole different matter. There could be no lapses now. Yes, yes, the police chief said compliantly.

To save time, the court sent Xuelian's son, Qin Youcai, to Beijing in a police car, straight through the night. Wang Gongdao said nothing to him when they met, but a deputy chief justice, who had accompanied him to Beijing, surprised Wang by telling him that while he and his men were looking for Li Xuelian, County Chief Zheng had also sent his security chief and dozens of police to Beijing to search for her. That damned Zheng Zhong had sent two teams to Beijing without telling him, proof that he did not trust him or anyone else associated with the court. On the other hand, it was comforting news, in that if Li was not caught before she crashed the Congress, the blame would not fall only on the court system; the security people would get their share, which ought to be greater than Wang's, since they had sent so many more people. Feeding and boarding a phalanx of security personnel added up to several times that expended by Wang in Beijing.

Despite the addition of Qin Youcai to the search, Wang held out little hope that they would be successful. If they managed to get through the three remaining days of the Congress with no incident, even if they did not find her, they could breathe easy. But Wang said nothing of this to his subordinates. Like Zheng Zhong, he demanded that his men keep up the search. He had started out with fourteen men ten days earlier. Two had taken ill eight days ago, but were back on the job. To this was added a deputy chief justice and a driver, making a total of seventeen, including Wang himself, a significant force. Zheng Zhong had commanded them to take Li into custody before the closing ceremony of the Congress, and he would not treat them lightly if she managed to cause an incident in the remaining three days. He'd sack every last one of them before he himself was shown the door. The force with which he said this made believers out of everyone, even though he did not really mean it. They searched for Li as never before. In three days it would all be over, they reflected, so this was no time to let down their guard, not after ten incident free days. Wang held out little hope that they'd actually catch Li, but since extra vigilance was ordered, he had his men make sweeps of certain locales twice a day instead of once every three days. Which made it even more surprising that two days later, Li was taken into custody at the Yuegezhuang farmer's market.

In strictest terms, she wasn't so much taken into custody as she fell into her pursuers' hands by accident. Wang Gongdao and his men played no role in the occurrence; they had the young Anjing, from the Bullhead Hospital to thank for that. If not for his persistent demand to be paid, she'd still be free. But that now meant nothing, and Wang Gongdao reveled in a sense of joyful relief. Hateful though Chief Zheng remained for his duplicity, it was Wang's people who had Li Xuelian in custody, which earned him richly deserved credit. Moreover, Wang's success meant those from the Security Bureau had wasted manpower, effort, and money with nothing to show for it.

While Li wept over her dashed hopes, Wang took out his phone and called County Chief Zheng to tell him that Li was in custody.

"We finally got her, Chief Zheng, after ten excruciating days. She's been told that Qin was killed in a truck accident. Can you hear her crying over the news? Her plans are useless now and she will never again crash the National People's Congress."

The news came as a relief to Zheng, though not in the same way it had come to Wang, who viewed the situation on its own merits, figuring whoever was involved in the capture deserved credit, and now everyone could return home. What pleased Zheng was that finding her was different this time. Now Qin Yuehe was dead and there would be no more trouble with Li in Beijing, not now, not ever. Qin himself had inadvertently seen to that. Li had gained fame as a modern-day Little Cabbage. Now the cabbage had turned to mush in the pot.

Never had someone's death brought a man so much joyful release. And because of that, Zheng was able to overlook Chief Justice Wang's mistakes. He said over the phone:

"Tell everyone I appreciate their hard work. When you're back home, I'll treat you all to a celebratory dinner."

Seeing how happy Zheng was, Wang knew that his disputes with the county chief had vanished like a puff of smoke.

"On behalf of the entire team," Wang said happily, "I thank Chief Zheng. We'll bring Li Xuelian back to the county as soon as she stops crying."

After hanging up, Zheng called to tell Mayor Ma that the matter was closed. His report differed from Wang's report to him, in that he mainly wanted to bring relief to Ma, whereas Wang had wanted to bring laurels onto himself. Zheng had not forgotten that Ma had been "somewhat disappointed" in him, and this was his chance to rescue his political reputation. In the Li Xuelian affair, this was his first opportunity to bring good news to his superior, who was still in Beijing taking part in the Congress, which would wrap up the next day.

When his call went through, he almost breathlessly explained how Li Xuelian's ex-husband had died in a traffic accident, bringing to an end any need for her to protest ever again. Ma Wenbin's relief was palpable, but his response lacked Zheng's excitement and jubilation when he heard the news.

"This is totally unexpected," he said.

Zheng assumed that he was referring to Qin's accidental death.

"It was to me, too," he said. "His truck went right into the river."

"That's not what I'm talking about," Ma said. "This affair was brought to a successful conclusion through unexpected events, not by anything we did. In other words, an inconclusive conclusion. That's what's unexpected."

Zheng hadn't expected that.

"The Li Xuelian affair may have ended," Ma said, his tone increasingly stern, "but we have not changed the way we think about things, and our leadership prowess has not been elevated. The quality of our mastery and guidance of events is stalled. We've struggled with his Li Xuelian business for twenty years, and why is that? If it had been caused by something major I wouldn't have minded. But as I've said time and again, it arose out of something very small. Take my advice, Zheng, and do not relax your vigilance. The Li Xuelian affair is not over. It will be over only when we have learned a profound lesson from the experience. If not, while this time it was a Li Xuelian, the next time it will be a Wang Xuelian."

Once again, Zheng Zhong's report had backfired. What had started out as good news only brought him a reprimand. He broke out in a cold sweat.

"Don't worry, Mayor Ma, we will take a profound lesson from this Li Xuelian affair, starting from the tiniest detail in order to make our work more thoroughgoing and down to earth."

"One more thing. Even though the woman did not carry out her plan, be sure to take her back home. The Congress runs one more day, and the last thing we want is for her to introduce any more complications in Beijing. That is another detail."

"Don't worry, Mayor Ma. She is with court personnel at this very moment, and I will tell them to bring her back without delay."

15

Ma Wenbin told Zheng Zhong to deliver Li Xuelian back home, an order that was passed on to Wang Gongdao, who did nothing of the kind. Not because he and his people did not want to or that she said she would die first and was unyielding in her desire to raise a stink, but because she'd passed out as a result of her incessant crying at the farmer's market. After forcing herself to travel to Beijing from Bullhead town when she was still in the grip of a serious illness, she remained in delicate physical condition. Already deeply troubled by the pressure to pay for her hospital stay and her inability to carry out her protest, plus the unexpected news of Qin Yuhe's death, she realized that she had endured the last ten bitter days and, for that matter, the hardships of the past twenty years, for nothing. Everything got under her skin; every new incident was worse than the one before.

Her collapse unnerved Wang. Her son, Qin Youcai, picked her up just as Yue Xiaoyi returned from the bank. Frantically, they carried her into the room Yue rented behind the market. The unconscious Xuelian immediately spiked a fever, a clear indication that she was in no shape to travel. Naturally, since she was unconscious, they could, if they wanted to, simply transport her without her knowledge. But that struck Wang as too risky. What if she died on the road? There had been no complications with Qin's death, a self-triggered traffic accident, but the possibility of her death spelled trouble for Wang, who would be seen as the cause. Faced with a dilemma, he phoned Zheng Zhong, who was not about to take the responsibility for moving Li back to the county.

"This is not good," he said after a thoughtful pause.

"Tell you what," he continued, "since the Congress only runs one more day and she's not up to traveling, assign someone the sole job of watching her till it's over. After that, you're free to leave."

At this point, that was about the only thing they could do. So Wang Gongdao summoned all seventeen courthouse personnel to Yuegezhuang and formed them into three-man squads to patrol the area around Yue Xiaoyi's room in four-hour shifts. They were to look in on Li Xuelian every half hour. Wang and his deputy were in charge of the operation, also on a four-hour rotating basis, though they spent their shifts in a police car outside, rejoicing over the fact that Xuelian remained unconscious for a full twenty-four hours, from noon one day to noon the next, at which time the gigantic TV screen on the building across the street from the farmer's market showed the closing ceremony of the National People's Congress; a new government administration was formally in place. Wang's shouts for joy echoed the thunderous applause from the Great Hall of the People. Nearly two weeks of hard work by all, from top to bottom, had been amply rewarded; their work, for this year and for the previous twenty, was done. A full stop had been placed at the end of Xuelian's protests, and all seventeen men, led by Wang Gongdao, began heading home from the Yuegezhuang farmer's market. After a discussion with Wang, Youcai stayed behind to care for his still unconscious mother.

Given her condition, Xuelian belonged in the hospital. But Yue Xiaoyi had nothing left after paying for her stay in the Bullhead Hospital, and Youcai was no better off. So Xiaoyi did the next best thing: he paid for a doctor at a local clinic to come hook Xuelian up to an IV. Two days later, she still had not come to, and Youcai was getting anxious, as he needed to return home to tend to his father's funeral, which he did after talking it over with Xiaoyi.

Xuelian finally regained consciousness two days after that. She had no idea where she was until she saw Xiaoyi's familiar face and surroundings. Recollections of what had happened before she lost consciousness filtered back, little by little, though everything felt like a lifetime ago. Xiaoyi was thrilled to see his cousin with her eyes open.

"You scared me half to death," he said as he handed her a bowl of millet porridge.

"Xiaoyi, I've been nothing but trouble for you," she said with difficulty.

Xiaoyi, true to his disposition, turned her comment aside.

"I'll have none of that," he said. "What could be more important than your life?"

"Don't worry about the money you spent, Xiaoyi," Xuelian said. "I still have a house back home, and I'll have enough to pay you back when I sell it."

"And none of that talk either," he said.

Tears sprang from Xuelian's eyes. Xiaoyi was well aware of her history of protests; he knew what had brought her to this difficult stage and could see what an awkward position she was in.

"Wait till you're well again, Sis. If you don't feel like going back there for the time being, you can stay here and sell ribbon fish with me."

That brought even more tears to her eyes.

"Xiaoyi," was all she could say.

The fever broke three days later, and she was able to get out of bed. In three more days she was walking and could help Xiaoyi with the meals. Once he was sure she could take care of herself, he went back to the farmer's market to sell his fish.

One morning, after breakfast, Xiaoyi went to work, leaving Xuelian to do the dishes and prepare lunch. That done, she set the lunch dishes out on the table and covered them with empty bowls, then sat down and wrote a brief note:

Thank you, Xiaoyi. I'm leaving now. I've already told you how I'll repay you, so I won't repeat it here.

She picked up her traveling bag and walked out the door, planning not to return home but to find a spot to end her life—to hang herself. Why? Not because her reason to protest had died in the river with Qin Yuhe, ending her quest to purge the stain on her name, but because Qin's death had made a travesty of that quest and a laughingstock of her. Tricked into soiling her body, an event that was known to all, Li Xuelian had in fact become a Pan Jinlian, and that too was a travesty. Failing to lodge her protest was an injustice, but the resulting travesty was humiliating. She could live on with an injustice, but not humiliation. Having made up her mind to kill herself, she was then confronted with the problem of where to do it. Ideally, she would hang herself in front of one of her adversaries: in front of Big Head Zhao's door or the courthouse or the county or municipal government building to give them one more dose of trouble before she died. But now that her protest had become a travesty, no purpose was served by killing herself in front of them. To do so would be yet another travesty. A travesty both in life and in death. Like dying with no place to be buried. Yet another travesty if word got out, for such ill-fated people are either hateful or wretchedly poor. For Li Xuelian, it would just be a humiliating travesty.

She left Yuegezhuang and headed not for the city, but the suburbs, feeling a sense of liberation, for now she could choose any spot she wanted to end her life. At noon she spotted a hill crowded with peach trees. After twenty days of struggle and unconsciousness, she had missed the riotous sight of early spring peach blossoms. She walked into the grove and spotted a little secluded hut, its open door revealing bedding and an array of pots and pans, plates and bowls, as well as pruning tools: saws, shears, a ladder, and more. An orchard tender's hut, in all likelihood. The peach trees were in need of a pruning. Xuelian continued walking, up one hill and down the next, where the peach blossoms were a fiery red in the bright sunlight.

"This is the place," she said, pleased with the surroundings.

"I said anyplace would do," she said to herself, "but this is more than that."

She unzipped her traveling bag and took out the rope she'd put there for this very purpose. After looking around, she found the tree she was looking for: tall with a sturdy, thick trunk. She tossed her rope over one of the limbs, sending a carpet of peach blossoms earthward. After forming a noose, she moved a rock over, stood on it, slipped her head through the noose, then kicked the rock out from under her, and was hanging by the neck.

But before Xuelian breathed her last, she felt a pair of arms wrap around her legs. Breathing hard as he lifted her up, a man shouted angrily:

"There's no bad blood between you and me, Cousin, so why are you doing this to me?"

He placed her on the ground. He was in his middle years.

"I've been watching you. I thought you meant to steal my things, never dreaming you were intent on killing yourself."

"I'll die if I want to," Xuelian said. "It's none of your business."

"That's what you think," he said, a hint of anger in his voice. "I contracted for this peach grove. Peaches aren't worth much in the fall, so I make my living from people paying to pick fruit themselves in the spring. Didn't you see the sign, 'PICKING ORCHARD' at the foot of the hill? Do you think people would come if they knew someone had hanged herself here?"

Xuelian did not know whether to laugh or cry at what he said.

"Where should I go then?" she asked after a moment.

"Are you really going to kill yourself?"

"Yes, and you can't stop me."

"Why are you doing it?"

"It would take more than a couple of sentences to make you understand. And if I understood it all, there'd be no need for me to die."

"If you're dead set on dying, then help me with something. See that hill over there, the other grove where the peach trees are blossoming? Old Cao has that contract, and he and I are rivals."

He paused, then added:

"As they say, if you can't hang yourself from one tree, try another. You won't lose much time doing that."

Xuelian had a good laugh over that.

Chapter Three

The Main Story: For Fun

1

On West Avenue in a certain county of a certain province there is a restaurant called Another Village, which has gained fame over its specialty dish, known as "meat on the bone." There are other dishes on Another Village's menu: offal soup, baked flatbreads, cold cuts, and an assortment of spirits. But these are little different than their counterparts in other restaurants. The preparation of their meat-on-the-bone, however, is unique. At other places, the meat is stewed until it falls off the bone; but not at Another Village, no matter how long it stews. The flavor penetrates both the meat and the marrow of the bone. And that flavor is unique as well: salty yet fragrant; fragrant yet sweet; sweet yet spicy; spicy yet bracing and smooth. Visitors to that county who crave a banquet will dine at Pacific Seafood City; those interested in less sumptuous meals will visit Another Village for its meat-on-the-bone. For full enjoyment it must be eaten straight from the pot, when it burns your hand. Strong liquor helps beat the heat, so you drink more than usual.

At Another Village, two cauldrons of meat-on-the-bone are prepared, one at noon and another in the evening. Eager customers queue up to partake of the specialty. The restaurant policy is that the meat is reserved for customers who eat at one of the tables; anyone wishing to buy takeout alone will be accommodated only if there is some left over after the diners have finished. And there is no guarantee there will be enough even for the regulars. It all depends on how many people are in line and each person's position in that line. Out-of-towners frequently ask, Why don't you make more, since it's in such demand? I don't want to tire myself out, proprietor Shi responds.

2

Shi, a man of sixty, plays mah-jongg when he isn't preparing meat-on-the-bone. Two cauldrons a day frees him to enjoy his favorite pastime. He won't let the restaurant tire him out, or, for that matter, mah-jongg, which he plays once a week, every Thursday, from three in the afternoon till eleven at night, a full eight hours. His playing partners are a distillery owner named Bu, a wholesaler of spirits and tobacco named Wang, and the owner of a bathhouse named Xie. Year in and year out, the seasons change, but not the players. They win some and they lose some, and it all evens out in the end. It's just four men killing time.

The game takes place in a private room at Another Village. In the afternoon an additional pot of meat-on-the-bone is prepared for their dinner. The distillery owner supplies the liquor. Once the meat and liquor are gone, the game begins.

3

One Friday, Shi received a phone call informing him that an aunt in the city of Liaoyang in Northeastern China had passed away. Her son, his cousin, asked him to come north for the funeral. Shi asked if she had spoken any last words. His cousin said no, that she had suffered a heart attack in the middle of the night, and when they discovered her body, it was already cold. With a sigh of regret, Shi decided to attend the funeral. That decision came not because she hadn't left any last words, but because he wanted to see her one last time. He thought back to his youth, when she had followed her soldier husband north to Liaoyang and found work in a textile mill. They did not return for five years, when Shi was eight, and came to visit his parents. When his cheapskate father saw how well they had done up north, he tried to borrow money. Shi's uncle held his tongue, but his aunt said no.

"Don't think I don't want to lend you some money," she said. "But we have so many poor relatives that if I said yes to you and no one else, I'd offend them all. But if I took care of them all, I'd have to sell my pants to survive."

At dinner that night, Shi's aunt took him aside and, without letting his parents see, handed him two yuan.

"I was the first person to hold you the day you were born," she said. "With these two hands."

Two yuan back then was a princely sum, and second-grader Shi held on to it till the sixth grade, a period during when he felt like a rich kid, when he fell for a girl in his class and spent twenty cents on a handkerchief that, he recalled, was embroidered with a pair of butterflies frolicking amid flowers.

Shi's cousin met him at the end of his two-thousand-li trip, where Shi expressed his condolences and reminisced about days past. After the funeral, he headed home, stopping in Beijing to switch trains. The sight of massive crowds trying to get to their far-flung homes reminded him that the year was coming to an end, a year that had passed almost without his knowing it. He stood in line for four hours, but was unable to buy a ticket for that day and the three days that followed; his aunt could not have picked a worse time to die. He decided to find a small hotel nearby and wait till after New Year's to buy a ticket home; by then there ought to be plenty of seats. Besides, he wasn't the anxious type, so why be put off by a forced delay away from home? He walked out of the station, heading south, and entered a lane to the east of the main road dotted with small hotels and a great many luggage-toting tourists, all speaking in different dialects. He was about to check on room rates when his cell phone chirped. It was his distillery owner friend at home. Old Bu told him he'd like to take home a bowl of Another Village's meat-on-the-bone for a visiting in-law. The man had asked specifically for the dish. Shi took a look at his watch. It was six o'clock. If it had been anything else, even a request for a loan, he'd have said yes unhesitatingly. Meat-on-the-bone was a different matter, for Another Village had its rule that they could not sell meat out the back door. People would be lined up at six o'clock. He couldn't make up his mind.

"My in-law isn't just anybody. I'm heading over to Another Village now. I'll see you there."

"You won't find me."

"Why's that?"

"I'm in Beijing."

Bad news. "That spells trouble," Bu said.

"It's only a bit of meat," Shi said. "Your in-law won't die without it."

"This isn't about meat," Bu said. "It's Wednesday. Tomorrow is our game day."

Shi had forgotten all about that. Tomorrow at three o'clock the four old friends were supposed to meet for their game of mah-jongg.

"I can't buy a train ticket," Shi said, "so I'm stuck here. We'll have to pass this week."

"We can't do that," Bu said. "It would mean big trouble."

"We're talking about mah-jongg," Shi said. "Missing a game won't kill us."

"Not me, maybe, but old Xie is a different matter."

"What does that mean?"

"After being bothered by a headache all month, yesterday he went to see a doctor, who found a growth in his head. They're going to operate right after the first. We don't know if it's malignant. We hope it's benign, but if not, old Xie will be in bad shape, and I'm worried that this could be his last game."

Bu hung up. Not another word, not even about the meat-on-the-bone. Shi snapped his phone shut. This was terrible news. Xie was the worst player of the four. When he won, he was over the top happy, whistling and singing opera; when he lost, he flung down his tiles and sputtered angry curses. But Shi really got to know Xie one night the winter before when he and his wife had had an argument, and he'd had too much to drink at dinner. The more he drank, the angrier he got, and the angrier he got, the more he drank, until he was roaring drunk. Wobbling unsteadily, he stumbled out the door; his upset wife did nothing to stop him. It was snowing heavily, and he had no idea where to go, as he weaved his way drunkenly from West Avenue to South Street. He spotted Xie's public bathhouse. As soon as he staggered into the compound he keeled over and was out like a light. The next morning he awoke to find himself in one of the bathhouse beds, Xie seated beside him. A couple of masseurs stood at the foot of his bed, towels over their shoulders. The next thing he saw was a needle stuck in his arm and an IV drip above his head.

"What's that for?" he asked, pointing with his free hand.

One of the masseurs said:

"When you wouldn't wake up last night, the boss sent for a doctor."

"I only had a little too much to drink," Shi said.

"The doctor said you're lucky he came," the other masseur said. "Your heartbeat was so accelerated you could have died."

"So what!" Shi said willfully. "Everyone has to die sometime."

Xie shook his head. "We couldn't let you die," he said. "We need a place to play mah-jongg."

Shi felt warm all over, not because Xie had saved his life, but because it had given him a chance to see the true worth of the man at a critical juncture. The momentous news that Xie suffered from a brain tumor, one from which he might not survive, and that the next day's game of mah-jongg could be his last, convinced Shi that he had to get home somehow, and no later than three o'clock the next day, when the game was scheduled to start. But how was he going to get a seat on the train if all the tickets had been sold? He walked out of the lane and headed to the station, going first to the ticket return window, despite knowing full well that at this time of the year, when there were no tickets to be had, no one would be returning theirs. Next he went to the stationmaster on duty, pleading for a ticket, saying that someone in the family was critically ill. The stationmaster looked at Shi sympathetically, informing that he'd already had more than thirty similar requests that day alone, and there simply were no seats available on any train. So Shi went out into the station square to find a scalper, but the overwhelming presence of police had kept them away. At that moment, the station lights came on, signaling the end of another day. All of a sudden, Shi knew what he had to do. He took a piece of paper out of his bag, and a pen, and wrote three words:

I DEMAND JUSTICE

He raised his new sign over his head.

Less than a minute later, four policemen rushed up and pushed petitioner Shi to the ground.

4

Two adjunct policemen, not regular cops, one named Dong, the other Xue, were charged with the responsibility of escorting Shi back to his hometown. The absence of seats on packed trains could not stop authorities from escorting petitioners out of Beijing. The end of the year was the worst time to air a grievance. The conductor on Shi's train freed up two bunks in the train's lounge for Shi and his escorts. Since petitioning was not illegal, not only did Shi's escorts avoid giving him a bad time, but in order to make sure he would not cause trouble, they gave him one of the bunks and shared the other. All three men breathed a sigh of relief when the train began to move. Once they were on their way, Dong and Xue kept an eye on Shi, who gazed out the window. After passing the city of Fengtai, Dong asked Shi:

"What took you to Beijing at this time of year, friend?"

"What good would it do to tell you? Could you solve my problem if I did?"

Dong and Xue exchanged glances. As unofficial escorts they could do nothing but try to talk him around:

"Whatever it was, if it occurred at home, that's where the solution lies," Dong said.

"Don't let it get you down," Xue said. "There isn't a problem in the world that can't be solved."

When mealtime came around, Dong went out and bought three boxed meals.

"Grievance or not, a man's got to eat," he said.

Old Shi dug in.

"This is how it should be," Dong was relieved.

After lunch, Xue poured tea for Shi.

"Have some tea, Elder Brother," he said. Shi complied.

Dinner eaten and tea drunk, Shi spread out on the bunk and went to sleep. Dong and Xue took turns watching him, three hours at a time, all the way till early the following morning. By then Xue, whose turn it was to watch Shi, was so sleepy he lay down next to Dong and fell asleep. When he woke up, with the sun streaming in the window, he broke out in a nervous sweat and hurriedly sized up the bunk opposite, where Shi lay, eyes open, lost in thought. Whew, he was still there. He gave Shi a thumbs-up.

"Good man, Elder Brother," he said.

5

When they reached the city, the three men boarded a bus for the two-hour ride to the police station. The station cops, frequent diners at Another Village on West Avenue, where they enjoyed the meat-on-the-bone, knew old Shi well. Liu, the man on duty that day, was puzzled to see two men escort him into the station. Reading the letter of introduction for Dong and Xue only mystified him further.

"Old Shi," he said, scratching his head, "what's this all about? What grievance took you to Beijing, and why did they send you back under escort?"

Shi decided to tell the truth.

"No grievance, none at all. I had to switch trains in Beijing, but couldn't buy a ticket. Since I needed to get home for a game of mah-jongg, this was the best I could come up with. A bit of a ruse."

"For fun?" He turned and walked off, leaving Liu standing there in wonder. He was not alone; Dong and Xue had the same look.

"What the hell is going on?" Dong stammered. "Did he say a ruse?"

"That took balls!" Xue said, banging the table with his palm.

"Who is he?" he asked, pointing to the vacated doorway.

Old Liu explained to them that Shi Weimin had been the chief of a county twenty years earlier, but was sacked over an incident involving a woman, either because of malpractice or of graft and corruption. Left with wages too sparse to support a family, he returned to his hometown and opened a restaurant on West Avenue called Another Village, where his grandfather, a one-time chef in

Taiyuan, had left the recipe for a specialty dish called meat-on-the-bone to him. Despite its popularity, he prepared only two cauldrons a day in order to free him for his favorite pastime, mah-jongg, which he played every Thursday afternoon, rain or shine.

6

Chief Liu's explanation both saddened and amused Dong and Xue. They were at a loss for words. They had to laugh over Shi's behavior, despite a bit of anger. Added to the mix was their curiosity over Another Village's meat-on-the-bone, dutifully related to them by the station chief; they might as well take advantage of their stay in town to give the dish a try. So they walked out of the station and asked directions to Another Village, where a waitress escorted them to a private room, in which four men were involved in a heated game of mah-jongg, Shi in the host's seat.

"You shouldn't have done that, Shi," Dong railed. "Tricking the Party and the government over a game of mah-jongg."

"Not to mention the two of us," Xue added.

"That's where you're wrong," Shi replied as he laid down a tile. "The Party and government should thank me."

"What for?"

"I was all set with my petition when the thought of mah-jongg occurred to me. If I hadn't changed my mind I'd have escaped on the train while you were asleep. Just think where that would have left the two of you."

Stuck momentarily for a response, Dong said:

"I don't believe you. A petitioner needs a reason."

Shi paused in mid-play.

"Some twenty years ago," he said, "I was a county chief."

"So we've heard," Xue said.

"Sacking me back then was the greatest injustice ever, and by rights I should have petitioned annually for the past twenty years. But I held back and swallowed the indignity, all for the sake of the Party and the government. I stayed home and cooked meat. I've let that go for a long time, and in the end you—the government—wouldn't let me off.

That stopped Dong and Xue. Meanwhile, the distillery owner waved the two visitors away impatiently.

"That's enough idle chatter," he said. "We've got business here."

Then he turned to Wang the wholesaler.

"No more bullshit," he said impatiently. "It's your turn, so play."

Tentatively, he laid down a tile.

"Double cake," he called out.

Xie, the bathhouse owner, grinned happily.

"Gotcha," he said, and broke into song, while Wang complained loudly to Bu. Shi's face lit up over the ensuing argument.

"This is great."

7

Dong and Xue walked out of the mah-jongg room and into the restaurant proper, where they planned to buy some meat-on-the-bone, only to discover a line of customers out the door. They'd missed that on the way in, but now they felt the power of meat-on-the-bone. A look into the kitchen revealed only one large cauldron in which meat was stewing, which meant that they'd be wasting their time lining up now. So Dong walked up to the manager and explained that the dish's fame had reached them all the way to Beijing, and they wondered if they could buy a taste of the meat. Their request was greeted with a shake of the head and an explanation that he could not sell them even a sliver. If he did, the people in line would beat him to a pulp. So the two of them walked out the door, shaking their heads and knowing they'd have to settle for another place to eat. They were stopped by a shout from the waitress who had taken them to see Shi.

"Please come on back," she said.

"What for?"

"Boss Shi says that since you bought him dinner on the train, he wants to return the favor."

After a brief exchanged look, they fell in behind the waitress, who escorted them into a private room, where a tub of steaming meat-on-the-bone and two bottles of colorless liquor were laid out on a table. They were ecstatic.

"Old Shi might have been a corrupt official in the past," Xue said, "but he's returned to the straight and narrow."

They sat down and began tearing off a piece to place on their tongues. They knew at once what made it special: It was salty yet fragrant; fragrant yet sweet; sweet yet spicy; spicy yet bracing and smooth. The flavor oozed from the meat but also the marrow of the bone. Most of the time neither man was much of a drinker, but the meat changed that for a day at least. They soon polished off one bottle. As Dong was opening the second bottle, Xue asked:

"What are we going to say to our superiors when we get back?"

"I don't think we can report truthfully. We'd be laughed at if we did."

"Not just that, they'd think we were idiots. We didn't spot a thing during a two-thousand-li trip. We could lose our rice bowls over that."

"We'll just say that everything went smoothly," Xue said. "We'll say that after we talked to him on the road, he wised up and said he'd never petition again. The case is closed and we'll be rewarded."

"Since he's promised to turn over a new leaf, we need to know what the old leaf was. How do we deal with that?"

"We tell the truth," Xue replied. "He wanted his sacking as county chief overturned. Something like that is very serious."

"You're right," Dong said. "We can't have something that serious turning into a travesty." He raised his glass.

"Bottoms up."

Xue raised his glass, they clinked glasses, and drained them.

Night had fallen. It was New Year's Eve. Firecrackers exploded and fireworks were set off outside the restaurant. They could see them through the window, a riot of purples and reds sending beams of light in all directions.